A WOLF AT THE DOOR

"Don't you dare come near this cabin, Jake Wolf." Renata glared at him. "From now on you can sleep in the bunkhouse."

"What's the matter? Afraid all this might appear to be just a bit improper?"

"You've ruined everything. You know that. You did it on purpose." Her eyes filled with tears.

Unfamiliar pangs of regret pricked at Jake. "I didn't mean—"

"Yes, you did. You deliberately let Mr. Boyle think...well, you know. And before the sun sets everybody in Silver Valley will be thinking the same thing. I'm ruined. I'll probably have to go to Texas to find myself a rancher now, and it gets so hot in Texas in the summertime."

"Still set on a rancher husband?" Jake asked coolly.

"Yes," Renata answered defiantly. "Perhaps you could introduce me to your father."

Jake didn't move, and his look was impassive, but he was certain she knew she had touched a nerve. "My father is already married. The Cheyenne often take more than one wife, but most ranchers only allow one bitch to a household."

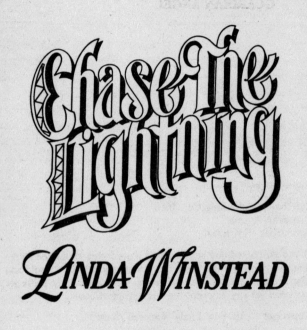

Chase The Lightning

LINDA WINSTEAD

LOVE SPELL   **NEW YORK CITY**

LOVE SPELL®

January 1995

Published by

Dorchester Publishing Co., Inc.
276 Fifth Avenue
New York, NY 10001

This is for my brother, Tom,
who's always known
how to make me laugh—
and when I needed it most.

Chapter One

Colorado, 1884

Renata Marie Parkhurst leaned over, trying her best to ignore the jostling and the dust that poured through the open windows of the stagecoach. The other six passengers in the Concord, seated comfortably in the coach built for nine, repeatedly wiped the sweat from their brows, covered their mouths with tightly clutched handkerchiefs, and moaned with every bounce.

Renata spoke loudly to the young woman across from her so she could be heard above the din of the vehicle that was practically flying down the rutted road. "I knew a woman once who fought with her husband on their wedding day." She nodded her head knowingly at the newlywed Margaret Tidwell, whom Renata thought of as young despite the fact that she was twenty-two and Renata was not yet twenty. "It was over some inconsequential insult to the bride's father, I believe. The bride absolutely refused to make amends, even when the poor groom begged for her forgiveness."

Margaret Tidwell cut suspicious eyes over to her own bridegroom. "It was my mother he insulted, and it was not inconsequential. He called her a shrew!"

Renata raised her eyebrows. "To her face?"

Margaret shook her head. "No, but it was an insult just the same."

Renata nodded her head in agreement. "This bride I was telling you about? The woman who refused to forgive her husband? She regretted it later, I can tell you." Renata continued to nod her head as she spoke, but the new bride looked skeptical.

"Well, I will never forgive Sam, and I will never regret it, either." Margaret's chin jutted forward defiantly.

Renata sighed deeply, wondering if she should even attempt to continue. The girl's mind was made up, but it pained Renata to see anyone suffer needlessly, particularly if she thought she could fix it. Her mother called it meddling and her father called it butting in, but Renata called it fixing. "I hope the same fate doesn't befall you and Sam as . . . well, never mind." Renata looked out of the window and sighed again, as dramatically as she dared.

There were several moments of strained silence. Sam was staring stubbornly out the window, two male passengers were trying with little success to sleep, and the other passengers, two spritely older women, were watching Renata intently.

Finally, Margaret broke down and asked, "What happened?"

"The groom took sick. His bride had locked him out of their house, but he was so distraught over her anger that he stayed outside, even in a cold March rain. He waited all night, and the next morning when his bride found him he was feverish and delirious. Naturally she felt bad, but it was too late. He never recovered, and she was left a widow at eighteen. The insult to her father seems very small when you consider . . ." Renata's voice trailed off wistfully.

She hoped her older sister wouldn't mind that she had taken liberties with the story. Of course, Amalie had been fourteen at the time, and instead of a groom it had been a small shaggy dog that had been put out of the house, punished for having had an accident on Amalie's favorite rug. The poor dog hadn't died, but it had gotten very wet, and Amalie had felt awful when she'd found it the next morning. Close enough to the truth, Renata decided.

Margaret looked over at her groom for the first time since they'd boarded the stage, and there was softness in her eyes. "That's very sad. Don't you think so, Sam?"

Sam Tidwell turned to Margaret with a lift

11

of his bushy eyebrows. "Yes," he said, reaching out to his wife and tentatively taking her hand. "I'm sorry I insulted your ma. Forgive me?"

As an answer, Margaret laid her head on Sam's shoulder, and squeezed his hand. Satisfied, Renata turned her attention once again to the landscape that was flying past. The train had been much more comfortable, but she only had half a day to spend on the stage . . . half a day to Silver Valley.

Her cousin Melanie had told her so much about Silver Valley and its inhabitants that Renata felt as if she would know everyone there the moment she stepped down from the Concord. The shy little man who put out the weekly paper, the dressmaker who mothered half the town, the couple who ran the general store . . . and Silver Valley itself, which Melanie had told her was not situated in a valley and contained no silver other than the silver dollars that were spent there. The town was supported primarily by the surrounding ranches, one of which belonged to Melanie and her husband Gabriel Maxwell.

Renata was so excited that she could feel her heart racing, the blood coursing through her veins. Leaving home had been her first act of defiance against her parents, and it was a doozy. She'd left a note saying that she was setting sail for Europe, which she thought should give her a little time to accomplish her mission before her parents figured out where she really was. When she had what she wanted she would send them a telegram, but by then it would be too late for them to stop her. Far too late.

Asking—no, *demanding*—that she marry that English fop was going just a bit too far, even for her mother. The man, whose name was Percival, for goodness sake, was almost old enough to be her father. Her mother said he was slender and elegant, but he was skinny! He didn't dance, he talked funny, and he wanted to take her away to England, away from everything and everyone she had ever known, and make her live in a drafty old castle. Amalie had said it sounded terribly romantic. Renata had suggested bluntly that her older sister leave her own ordinary American husband for the earl, or whatever he was, and Amalie had been shocked. She loved her husband, she had protested, and she would never . . . and then she had seen Renata's point. There was no substitute for love, not even a title and a castle that had been standing for three or four hundred years.

Renata knew what she wanted. Her objective had been vague in her mind until Melanie and Gabriel's visit the previous summer. They clearly adored one another, even after three years of marriage—four years, now—and rambunctious twin daughters. The way Gabriel looked at Melanie when he thought no one was watching, the way Melanie's eyes lit up when Gabriel entered the room. That was what Renata wanted. She hadn't been able to find a relationship like that in Philadelphia, and she certainly wouldn't find it in England with Percival.

So she had decided she had to look elsewhere, to find herself a rancher, a rancher like Gabriel. They would fall madly in love, at first sight of course, and they would live happily ever after.

Melanie would be surprised to see her, but Renata didn't think her cousin would mind. She had given the entire family an open invitation to visit the ranch in Colorado, and Renata had simply decided to take Melanie up on her offer. Of course, she should have written or wired first, but she hadn't dared. She didn't want Melanie to have the opportunity to let the rest of the family know what had become of her. Renata was certain that once she explained her mission to her cousin, Melanie would understand. And Renata didn't plan on speaking to her parents again until after she was married, when it was too late.

One of the older ladies sitting next to Renata leaned over and whispered into her ear. "Was that story true?"

"Of course." Renata's whispered reply was serious. "Most of it, at least." She cast a sly glance at the newlyweds. "They are a lovely couple, aren't they?"

The gray-haired lady smiled and nodded her head. "And what about you, young lady?" She turned away from the Tidwells and studied Renata intently. "Do you have a young man

14

waiting for you in . . . where are you going?"

"Silver Valley." Renata supplied the name of her destination. "You're going on farther, aren't you?"

"Yes. My sister and I won't arrive until tomorrow." She tilted her head toward the woman on her left, who was asleep. "Do you have a beau waiting for you in Silver Valley?"

Renata smiled. In spite of the trip's discomforts she was filled with hope and wonder. "Yes," she answered finally. "Yes, I do."

The older lady, who had introduced herself earlier as Mrs. Hundley of St. Louis, returned Renata's smile warmly. "How wonderful for you. What does he do there?"

"He's a rancher," Renata said assuredly, with an unexpected swelling of her heart. Her future was bright and exciting and she had everything planned perfectly.

"That will be quite a change for you, won't it? Didn't you say you were from Philadelphia?"

"Yes. I've lived there all my life. I'm sure the life of a rancher's wife is very different from that of a physician's daughter, but I look forward to the challenge. I'll have a cousin living nearby, and I'm sure she'll be of great help to me."

Mrs. Hundley patted Renata's arm just as they hit a particularly nasty rut in the road. "I wish you the best of luck, my dear. You're a sweet, beautiful girl. Your young man is very lucky."

"That's very kind of you, Mrs. Hundley,"

Renata said sincerely as a loose strand of hair fell over Renata's cheek when they landed roughly. Sweet, of course. Renata had never met anyone she couldn't get along with. She was certain that was why she had received so many proposals of marriage. But none of her suitors had sparked any passion in her. Their kisses had been pleasant, but they hadn't left her breathless or even half as excited as she was as she approached Silver Valley at a breakneck pace.

Beautiful? She thought not. Melanie was beautiful, with her blond hair and blue eyes. Amalie was beautiful, with dark hair, their father's legacy to his oldest daughter, and deep blue eyes. Renata had no illusions about her own looks. She wasn't ugly, of course, but her hair was neither pale nor dark. She didn't have blue eyes like her sister and her cousin, but green ones that had a tendency to turn gray when she was angry. Amalie was tall, lean, and graceful, and Melanie moved with an inbred elegance, tempered with careless assurance. Renata sometimes felt clumsy and always too short, at barely five-foot-two.

Of course, she was the youngest of the girls, and had been comparing herself to her older sister and her beautiful cousin for years . . . always unfavorably.

"What's your young man's name?" Mrs. Hundley asked. "Perhaps I know him. We've visited this area several times over the past ten years. Our older sister lives just a day's ride from Silver Valley."

"His name?"

"Yes. Unless I'm being too forward." Mrs. Hundley backed off. "I didn't mean to pry."

"It's not that," Renata reassured the woman quickly. "It's just that . . . well, I don't know his name yet."

Mrs. Hundley didn't question Renata further, as she obviously would have liked to do.

Renata looked out the window and caught a glimpse of her destination. She could hardly contain her excitement. "There it is! Silver Valley! Isn't that a lovely name? Silver Valley. It just sort of rolls off the tongue, much more poetically than Philadelphia." Renata bit her bottom lip. He was there, somewhere; she was certain. Would he be watching her arrival, unaware that she was his destiny? Perhaps. The idea was exciting.

The Concord pulled to a stop, and Renata suddenly became nervous. She chewed her lower lip, a habit her mother detested, and tried to straighten her hair to smooth her errant curls. Brushing the skirt of her gray traveling suit, she took a deep breath.

"My dear." Mrs. Hundley leaned forward and clasped Renata's hand, giving her a soft yet somehow stern look of concern. "It's none of my business, I know, but you're such a sweet girl. Did I hear you correctly? You don't know the name of your intended?"

Renata nodded.

Mrs. Hundley pursed her lips. "Why is that? Is it an arranged marriage? Are you—"she blushed, bringing high color to her wrinkled cheeks—"a mail-order bride?"

Renata raised her head and met the woman's curious stare with determination. "Nothing like that, Mrs. Hundley. I just haven't found him yet."

Silver Valley was just as Melanie had described it, the dust rising from the main street on a dry summer day, the two old men sitting in front of the general store arguing. Horses were tethered in front of the single saloon, and men in sturdy work clothes and serviceable, wide-brimmed hats milled about in front of the saloon, the general store, and the livery. Cowboys. Ranchers. Her rancher? Renata wondered as she stepped down from the coach.

The single dirt-packed street was lined with businesses, an occasional two-story building rising above the rest. The only hotel had three stories, and the dress shop had two. Renata remembered that the dressmaker had her rooms above her shop. The livery was at the far end of the street, and when Renata turned around she saw the pristine white church at the east end, a building set apart from the dusty town and yet an integral part of it. Tall trees surrounded the church, towering even above the steeple that reached for the sky.

Renata supervised the unloading of her Saratoga trunk and two slightly smaller ones.

Almost everything she owned was in those trunks. She was never going back to Philadelphia, except to visit with her future husband and their children, just as Melanie and Gabriel had the summer before.

She was the only one of the passengers departing at Silver Valley and she received her fair share of stares from the cowboys and the old men in front of the general store.

"Good afternoon," Renata said cheerfully as she entered the general store and approached the sour-looking woman behind the counter. "You must be Mrs. Boyle. Melanie has spoken so kindly of you, I believe I would know you anywhere. What a lovely store you have." Renata looked around appreciatively. "I'm certain I'll be doing lots of business here."

Mrs. Boyle looked Renata up and down blatantly. "Are you plannin' on stayin' in Silver Valley, miss?"

"For a while, certainly. First I need to hire a carriage to take me to Melanie Maxwell's house. Who might I see about that?"

Mrs. Boyle smiled. "So you're a friend of Mel's, are ya?"

Renata pursed her lips. She had never cared for Melanie's nickname. Mel, indeed. "She's my cousin. I've come to visit."

Mrs. Boyle knit her heavy brows and her lips thinned. "Did she know you were comin'?"

"No. It's a bit of a surprise. I'd promised to visit soon, but I never—"

"She's not here," Mrs. Boyle interrupted.

"Her and Gabe and the twins left last week for Texas. No tellin' when they'll be back."

Renata frowned. If she had known they would be at Uncle Richard's, she could have gone directly there. After all, there were ranchers in Texas, too. Lots of them. "Well, I suppose there's nothing to do but wait," she said, pushing her disappointment aside. "Surely they won't be gone too long. They have a ranch to run."

"Gabe pretty much leaves the runnin' of the ranch to Lester Patton, and that Jake Wolf." She said the last name as if it left a sour taste in her mouth, pursing her lips and transforming her already stern visage to one of obvious distaste.

"I can't wait to meet them." Renata straightened her skirt and smoothed a wayward strand of hair. "And everyone else Melanie has told me so much about. The first order of business will be to get to the ranch and clean up a bit. I'm afraid I'm not much of a traveler."

Mrs. Boyle met Renata's friendly smile with a calculating stare, then cracked a tiny smile of her own. "You look a bit better than most who step off the stage. That bumpy, dusty ride usually manages to get the best of even the toughest men. My husband Donnie will be happy to take you out to the Maxwell ranch. Will you be wantin' to go to the new house or the old cabin?"

"New house?"

"Yep. It's not quite finished. Lester has some

of the boys workin' on it so it will be done by the time Mel and Gabe get back. It might be a tad quieter for you at the cabin."

Renata smiled. Melanie had told her stories about life in that cabin, and she knew that was where she wanted to go.

Donnie Boyle loaded Renata's trunks onto the back of a buckboard. A short, stocky man, he lifted the heavy trunks as if they weighed nothing at all. Renata decided that Janie and Donnie Boyle looked so much alike that they could have been brother and sister, instead of man and wife.

After he helped her into the buckboard, offering Renata his meaty hand, neither of them said a word as they settled themselves on the wide, unpadded seat.

"I hope you're not too uncomfortable," Donnie offered as they started down the dusty street.

Renata looked at him and smiled. "Mr. Boyle, after spending an entire morning in a stuffy coach I am certainly enjoying the fresh air. Why, this way I can see everything. The countryside is lovely, isn't it? So green."

She looked him right in the eye and smiled widely. The discomforts and inconveniences she'd endured to get to Silver Valley were small compared to the exhilaration she felt now.

Donnie Boyle relaxed visibly and returned her smile. "Now, that's the prettiest smile I ever did see. Makes me feel like a young whippersnapper again. If I wasn't married, I'd propose to you right this minute."

Renata laughed at his joke. She'd received dozens of marriage proposals, but none quite so informal. She believed that her many offers had come because Amalie was already married, and because Renata would make any man a good wife with her pleasant personality, her slowness to anger, and her ability to entertain as well as her mother. But she had taken those offers as seriously as she took Donnie Boyle's lighthearted teasing.

She lulled Donnie into a conversation about Silver Valley, and he confirmed much of what Renata already knew. Melanie had told her about everyone in the town and the surrounding area, but it had been a year since Melanie and Gabriel's visit to Philadelphia, and Renata wanted to hear all the current news: who had gotten married, had babies, made or lost fortunes.

"What about Jake Wolf?" Renata asked innocently, after Donnie had exhausted his supply of information.

"Humph." Donnie frowned. "You just better hope he's on one of his long treks to God only knows where."

"Why?" Renata asked, puzzled, as she turned to him. Melanie and Gabriel had spoken so fondly of Jake, and even the girls had asked time and time again for "Unca Jake," as Renata held them close and told them fanciful stories.

Donnie turned dark, serious eyes toward her,

and his frown deepened. Renata looked at him expectantly. What could be the problem with the man Melanie and Gabriel talked about as if he were a part of their family?

"Jake Wolf is a mean, dangerous half-breed son of a bitch, pardon my language. If he wasn't a friend of Gabe's, we probably woulda strung him up years ago," Donnie answered angrily.

"For what?"

"I just told you that he's mean . . . danger-ous . . . a damn half-breed."

Renata turned away from him and stared at the enchanting hills and green landscape that rolled past. "How unusual. Why, in Philadel-phia if we hung men just for being mean, there would be a hanging every day."

Donnie shook his head. "You're not takin' me seriouslike. You just be on the lookout, you hear? I'll come out and check on you in a week or two. If you need anything before then, just head on over to the big house." He pointed to the west, and Renata saw it in the distance, white and tall and much like Melanie's descrip-tion of her Texas home. The most distinctive feature, the element Melanie had probably insisted upon, was the gallery that wrapped around the first and second stories.

"Lester and some of the boys will be there most every day, tryin' to finish up before Gabe and Mel get back."

"You really needn't check on me," Renata assured him as he helped her down from the buckboard when they reached the cabin. "I'm sure I'll be just fine. But it is very kind of you to offer." She gave him another bright smile.

Glancing away from Donnie, she appraised the sturdy structure with a careful eye. The cabin was rustic, its glass windows sparkling in the sun, and the front porch looked as if it had been recently swept clean. After all she had heard about the cabin, Renata felt an immediate rush of warmth and comfort, almost a sense of homecoming.

When she went inside, she saw that the front room was spacious and immaculate. A rocking chair sat in front of a cold fireplace that dominated the main room. A worn but not yet tattered rug covered the floor, and Renata stepped across it to reach the dining-room table and peeked into the kitchen.

Donnie carried her trunks to the larger of the two bedrooms, which was separated from the hallway by a green calico curtain. The smaller bedroom was across the hall, and a curtain of blue hung there.

He took her out back and showed her the well and how to operate it, drawing and carrying in several buckets of water for her. They found the pantry well stocked, but Donnie offered to make another trip with supplies for Renata. She declined, as she was obviously set for weeks.

As Donnie Boyle pulled away from the cabin, Renata stood on the front porch and waved good-bye, a satisfied and victorious smile on her face and in her heart.

Chapter Two

Somebody had cut the fence on purpose. Jake pulled on a pair of gloves and started repairing the barbed wire. He hated this . . . barbed wire and riding the boundaries of Gabe's ranch looking for damage. There had been a lot of breaks in the fence lately. Deliberate damage.

It was time. Time to leave it all behind and disappear into the mountains. To trap for his food, travel into reaches of the Rocky Mountains where no white man had ever been . . . where *no* man had ever been. To wake in the morning to the absolute quiet of the mountains, to watch the stars at night unencumbered by the sound of another human voice.

Jake had admitted to himself long ago that he didn't really like people much, and they certainly didn't like him. Gabe and Mel Maxwell and their twins were the exceptions. They were the only family he had, the only family he wanted . . . and that was why he would be stuck on the ranch for another couple of months, at least. He had promised Gabe he would stay to look after the place.

A shot rang out, and Jake knew he was hit even before the burning sensation in his side began to grow. He looked down as he dropped to the ground. The bullet had passed through cleanly, and blood was pouring from his wound. Another shot was fired from the heavy cover of the trees, the bullet whizzing over Jake's head as he lay in the grass.

Jake blew a low whistle, and his black stallion galloped to his side. A rifle was slung from the saddle, and after a third shot was fired Jake pulled himself to his feet and slid the rifle from its boot. Absently, he stroked the animal's neck. The stallion was a good mount, well trained and unafraid of gunfire. It would have made a good battle horse, in the old days.

Jake slapped the horse's rump and watched it trot away as he dropped into the tall grass. A fourth shot went wild as Jake aimed blindly into the stand of trees and fired.

After his third unanswered shot, Jake knew his attacker had fled. Whoever had ambushed him was a coward who was unwilling to be fired on in return.

He sat in the grass and pulled his buckskin

shirt over his head. The flow of blood was steady, and Jake wrapped his shirt around his midsection, tying the long sleeves together as tightly as he could. Ambushed. He wasn't even surprised . . . not really. Most everybody wanted him dead.

Rising slowly, Jake whistled again for his horse and with silent effort he pulled himself into the saddle and turned toward the ranch. Knowing his wound was just above his waist, he figured he should be able to doctor it himself. He'd never asked anyone for help before—ever—and he wasn't going to start now. There were bandages and fresh water for cleaning the wound at the cabin.

His makeshift bandage had slowed the flow of blood, though it continued, and after a short while Jake became dizzy. For a split second he believed he saw Lita ahead of him, guiding him to the cabin, but his loyal companion was dead, shot in the head by some cowboy who didn't like the idea of wolves mixing with people. But Jake had liked that wolf better than most people.

Mel had cried for three days, had insisted on burying the wolf she had named Lita and placing a marker on the grave. Jake never admitted to anyone, not even to Mel, how much he missed that animal, but he did.

The sun was setting, and Jake began to believe that if he didn't reach the cabin before dark he would bleed to death. There in the distance, barely more than a silhouette against the setting sun, was Beryl Garrett, her hand held high as she waved to him. Of course it wasn't really Beryl . . . She was still in Denver, probably married by now to some well-bred gentleman with pure blood.

As Jake watched, the woman who had waved to him changed into a sapling, a young tree bending in the wind, and his hallucination was replaced by reality.

No one in Silver Valley, not even Gabe, knew what had happened during Jake's trips to Denver, where he exchanged his buckskins for a plain black suit and clubbed his straight black hair, securing it with a leather strap at his nape. He had plenty of money for his brief forays to the city; he had allowed Gabe to invest his share of the profits from the sale of their silver mines, and Gabe had made them both a small fortune. Jake knew that in a way Gabe hated the fact that he had a talent for making money, a talent Gabe's grandfather had, for Gabe had broken away from his grandfather's influence and his stifling Bostonian background.

But like it or not, Gabe had the golden touch, and Jake was grateful he did. The money had helped Jake gain entry into Denver society, which treated him differently than the people of Silver Valley.

His bankers invited him to dances and dinner parties, and he attended, curious about these people who seemed so happy and carefree, and to get a glimpse of a world so foreign to him, where everything was clean, peaceful, and free of hate. Of course, Jake never danced and said little, which he realized only added to his air of mystery, especially with the women who behaved differently toward him, too, flirting with him and sending seductive, sidelong glances his way.

Then the prominent, wealthy Marcus Garrett decided that Jake would make good husband material for his 18-year-old daughter, Beryl, who had hair as black as Jake's, eyes a sweet honey-brown, and milky-white skin that obviously had never been touched by the rays of a hot sun.

Beryl's life had been so unlike Jake's that he found himself entranced by her. She was always smiling, always happy, and it was obvious that she was intrigued by the quiet Jake, whom her father brought home for dinner more and more often. Jake knew she liked him a lot, as she showed him with glances that hinted at passion and frequent touches. Her hand on his arm, on his back. Feathery touches.

Jake never would have proposed to the girl, he had told himself, and if he had ever planned to, he would have told her first about his Cheyenne blood. Though only one-quarter Cheyenne, in his heart he was more Indian than white. How could he not be, after seeing his mother shot at Sand Creek, his grandfather murdered at the Washita River Massacre?

But Marcus Garrett and his lovely daughter Beryl found out about Jake's background on their own, and were shocked to learn that Wolf was not an old English name, but part of Jake's Cheyenne name.

Jake would never forget the way old man Garrett had looked at him—the disgust in the man's eyes—but even worse was the look in Beryl's. The girl who had flirted and teased him was suddenly afraid of him, as though he might show up at her door one day in a breechclout to take her scalp.

That had been nearly two years ago, and Jake had told no one—not Gabe, not even Mel. He tried to forget it himself. The experience only reinforced his belief that he was meant to live his life alone. One day he would go into the mountains and not come back because he knew that Gabe's family was not really his . . . though he tried hard at times to pretend that they were.

He tried, too, to forget that he'd almost fallen in love with Mel when they'd both believed Gabe was dead. Maybe he actually had loved her a little, but her heart had been for Gabe alone, even when she thought she'd lost him forever.

Jake lifted a blood-soaked gloved hand from his side. He was losing too much blood, too fast. The cabin was in sight now, and none too soon. There was precious little light left in the sky, and—Jake narrowed his eyes—there was a soft yellow light at a window. Someone had lit a lantern and was in the cabin. Jake cursed under his breath. If he hadn't been injured, he would have turned away. Maybe it was Lester or one of the hands. It was much too soon for Gabe and Mel to be back.

Jake slid from the stallion's back slowly, knowing that it was essential that he keep his footing. He could have called out to whoever was in the cabin for help . . . but he wouldn't. Although he wouldn't admit it, he would prefer to bleed to death on the steps than ask Gabe's foreman or one of his hands for help.

His stallion would find its own way to the stable, and Jake hit it on its rump. He took the first of the several difficult steps it would take just to reach the front door. He held his hand pressed over the wound. Though slowed to a trickle, he felt that if he lost another drop of blood it would be his last. The door swam before him, and he shook his head in disgust. Ambushed. By morning he'd be dead and the residents of Silver Valley would throw the biggest party the town had ever seen.

He laid his hand on the doorknob and noticed as an afterthought that he was still wearing his kid gloves. He didn't usually wear them, but working with the barbed wire made it necessary. He stood there looking at his hand for several long seconds before he twisted the doorknob and pushed against the heavy door. Falling inside, he felt everything spin around him. Only one element pierced through his rapidly fading consciousness, and that was a woman's high-pitched scream reverberating through his brain.

*   *   *

Renata stopped screaming the moment she realized that the savage-looking man who burst through the front door was in no condition to be any danger to her. A big man, tall and broad in the shoulders, his shoulder-length hair was as black as midnight. His blood-soaked shirt, wrapped around his midsection, was the last thing she noticed, as he landed half in and half out of the doorway.

One look outside told her that he was alone, and in the distance, galloping into the last tinges of a lavender-gray sky, was a horse. His horse?

Seeing it was too dark for her to walk to the big house, she knew what she had to do.

"Only one way to deal with you." Renata talked to the unconscious man who lay facedown as she knelt beside his still body. She grabbed him under the arms and dragged him into the room, then closed the cabin door. She then bent down and pulled him across the floor. Her progress was slow as the injured man was heavy and no help to her at all.

Once she had him on the rug she rolled him over, very gently, onto his back, and when she got a good look at his face she smiled. "You must be Jake Wolf," she said to the unresponsive man. "Melanie described you perfectly." Her voice was little more than a whisper. "But she didn't say that you were beautiful."

Renata shook her head. How ridiculous. Men

weren't beautiful, and this one had too hard a face to be called fair. His chiseled features were strong, his cheeks smooth-shaven and bronzed, his nose aristocratic and perfectly straight. She made herself pull her eyes away from his face. He was badly wounded and had evidently lost a lot of blood. The left side of his buckskin trousers was soaked, as well as the shirt around his waist.

Leaving him on the rug, Renata rushed to the kitchen and soaked several clean rags in one of the buckets Donnie Boyle had drawn for her. She searched the pantry and finally found what she was looking for. Only then did she return to his side, as prepared as she would ever be.

Jake opened his eyes to find a woman leaning over him, washing his face with a cool cloth as though he might break if she pressed too hard against his skin. The lantern was behind her, and he couldn't make out her face, but it was her hair, a pale red-gold, that made him certain he didn't know her.

"Oh, good. You're awake," she whispered. "How do you feel?"

Jake squinted and tried to see her face better, but he couldn't, no matter how hard he tried. "Like I've been shot."

"It seems you were," she said simply, leaving his face alone for the moment. "Do you think you can move? I hate to leave you on the floor, but I can't get you into a bed by myself."

"Of course I can move," Jake said sharply.

What did she think? That he was helpless? He rolled up slowly, surprised to discover how difficult that was, and found the woman's arm around his back as she lifted him gently.

"I don't need any help."

"Yes, you do," she insisted pleasantly, half supporting him as he rose to his feet. "You've lost a lot of blood, and you'll have to spend several days—maybe even weeks—in bed recuperating. The bleeding has stopped, but if it starts up again, you'll be in a lot of trouble."

Jake looked down at his midsection. The woman had bandaged him tightly with a length 'of lavender calico dotted with pink flowers.

"I know, I know," she said softly as they started down the hallway. "It was all I could find, and it seems to be working well enough."

Jake wanted to argue with her, but he couldn't. He was too weak, and all he could think about was dropping into the bed and staying there for a couple of days. Tomorrow he would worry about who this woman was, and why she was in Gabe's cabin.

"Come on." She tightened her grip on him as he faltered just a little. "Don't give up on me now, Jake. Not unless you want to spend the night on the floor in the hall."

Her use of his name caught his attention, allowing him to stay alert as she led him into a dark bedroom and helped him into the bed. She pulled off his moccasins, studied his bloodstained pants for a moment, and decided to leave them on him. Gently, she covered him

34

with a quilt and tucked him in as though he
were a small child, helpless and frightened of
the approaching night.

He wanted to ask her who she was, where
she had come from, if he could touch her hair.
It was all he had really been able to see of her,
and it looked soft and warm . . . but that could
wait for tomorrow. He realized as he drifted
into a deep sleep that it would have to wait;
he didn't have the strength to speak.

He knew even as he fell asleep that she was
still watching over him, and that should have
irritated him. But it didn't. It felt strangely . . .
right.

Chapter Three

Renata paced at the foot of the bed, clasping her hands together and frowning whenever she looked down at the still figure. As far as she could tell, Jake hadn't moved at all since she'd helped him into the bed the night before, and it was nearly midday. What if he died? What if she'd done something wrong? To reassure herself, she lifted the quilt and checked the lavender bandage. She was pleased to see that it was clean and dry, with no sign of blood seeping through.

So this was Jake: the man Melanie had spoken of so fondly . . . the man everyone else in town apparently hated. Why? Simply because he had some Cheyenne blood in his veins? That didn't make any sense to her. Donnie Boyle had told her Jake was mean, and dangerous.

Sleeping, he looked perfectly safe and tame. He was, perhaps, the handsomest man she had ever seen. His skin was bronzed from the sun, and his hair was thick and straight, black as night. Renata continued to hold the quilt high even after she'd been assured that Jake's wound hadn't started bleeding during the night. She'd never seen a man bare-chested before, but she was certain they didn't all look like him. Renata was fascinated by the corded muscles in his shoulders and arms, and the smooth bronze chest that rose and fell with every breath he took. Even his neck was well formed, sinewy and brown and . . . she saw a thin white scar beneath his jaw and reached out to touch it. It was long but wouldn't show unless he turned his face to the side.

Her fingers had barely touched his skin when he came awake, grasping her wrist in a sudden movement that shocked her. Then his eyes opened—deep blue eyes that caused her to freeze. She was so scared, she could barely manage to breathe, much less move.

"Who are you?" he rasped.

"Let me go," she demanded weakly.

"Answer me first."

Renata found herself in an awkward position, half leaning, half standing, her arm slightly twisted. "Renata Marie Parkhurst," she said primly. "Now will you kindly release me?"

Jake loosened his grip but continued to hold her. "What are you doing here?" He studied her so intently, Renata had to wonder if he even remembered what had happened the night before. He shifted his attention from her, and his eyes wandered to the calico bandage at his midsection.

"Well, I came to see Melanie, but she's not here. She and Gabriel have gone to Texas, so I'm just going to wait until they come home."

"They won't be back for another two months or more."

"Two months? Are you certain?" She felt distressed suddenly, but that quickly changed to acceptance. "Well, I can wait. Perhaps I can start without Melanie."

"Start what?"

Renata tried to work her hand free, and he released her easily. "That's none of your business, Mr. Wolf."

He closed his eyes again. "Last night you called me Jake. Nobody calls me Mr. Wolf."

"Last night was different. It was an emergency." Renata tucked Jake in, covering him nearly to his chin and patting the quilt alongside his body. "I'm going to make you some tea."

"I don't want any."

"Well, you'll drink it or I'll pour it down your throat, Mr. Wolf," Renata warned, and he opened his eyes again.

"Yes, ma'am," he agreed meekly. "Thank you for bandaging me up and all. You did a good job."

"Thank you. My father is a doctor."

Renata moved around the bed, staying just

out of his reach and pretending not to notice that he stared.

"So you helped your father in his work?" he asked.

Renata laughed, and Jake gave her a small grin. "Good heavens, no. My mother never would have allowed that. But he did talk about his work a lot, and I usually remember what I hear."

She leaned over him again and felt his forehead. "No fever, Mr. Wolf. That's good." She looked at him then, right into those marvelous dark blue eyes.

"I know who you are," he said, a triumphant ring to his voice.

"Of course you do. I told you exactly . . ."

"You're Red Rennie."

Renata pulled back from him hastily. "Oh, I hate that nickname. Melanie insists on calling me that, even though my hair isn't red, and no one's called me Rennie since I turned twelve."

"Looks red to me," Jake insisted. "Sort of."

Renata placed her hands on the bed and leaned over Jake. "My hair is not red." It couldn't be. Red hair was very unfashionable. "It is . . . strawberry blond, Mr. Wolf, and if you expect me to continue to tend you, you will refrain from calling me by that name. You may call me Miss Parkhurst, or perhaps Renata, since you're such good friends with my cousin and her husband, but never again call me . . ."

"Red Rennie," he finished for her.

Renata did her best to glare at him, but she had never been particularly good at holding on to her anger. Jake was glaring right back at her, with eyes as hard and cold as sapphires.

Renata relaxed slightly as she distanced herself from Jake Wolf, drawing herself to her full height and folding her hands in front of her. He was, after all, just a man. She wouldn't allow him to intimidate her.

"Would you care for sugar in that tea, Mr. Wolf?" she asked, then went on when he looked as if he was going to refuse. "Never mind. You need the sugar to get your energy back." She spun around and left him before he had a chance to answer her, before he could catch and hold her with those deep blue eyes again.

Jake had finished the tea at her insistence and had fallen almost immediately into a deep sleep. Every few minutes she had looked in on him, glancing through the parted calico curtain to assure herself that his chest still rose and fell steadily, and now, as she moved away from the doorway to his room, she heard a horse approaching. She went to the window in the main room and saw a man riding toward the cabin. Obviously he had come from the direction of the big house, and with a purpose indicated by his horse's hurried gait. Renata smoothed the skirt of her pale blue gown and patted her softly curling hair as she walked out the door. She was about to receive her first visitor.

The cowboy jumped spryly from the horse, but Renata saw even from where she stood on the front porch, the cabin door open behind her, that he was much too old for her, and the word "grizzled" came to mind as he tramped toward her. The man removed his dusty wide-brimmed hat and held it in both hands, as he looked almost nervously from the ground up to Renata and then to the ground again.

"You must be Miz Maxwell's cousin," he said as he stopped at the bottom of the stairs, one booted foot on the first step, one on the ground.

"Yes." Renata stepped forward. "Renata Marie Parkhurst."

"Lester Patton." He plodded up the steps and offered Renata a filthy hand. She smiled and took it as if it were an everyday occurrence to clutch a dirt-encrusted palm in her own.

"I hate to bother you," Lester continued, releasing her hand at long last. "Donnie Boyle stopped by yesterday afternoon and let me know you were stayin' here . . . suggested that I might look in on you now and again, but I'm afraid that's not what brung me here today. I got me a little problem."

Renata released the breath she had been holding. Lester Patton not only looked as if he'd been rolling in the dirt; he smelled as if he hadn't had a bath since springtime. "A problem? Is there anything I can do?" She tried not to let her voice or face show her discomfort.

"I don't suppose you've seen a half-breed son of a—uh, fella here abouts?" Lester's leathery face was crinkled into a puzzled frown.

Renata managed to maintain a calm expression. "Do you by chance mean Jake Wolf?"

Lester stepped back. "Why, yes, ma'am. His horse showed up at the stable last night with blood all over the saddle, and Jake never goes anywhere without that stallion. I reckon he's lyin' dead out there somewhere." There was a decided lack of concern in Lester's voice that pricked at Renata's usually serene disposition. This man had discovered Jake's horse the night before, and he was just now getting around to looking for him?

"Jake Wolf is here," Renata said demurely. "He was shot yesterday, and he's sleeping right now. If you'd like to arrange for a doctor to come out and have a look at him—"

Lester took another step back. "A doctor? For Jake? Hell, he wouldn't have nothin' to do with no doctor. I'll just haul him on up to the bunkhouse and we'll keep an eye on him."

Until he was dead. Renata knew what the man was thinking. There was no way she was going to allow this man to haul Jake anywhere.

"No. I think he should remain here. He shouldn't be moved."

"Ma'am, I can't let you do that." Lester shook his graying head. "Ain't right."

"My father is a respected Philadelphia physician," Renata said, raising her voice slightly.

42

"I have assisted him for years in his practice, and I can assure you I know how to care for a gunshot wound." That wasn't exactly a lie. Her father had spoken once about a particularly nasty case, before her mother had insisted on dropping the unpleasant subject. Even if it was a lie, it was a necessary one. She knew Lester Patton would sit back and watch Jake die, if it came to that. What was wrong with these people?

"I'm sure you can, ma'am, but I reckon I better—"

Renata was very close to losing her temper, something she rarely did. So she took a deep breath and looked Lester Patton squarely in the eye. "The last time I handed a patient over to someone else the poor man died days later. I've never forgiven myself. So many nights I've wondered—" She sighed deeply. "Surely you can understand why I'm reluctant to turn this man's care over to anyone else."

"Yes, ma'am," Lester said. "But I—"

"Please, Mr. Patton," Renata pleaded, training saucerlike eyes on him. "I promise I'll go up to the big house and ask for you if Mr. Wolf's injury turns out to be more than I can handle."

Lester was still unsure, but Renata saw a bit of relief on his face. "Well," he finally said, "I do have my hands full at the moment, what with finishing the house and running the ranch. I reckon if you insist, Miz Parkhurst, we can leave Jake where he is."

"I'm so grateful to you, Mr. Patton." Renata smiled warmly as Lester backed away. Her opportunity to be rid of Jake Wolf had come and gone. Should she have handed Jake over to Lester Patton? Her instincts told her no. He was her responsibility, and no one would watch over him the way she would.

Renata bent over the stove in earnest, sniffing the stew to make sure it smelled edible. Her first meal; at least the first she had prepared alone. Her mother had never allowed her or Amalie near the kitchen, though they'd managed to sneak in and watch the cook now and again.

Fortunately, Melanie had a cookbook in her pantry, though it looked as if it had never been touched. Renata had followed the instructions to the letter, and her stew actually smelled good.

Jake hadn't made a sound, but Renata sensed he was watching her. She spun around and saw her patient standing in the doorway, leaning casually against the doorjamb.

"What are you doing out of bed?" she snapped, more irritated at being surprised than shocked to see him up and about. "You need several more days in bed, Mr. Wolf."

"Jake."

"What are you doing up?" she repeated, her anger fading rapidly.

"I smelled your cooking and it made me hungry," Jake said, not moving an inch. She wondered if he was really as casual as his stance implied, or if the doorjamb was holding him up. "I hope you're a better cook than Mel."

"I don't know if I am or not," Renata admitted. "This is the first meal I've ever prepared."

Jake grimaced. "I'm sorry to hear that."

Renata saw the subtle shaking of his legs and in a few short steps was beside him, wrapping her arm around his waist and drawing his arm over her shoulders. She hadn't remembered that he was so tall—at least a foot taller than she.

"Back to bed with you, Mr. Wolf."

"Jake."

Renata took small steps toward the hallway that led to the two bedrooms. "Are you going to be a difficult patient Mr. Wolf?"

He put very little weight on her, but he seemed steady, so she wasn't afraid he would fall.

"Probably, Red Rennie."

"I told you not to call me that."

"I told you not to call me Mr. Wolf."

Her head barely came to his shoulder, and Renata kept her eyes straight ahead so she wouldn't have to look at his chest.

"Red," he muttered. "Definitely, sort of . . . red."

"All right, Jake," Renata conceded, lowering him onto the bed. She'd been trying to avoid looking at him too closely. That bare chest was too disconcerting, and his face was even worse.

She hadn't come all the way to Colorado to become infatuated with a pretty face; she could have done that in Philadelphia.

Her eyes fell to the bloodstained trousers and she frowned. "We're going to have to get you a change of clothes."

"I've got clean clothes in the bunkhouse . . . the old bunkhouse out back." Jake laid his head back, closed his eyes, and let out a long breath.

"The long building by the barn?" Renata asked, leaning over him and feeling his forehead.

Jake cracked open one eye. "Yes," he said curtly. "No one else uses it anymore. There's a new bunkhouse closer to the big house."

Renata pulled her hand away. No fever, and that was a good sign. He'd be healed and gone before she knew it, and then she could concentrate on finding that rancher and her love at first sight.

"I'll bring you a change of clothes, and if the stew turns out to be edible, I'll bring you a bowl for dinner. If it doesn't . . . well, there are some canned goods in the pantry. I think I can make a meal out of . . ."

"What are you doing here, Renata Marie Parkhurst?" Jake asked tiredly.

"I told you; I came to see Melanie, but she wasn't here," Renata answered him shortly.

"You didn't write or send a telegram. If you had, they would have let you know that they wouldn't be here. Philadelphia is a long way away to just drop by." Jake looked up at her, and she frowned, pursing her lips. "Did you run away from home, Miss Parkhurst?"

"What if I did?" Renata looked away from him and out the window. "You should be thankful I decided to run away when I did. Otherwise you'd be in a sorry state right now."

Jake looked down at his calico bandage. "I guess that's true. But I wonder why a little girl with soft white skin who's never had to dirty her hands in the kitchen ran away from home."

Renata turned away from the window and frowned down at him. "I'm beginning to understand why who no one likes you, Mister—Jake. It's none of your business, but, yes, I did run away. And I have my reasons. My father was about to force me to marry a man I detest."

"Force you? I can't imagine," Jake said dryly.

"Neither could I. It was so unlike Daddy." Renata forgot for a moment that Jake was making fun of her, that he cared nothing for her problem, her dire dilemma. "Lord Edenworth is too old and too thin, and he can't dance at all," she said vehemently. "Daddy said I needed the discipline."

"No."

"Yes."

"How barbaric. To force you to marry a man who is thin and can't dance." Jake shook his head. "And old. How old is this ancient Lord Edenworth?"

"I'm not sure. Nearly forty, I would guess." Renata looked down at the wry smile on Jake's face and realized he was teasing her. "You despicable cad."

Jake closed his eyes, effectively shutting her out.

"I've been called worse."

When Jake opened his eyes he saw that he'd spoken to an empty room. Renata Marie Parkhurst had disappeared silently, leaving only a trace of her scent behind—a scent like crushed flowers—probably some expensive perfume that her daddy had bought to lure Lord Edenworth to his marital doom.

What on earth had driven him to get out of bed and search for her? It hadn't been any tantalizing smells that had lured him. It had been his own damn curiosity. He'd heard her in the kitchen, and he'd wanted . . . he'd needed another look at her. He'd wanted to know if she really was as pretty as he remembered.

He'd also wondered if she'd tell him that Lester Patton had stopped by that afternoon, and that she had sent Gabe's foreman away with a preposterous lie. Why had she done that and what did she want from him?

He was disgusted with himself, that he liked the feel of her hand on his forehead, that he liked the way the sun came through the window and lit her hair. She was just another spoiled little rich girl who judged people by appearances and broke men's hearts for her own amusement. But she smelled like crushed flowers . . .

He was still thinking about that scent when she reappeared in the doorway and tossed a clean pair of pants and a white shirt on the bed. "If you're capable of walking from here to the kitchen, you're certainly capable of dressing yourself."

Before Jake could think of a clever reply she was gone again, leaving only a hint of her fragrance behind.

The stew was not just edible; it was delicious. Jake didn't tell her that, but he finished the bowl and didn't complain. She knew it was good. He could tell by the triumphant look on her face.

She had obviously forgiven him for teasing her, because she smiled as she fed him. Renata lifted spoonfuls of stew to his lips, ignoring his protests that he was perfectly capable of feeding himself. It wasn't until the bowl was empty that he wondered if perhaps she had poisoned him . . . maybe that was the reason for her satisfied smile.

Jake gave her his best and coldest glare, a look guaranteed to frighten young girls and to keep anyone at a distance. But she met his gaze fully and continued to smile, and he found he couldn't maintain his icy look. There was something about the way she was looking at him that melted his determination. She had the greenest eyes, and the milkiest skin . . .

Jake looked away from her. She might be Mel's cousin, but under the skin she was Beryl Garrett's sister. Calculating. Shallow. Daddy's little girl, running away from the horrible fate of marrying a man who couldn't dance.

Renata sat silently through the meal, and for a few moments afterward Jake stared her down in an obvious attempt to frighten her. But it didn't work. She knew him better than he would ever know. So he liked to scare people; that was none of her concern. She didn't like to admit that it bothered her to sit at his bedside and feed a man who obviously didn't like her. She'd never in her life met anyone who openly disliked her. It was as disconcerting as his chiseled face and bare chest, a chest that was, thankfully, covered with a clean shirt by the time she'd returned to the bedroom with his dinner.

If he didn't want to talk to her, that was fine. She would do her Christian duty and see that he healed, and then she would go about her own business.

But the silence became awkward, and she decided to try to carry on a decent conversation with him. "Jake?" Renata leaned forward and ran her finger under his jaw. "How did you get that scar?"

Jake grabbed her by the wrist and pulled her hand away from his face. "That's none of your business, Renata Marie Parkhurst."

She gave him a dazzling smile, ignoring the

tight grip on her wrist. "You might as well call me Renata." She had decided there was nothing he could do to upset her. Nothing at all. He released her hand and she returned it to her lap. It was evident that Jake did not find conversation about himself acceptable.

"You know, you could be a great help to me, Jake."

Jake simply raised his eyebrows in response.

"You know this area fairly well, I would think. Are there very many unattached ranchers near Silver Valley?" She cocked her head to one side and kept her eyes on Jake's impassive face.

"Unattached as in unmarried?" Jake asked coldly.

Renata nodded.

"Is that why you're here? You're looking for a husband?"

She nodded again. "Yes. A rancher."

Jake shook his head in wonder and disbelief. "Why a rancher?"

Renata bit her lower lip and leaned a bit closer to the bed. "Have you seen the way Gabriel looks at Melanie?"

"Sure. I live here most of the time, or close by, anyway."

She whispered, forgetting who she was talking to, "I want someone to look at me that way. Since Gabriel's a rancher, I thought—"

"You can't go by that," Jake interrupted. "First of all, Gabe's a lousy rancher. Getting married and having a family didn't cure his

51

itchy feet. It's just that now when he gets the urge to wander he packs up Mel and the twins and takes them with him. Lester Patton does all the work when it comes to running the ranch, and I guarantee you, Lester is not your type."

"I'm certain there are other—"

"Trust me, Renata Marie Parkhurst. I hate to tell you, but I think what Mel and Gabe have is a one-in-a-million marriage. You're probably more likely to be struck by lightning than to find what you're looking for . . . especially in Silver Valley."

Renata stood suddenly. He was coming very close to irritating her, and she'd promised herself that wouldn't happen. "As likely as my taking advice from a man who's managed to alienate the entire town," she said crisply, her smile fading but never disappearing completely. "From what I've heard, nobody likes you, Jake, and I'm beginning to understand why."

"Nobody likes the truth, Renata Marie Parkhurst," Jake said coldly. "It's much too hard to take."

Chapter Four

Renata stood in the hallway as she peeked through the calico curtain she parted with her fingers. He certainly did sleep a lot, but she supposed that was good. At least there was still no fever, and for that she was grateful.

She held her breath and stepped into the room. There was something about Jake Wolf that drew her to him: a strength that made him powerful, even in his current condition; an energy that surpassed what Renata had ever known.

Renata was well aware of the fact that she had lived a charmed life. She'd wanted for nothing, had never endured any hardship. She had friends and a loving sister, and parents who loved her, though they sometimes demonstrated that love in domineering ways. Her life in Philadelphia had been very comfortable—and completely devoid of the energy she sensed in Jake. Some might call him dangerous—and they might be correct—but Renata sensed something more. Something beneath the danger and the power and the palpable energy.

Without thinking about it, Renata found herself beside the bed. Watching Jake sleep was fascinating, and she cocked her head as she boldly studied his face. Even in sleep there was a tension in it, a hardness that he never seemed to lose. What made a man so harsh?

She decided that her natural maternal instinct made her want to take away his pain, but what she felt as she looked down at him was anything but motherly. Why had none of the men who'd courted her in Philadelphia made her heart beat like this? Why had they been so . . . ordinary? Though anything but ordinary, Jake was also completely unacceptable as marriage material. Melanie and Gabriel had said kind words about Jake Wolf, but they had also mentioned that the man preferred wolves to people and was prone to disappear on a whim, often staying away for weeks at a time.

Renata had always been able to rationalize what she wanted, and she practiced that art as she watched Jake sleep. Yes, he was attractive, even with that awful stubbly beard on his face, and yes, she felt a strange urge to place her hands on that face. It was an urge so strong, she found herself clasping her hands tightly. Perhaps he did make her heart beat fast and her face feel warm. That could very well be fear she was feeling . . . though in all honesty she knew it wasn't.

But *he* wasn't what she had come to Colorado looking for.

Without warning, he opened his eyes, dark blue eyes that settled on her immediately. Why didn't he wake like normal people? Why didn't he stretch and yawn and blink his eyes as they slowly began to focus? His breathing hadn't even changed, for goodness sake. He'd just opened his eyes and looked at her in that piercing way he had.

"Well, it's about time," she said primly. "I was just wondering if I should have Lester Patton fetch a doctor for you."

"No doctor," Jake said gruffly. "You're doing fine."

Renata gave him a false smile to hide her consternation. "You're not afraid of doctors, are you, Jake?"

He shook his head in a way that made Renata wonder if he was afraid of anything.

"Are you afraid to let me take a razor to your face?" she asked as her hand reached out and touched the stubble on his chin. Her fingers barely touched him before she drew them back again.

He raised his eyebrows slightly at her question and touched his palm to a cheek. "I can shave myself."

Renata allowed herself a real smile, re-strained as it was. "So you are afraid," she said softly.

"Hell, why not." Jake slowly pushed himself into a sitting position. The muscles in his arms tightened and hardened until Renata had to force her eyes away. If only she could convince him to wear a shirt while he slept, perhaps she wouldn't be so distracted. His nakedness was positively decadent. She could feel her face growing warmer and knew she was blushing as Jake sat up and the sheet fell to his waist.

"I saw some of Gabriel's shaving implements in the other room," Renata said a bit too hastily. "I'll get them." She turned on her heel and hurried from the room, leaving a silent Jake Wolf.

Renata sat on the edge of the bed and worked a brush through the lather she'd prepared. Jake hadn't moved. He just watched with those cold eyes as she tried to avoid looking at him. That would be difficult to do once she began to shave him. What on earth had she been thinking when she'd offered to shave him? Obviously she hadn't been thinking at all, and anyway she had expected him to decline her offer. But he hadn't.

They were too close. All he would have to do was reach up and he could touch her. If he leaned forward, his face would be directly next to hers. She could only hope that he would do neither of those things.

With a slightly trembling hand, Renata began to lather his beard. Jake didn't move at all, but his eyes hardened.

"How many times have you done this?"

She lifted her eyes and looked into his as she finished and set the mug of lather aside. "Actually, to be honest, I never have. But I've watched my father shave once or twice, so I'm pretty sure I can do it—if you're very still."

Jake groaned. "You're trying to kill me, aren't you?"

His wry comment made her smile, and she forgot for a moment that he threatened to turn her world upside down. "I do imagine that if I wanted you dead I could think of a better and less messy way than this." She held the razor aloft.

Renata leaned forward slightly, and with a suddenly steady hand she scraped away a small section of the lathered beard. So far, so good. She wiped the razor on the linen towel that rested in her lap and tried again. Jake was a good customer, remaining perfectly still as she slowly shaved away his beard.

Jake cursed himself silently. Renata was painstakingly unhurried as she removed the week's growth from his face. At least she had quit chewing her lip, and her hands no longer trembled. All of her attention was on her task, and he could study her openly.

Her hands were so soft. Occasionally she rested her idle hand against his shoulder, an unconscious movement, until she realized that she was touching him and pulled her hand away. She was so close. He could smell her hair, that flowery fragrance he couldn't identify but had come to associate with her.

She scraped away another tiny section of lathered beard, and Jake cursed himself again. He could have done this, or he could have allowed his beard to grow for a while longer. But her assertion that he might be afraid to allow her to touch his face with a razor had challenged him in some way. Stupid. Now she was so close to him that he could feel her breath on his skin. Her fingers brushed against his cheek and her brilliant green eyes were fastened on his face.

She was so intent on her task that she didn't realize he was studying her so raptly . . . of that he was certain. What was it about her that bothered him so? Her smile? No one had ever smiled at him like that before. Her voice? She was silent now, as she focused all her attention on her efforts, but normally she talked to him incessantly. The way she looked at him when she thought he was sleeping?

"There now," she announced with satisfaction in her voice. "All done, and not a single scratch." Renata took a clean towel and wiped his face, brushing away the remnants of soap that dotted his cheeks. "You look much better."

Jake ran his hand over his cheeks, feeling for places she might have missed. But his face was smoothly shaven, and she hadn't nicked him once.

"Not bad," he declared glumly.

"You sound almost disappointed that I didn't cut you."

He watched her as she gathered her tools and prepared to leave the room. Her movements were just a bit too quick and her face was flushed, pink with evident embarrassment, as she looked all around the small room, looked everywhere but at him.

"Surprised," he assured her in a low voice. "Not disappointed."

Renata pulled herself to her full height and looked down at Jake, giving him her haughtiest stare. "From now on you can shave yourself."

Jake sighed with relief. "Good idea."

Renata's face fell as she turned away from him, and he had a brief glimpse of her flustered expression before she practically flew from the room.

Jake lay in the soft bed, caught between sleep and full awareness. He'd slept far too much in the past two weeks and now, even though it was the middle of the night and the cabin was quiet, he couldn't ease into a deep sleep.

His side was healing nicely, bound now by a plain white bandage. Renata was finally allowing him to eat at the table and to walk around the cabin for a short time in the afternoon. Allowing him—that was what she said and, God help him, that was how it felt. It was taking him much longer than he liked to get his strength back. He must have been nearer death than he'd imagined for his body to be so slow to heal.

Renata fussed over him all day, cleaning his wound with only a bit of squeamishness passing over her face, her hands as soft and gentle as a passing breeze. Her touch was feathery, never lingering against his skin.

She hadn't mentioned her reason for coming to Colorado again, her manhunt for some poor rancher who would no doubt be blindsided by her charm and her eyes and her hair. Jake couldn't decide who he pitied most, the rancher she was after or Renata herself. She was bound to be disappointed in her search for the perfect husband.

He had managed, with some great effort, to remain silent for the better part of the past two weeks, but she didn't seem to mind. Renata talked more than enough for the two of them, sometimes prattling on about people in Philadelphia he didn't know and would never meet. Normally, Jake became irritated at the sound of a ceaseless voice, particularly a woman's ceaseless voice, but after a while he became accustomed to Renata's timbre. It had a soothing quality, and he lay back and let it wash over him.

For the past week he had been shaving himself every day, afraid that if he neglected that chore, Renata would offer to do it for him. He couldn't take that again.

The low rumbling of thunder in the distance foretold a coming storm. It had been several weeks since they'd had a really good rain, and a summer that was too hot and dry wasn't healthy for man or beast. A good rain was just what the ranch needed . . . just what he needed. Jake rolled from the bed and opened the window, propping up the glazed pane with a stick that lay on the windowsill for that purpose. He wanted to smell the coming rain.

The breeze picked up, and a rush of cool air ruffled the curtains and rushed over his body. Jake closed his eyes and took a deep breath. Wounded or not, he'd been inside too long. It was stifling.

"What are you doing out of bed?" Renata asked, and Jake turned to see her watching him from the doorway. It was a question he was becoming accustomed to, but it was usually delivered with a bit more energy. This was a whispered inquiry, low and only slightly curious.

"Letting in some fresh air. Do you approve, doctor?"

She didn't answer, hugging her dressing gown to her body.

"There's a storm coming." Jake moved away from the window, and the slice of moonlight that peeked through the clouds lit the ghostly figure in the doorway.

There was another long, low rumble of thunder, and Renata shivered visibly. "I don't like storms," she said softly. "Before my sister

Amalie married I would sneak into her room when a storm came at night. After she left home I had to wait out the storms in my room. I was far too old to run to Daddy and hide my face in his shoulder . . . as I did when I was a little girl." She looked him square in the eye, unsmiling and undaunted. "I should have stayed in my own bed and buried my head under the covers, but I thought I would come sit with you for a little while. I did think you would be asleep, so I guess it was a silly notion."

Jake returned to the bed, but he placed his plumped pillows against the headboard and sat up, his legs stretched in front of him. She was truly afraid; that much was clear.

"This is a good, sturdy cabin," he reassured her. "A little wind and rain won't wash us away."

Renata stepped into the room, her eyes on the window as a distant streak of lightning lit the sky. "I know," she whispered. "I'm not afraid."

"You're not a very good liar, Renata Marie Parkhurst." Jake watched her walk slowly toward the window, a woman drawn to that which frightened and yet fascinated her.

Another flash of lightning lit the room, and he saw a quick smile pass over her face.

"Actually, I'm a very good liar, as long as there's a bit of truth in what I say. I can almost convince myself of anything . . . for a while. Will it be very bad, do you think?" She looked over at him, a question in her eyes, trusting and guileless. A long braid fell over her shoulder, and a few loose curls framed her face. Her dressing gown was belted at the waist, accentuating a figure that made him shiver as surely as the thunder had made her shiver. The thunder was growing closer, following the flashes of lightning more closely.

"Don't get too close to the window," he warned. "If you have to watch, move the chair back a little and have a seat."

"I don't want to watch," Renata said, but she placed the single chair in the room directly in front of the window, then pulled it back several feet before she sat down gingerly.

The thunder and lightning that followed were closer, much closer, and Renata jumped. The first drops of rain fell, large and driven by the wind, a few errant drops blowing through the open window and landing at Renata's feet. The wind that had cooled Jake earlier rushed over her, pushing back the tendrils of hair that framed her face and pressing her dressing gown to her body.

"It's beautiful, though," she said, her voice still low. "Bright and beautiful and dangerous."

"Yes, it is," Jake agreed, his eyes never leaving her. "Very beautiful. Very dangerous."

She turned to look at him. "This is highly improper, you know," she said with a small smile. "Sitting here in the middle of the night, staying in this cabin without a chaperon. Very improper. But this is Colorado, not Philadelphia."

Jake thought it best to change the subject. "Why are you so afraid of storms?"

Renata laughed. "I don't know. It's not a rational fear. I don't really believe that I'll be struck by lightning, or that the cabin will be washed away by a terrific storm. It just stirs up something inside me that I can't control. My heart beats fast, I shiver all over, and every time the thunder crashes my heart skips a beat." As if on cue, a loud boom sounded above their heads. "Like that."

Jake watched her as she stared out the window, the lightning playing across her face, dancing across her hair like fire, proving to him that her face was as white as the lightning itself.

He stared at her for so long, he almost jumped when she turned to look at him. "Tell me a story, Jake."

"What?"

"A story." She smiled, ghostly in the moonlight. "Melanie told me that you tell wonderful stories that your grandfather told you when you were a little boy."

"My grandfather was a full-blooded Cheyenne," Jake said defensively.

"I know," Renata said softly, returning her gaze to the window.

"You do?"

"Melanie told me."

"He was killed at the Washita River Massacre," Jake said sharply.

"I know."

"Mel talks too much."

Renata sighed deeply. "If you'd rather not tell a story, just say so. For goodness sake, Jake."

He sat silently in the middle of the bed for several minutes. Why did she never act as he expected her to? She should have sent him away with Lester that first afternoon. She should have trembled with fear when he glared at her. She should have shuddered in distaste when he mentioned his heritage. But she'd done none of those things. In fact, she continued to look at him as if she expected something more.

He told her the tale of Sweet Grass, the boy, who grew to be called Sweet Medicine, and the four sacred arrows. It was a tale every Cheyenne youth heard at an early age, and the words flowed off Jake's tongue as his grandfather's own telling came back to him. The worst of the storm passed as frequent flashes of lightning filled the room with light, and the thunder, not rumbling, cracked above their heads.

Renata turned her attention from the storm to Jake. She listened, no longer jumping every time the thunder crashed.

By the time Jake finished his story the thunder and lightning had abated, and the rain had begun to fall even harder than before, landing on the cabin floor near the open window in a near torrent.

"You have a good voice for telling a story," Renata said when he was finished, her relief that the storm was passing evident in her voice and in her calm face.

Jake jumped from the bed—too fast—and felt pain in his side. He tried not to show it, but Renata seemed to see everything.

"What are you doing?"

"I was going to close the window," he said through clenched teeth.

Renata lowered the window, putting an edge of the stick under the window to allow a little fresh air in. "For goodness sake, I was going to do that."

The old Renata was back. In charge. Unafraid. Ordering him back to bed. She moved the chair against the wall and turned to leave the room.

"Aren't you going to tuck me in?" Jake asked wryly, expecting a haughty glare in reply. But Renata did an about-face and hovered over him, straightening his quilt and roughly plumping his pillows.

"I swear. A twenty-nine-year-old baby is what I've got on my hands." She looked all around him. At the quilt, at the pillows, even at the floor.

"It seems Mel told you a lot about me." He was half angry and half curious. "Didn't the two of you have anything better to talk about when she visited you?"

"I assure you, we had many conversations about more interesting subjects than yourself, Mr. Wolf."

"How unkind you are, Red Rennie. What

else did Mel tell you about me, besides my family history, my age, and my talent for telling a tale?"

Renata looked down at him then. "She said you couldn't seem to get along with anybody, and as I told you before, I can see why."

Jake grabbed her wrist when she tried to walk away from him. "What? No kiss good night?" His voice was gruff, with no hint of tenderness.

"Don't be ridiculous." Renata was trying to sound determined and cold but fell short on both counts. He could feel the small, deep tremor that passed through her body. "You know why I came to Colorado, and my plans don't include a . . . a . . . half-civilized, moody . . ."

"Say it, Renata." He released her hand abruptly. "Half-breed. Was that the word on the tip of your tongue?"

She pursed her lips and didn't confirm or deny his accusation.

"Good night, Jake." She turned her back on him and walked out of the room.

Chapter Five

Renata finished her morning chores frowning. She had pulled her hair back and tied it with a pink ribbon that matched her deep rose day dress. She'd found most of her wardrobe unsuitable for her new life, but a few of her simpler dresses served her quite well. But her clothes were not the reason for the frown that marred her usually happy face. It was her patient. Apparently, Jake was a fast healer, though he moved around the cabin a bit slowly. But still, his movements were steady and purposeful, and she knew he'd be ready to leave any day now, and would as soon as he was able.

Jake had hardly spoken to her since the night of the storm a week ago, the night he had believed she had rejected him because of his

Indian blood. He had said that, not she, and she had allowed him to believe it simply by not denying his accusation. That had been easier at the time than trying to explain the truth.

But what was the truth? she asked herself, and not for the first time. That she was attracted to him? Definitely. And why not? He was handsome, and muscular, and she knew enough about him to see through his scowls and frowns. That she was falling in love with him? Impossible. Out of the question. Definitely not in her plans.

So why did the thought of him leaving upset her?

An unexpected sound close to the house made her jump, yanking her from her reverie. A thud, followed by a cracking sound, and then another loud thud. One of the hands from the big house? Doing what?

She wiped her hands on a freshly cleaned linen towel and walked through the main room to the front door, stepping onto the porch and catching the late morning sun in her eyes. She had but to turn her head slightly to see the source of the noise.

Jake was standing near the barn, his arms raised, an ax handle gripped in both hands. He was wearing nothing but his buckskin trousers and an old pair of boots, and the thin white bandage that Renata insisted he wear wrapped around his waist a even though he no longer needed it.

Muscles rippled across his back. Sweat was

already glistening on his shoulders, his back, and his arms, and as he lowered the ax she heard a low grunt just before the ax met the log that was standing on end. The log split in two and a cracking sound filled the air.

"What do you think you're doing?" Renata ran down the steps and toward her stubborn patient. She stopped several feet short of him when he turned and gave her his familiar scowl. He hadn't been exerting himself for very long, and it wasn't all that hot, but there were already drops of sweat on his face. A bead ran from his temple to his jaw, snaking slowly across his cheek. The sight of that simple bead of sweat angered her.

"Chopping wood. Getting my strength back." His words were harsh, his eyes fierce.

Renata shook her head. "That look doesn't scare me, Jake. We already have plenty of wood, and you're not getting your strength back; you're sapping what little you have. Now, get back into your bed this instant."

Jake glared at her, and she glared right back. It was clear he was unaccustomed to allowing anyone to tell him what to do, and he didn't like it one bit. Those dark blue eyes tried to burn her, but she didn't back down.

"I'm fine. A little exercise will do me good."

"No."

Jake raised his eyebrows, and Renata felt her face grow warm as he watched her. "No?" He took a step forward, and Renata took a small step back. "No?"

Renata watched as his face changed, from angry to irritated to amused. He wasn't actually smiling, but his mouth turned up at the corners. He took another step toward her, and she unconsciously stepped back as he approached her. "Stop that, Jake Wolf!" she said sharply.

"Stop what?" He took another step forward. "You said yourself that I'm nothing more than a sickly, old, weak man who should be confined to his bed."

Renata knew what he was thinking as an unexpected sparkle lit his eyes. It was a challenge . . . a dare. "You couldn't catch me even if I did agree to participate in your childish, foolish game."

"Are you sure, little girl?"

Renata needed only a moment to think about it. He couldn't possibly run very far. So she turned on her heel and ran as fast as she could, which admittedly wasn't very fast. She lifted her skirts in her hands and dashed across the lawn, laughing in spite of herself. It had been ages since she'd allowed herself to frolic like a child.

She could hear him behind her, his booted feet landing on the grassy earth, his harsh breathing growing closer and closer. She wanted to turn her head and see how near he was, but she knew if she did, he'd have her for sure. She expected him to stop at any moment, but he stayed with her, drawing closer and closer until she felt his long arm snake around her waist and they both fell into the grass.

The very breath was knocked out of her as she hit the ground, and Jake covered her body with his, his labored breathing in her ear. For a moment he didn't move, and Renata twisted beneath him until she could see his face.

"Jake? Are you all right?"

His face was inches from hers and his dark blue eyes were half closed as he studied her intently. She could see the pain and distress in his eyes, in the lines of the face, which was so close.

"I'm fine."

She took a deep breath and felt her body expand against his. "Well then, you were right. You're all better."

Renata wondered, for a moment, if he was going to kiss her. He hadn't moved to get up, and she was pinned to the ground by his weight. He was giving her the strangest look, one without his usual stoic iciness or his stubborn willfulness. His black hair fell around his face, and if she could have moved her hands she would have brushed it away so she could see him better. It should be against the law for a man to be so beautiful.

"No," Jake said when he finally spoke. "You were right. I can't move."

Renata's look was more than slightly triumphant. "I told you so. Next time I tell you . . ."

"Can you gloat later?" Jake interrupted her.

"Of course. Can you move at all? Are you bleeding again? Try to take a deep breath." Renata said it all in one long, fast breath, not waiting for any answers as she worked her arms up and around Jake's neck. "Move very slowly to your right. Just roll slightly. Stop if it hurts too much."

She pressed against him and they rolled together, slowly and deliberately, until his weight was off her and Renata was lying on top of him. Jake closed his eyes and took a deep breath, and Renata could see that it pained him. But he said nothing.

She could feel his heart beating against hers, could feel his breath on her face. Jake was so strong, but still he needed her. Melanie had told her so much about him, and one thing came to mind now. Melanie said that one day Jake Wolf would meet a woman who wasn't frightened half to death even of his fiercest stare . . . and heaven help them both when that happened. Renata had been on the receiving end of more than a few of those stares, and they didn't scare her . . . not in the least.

She kissed him and pulled away before he had a chance to react. She wasn't certain why she had done it. It was an impulse she had given in to, as she often did.

Jake's eyes flew open. "What the hell did you do that for?"

Renata pouted. That was not the reaction she had expected. "You just . . . looked like you needed a kiss."

They might have remained there a while longer, and Renata might even have decided to kiss Jake again, but the sound of an embarrassed man clearing his throat brought Renata to her feet. Donnie Boyle was standing several feet away, close to the porch, with an armful of supplies.

"I brung you a few groceries, Miss Parkhurst," Donnie said glumly, refusing to look directly at her. "I'll just leave them in the kitchen." He turned away and strode into the house, and Renata turned to look at her patient lounging in the grass.

"This is all your fault," she hissed. "Can you imagine what Mr. Boyle must think?"

Jake rolled slowly into a sitting position. "He probably thinks we were rolling around in the grass and you decided I looked like I needed a kiss. Pretty accurate, wouldn't you say?"

Renata didn't have a chance to reply before Donnie Boyle came out of the house, his head down as he headed for his buckboard. Renata realized that she should have heard the conveyance approaching the cabin, but she hadn't.

"Thank you, Mr. Boyle." Renata moved quickly to catch up with him. "It's very kind of you . . ."

Donnie Boyle turned to her, frowning. "I warned you about Jake Wolf," he said in a low voice, his disappointment evident.

"I know you did, but . . ." Renata stopped. Boyle's eyes widened as he looked over her shoulder. She turned her head and saw that Jake was approaching them, very slowly.

"I see you can move again," she snapped.

"Yes, sugar," he answered, to her mortification. "I finally got my strength back." His words seemed to have a double meaning, and he delivered them with a sardonic lift of his brows. He reached out and plucked a long blade of grass from her hair, dropping it to the ground as he placed his arm around her shoulders familiarly.

Donnie Boyle paled and turned away.

"Sugar?" Renata pushed Jake's arm off her.

"Yes, dear?" Jake responded, and Renata realized that it was too late. Donnie Boyle was leaving.

Renata watched the buckboard disappear with a sinking heart. Her reputation was ruined. She would never find a respectable rancher anywhere near Silver Valley who would have her for a wife. All her plans . . . for nothing.

Jake watched her storm into the cabin, her red-gold hair dancing down her back, blades of grass in her hair and sticking to her rose-colored dress. He wasn't certain why he'd done it . . . why he made certain Donnie Boyle left the ranch under the wrong impression. Actually, he did know, but it made no sense.

He didn't want Renata Marie Parkhurst to marry a rancher and settle near Silver Valley. Somewhere deep inside he had begun to think of her as his . . . though he knew it was a foolish delusion. He didn't want to see her and her husband come to Sunday dinner with Mel and

Gabe, or to watch her grow fat with another man's child. . . .

That thought stopped him completely. It was time for him to get away from the ranch, away from Silver Valley and the invisible bonds that had held him there too long. What did it matter who she married? It didn't. Not at all. He took a painful step toward the cabin, and Renata burst through the door, as if she'd been waiting for him to make a move.

"Don't you dare come near this cabin, Jake Wolf." He saw real anger in her eyes as she glared at him. "From now on you can sleep in the bunkhouse."

"What's the matter? Afraid all this might appear to be just a bit improper?"

"You've ruined everything. You know that. You did it on purpose." She stamped her foot, and he could see, even from where he stood, that her eyes were filling with tears. Unfamiliar pangs of regret pricked at Jake.

"I didn't mean . . ."

"Yes, you did. You deliberately let Mr. Boyle think . . . well, you know. Before the sun sets everybody in Silver Valley will be thinking the same thing. I'm ruined. I'll probably have to go to Texas to find myself a rancher now, and it gets so hot in Texas in the summertime."

"Still set on a rancher husband?" Jake asked coolly.

"Yes," Renata answered defiantly. "Perhaps you could introduce me to your father."

Jake didn't move, and his look was impassive,

but he was certain she knew she had touched a nerve. "My father is already married. The Cheyenne often take more than one wife, but most ranchers only allow one bitch to a household." Jake didn't give her a chance to respond. The shocked look on her face was satisfaction enough. She deserved it. Surely she knew. Surely Mel had told her the whole story—or at least what Mel knew of it. Nobody knew it all. Nobody knew it all but Jake and his father and a few ghosts. Ghosts he'd tried in vain to bury.

But Renata Marie Parkhurst certainly understood that he didn't see, or speak of, or acknowledge his father in any way. He hadn't in fourteen years. As he walked toward the bunkhouse, he heard the front door of the cabin slam, and his thumb unconsciously went to the scar beneath his jaw. He rubbed it several times without thinking about what he was doing. It was faded now, white and thin, and he often caught himself rubbing his thumb against the rough texture when he was lost in thought. It was an old scar. A fourteen-year-old one, to be exact.

Jake slowly sank onto the bunk and let his mind wander back through the years. His earliest memory was of his mother, Snow Flower Woman, who was the daughter of the great Cheyenne warrior Six Bears and a white captive who had chosen to stay with the tribe. He remembered his mother as being very beautiful, with straight black hair and twinkling brown eyes. His grandfather, Six

Bears, had told Jake that Snow Flower Woman had always been a willful child, and that once she'd met Harrison Summers she would have no other man as a husband.

Of course, Harrison Summers and Snow Flower Woman were never really married, at least not in any white man's ceremony. Not even after Jake was born.

His mother called him Little Wolf, and his father called him Jake Summers. He remembered the morning his mother woke him and took him from his bed, holding a finger to her lips to silence him, slipping from the Summers ranch before the sun was up and the hands were about. She told him it was time for his father to take a new wife, and time for them to return to the village where she had grown up. Jake knew this could mean only one thing: His father had thrown them out so he could take a white wife.

For several years Jake was taken to the Summers ranch for summertime visits. It was never his mother who accompanied him on the long trip, but a relative who left Jake with his father. Snow Flower Woman never saw Harrison Summers again after her early morning escape from his ranch.

When the weather turned cool another Cheyenne cousin would fetch Jake, Little Wolf, and together they would return to the Indian village before they moved to their winter camp. Always his father would ask him to stay. Always a sullen Jake would say no.

One summer she was there ... the white woman who was his father's new wife. She hated Jake. He knew it even as she smiled at him with hate in her eyes and in her heart. His father said to call her Mother Summers, but Jake refused. She said he could call her Miss Corinne, and he had nodded silently. He tried never to speak to her or of her, and he couldn't remember ever actually speaking her name.

When Jake was nine he had seen his mother killed at the Sand Creek Massacre. He almost died himself that day but was pulled away from his mother's body by an older cousin. He survived, and so had his grandfather.

The following summer Jake was taken to his father's ranch as usual, and he had told Harrison Summers of his mother's death in an emotionless, tearless voice. Summers was a tough man, a hard man, but there were tears in his eyes. Jake thought they were tears of guilt, since he had sent Snow Flower Woman away.

That year, when his Cheyenne uncle came to take Jake back to the village, Harrison Summers practically begged his son to stay. Jake refused, as he always did, and for a moment he thought his father was going to try to force him to stay. He didn't realize until much later that his father had been terrifed for his only son. The life of the Indian at that time was changing. Food was growing scarce, as the buffalo were killed off in a deliberate attempt to starve the remaining independent Indians. Army officers, career Indian killers, came to the West looking to make names for themselves.

Four years after his mother's death, Jake had seen his grandfather shot and scalped at the Washita River. Jake had made another narrow escape, but this time there was no village to return to . . . no relatives for Jake except his father and Miss Corinne.

So Jake returned to his father's ranch, this time to stay. He found Miss Corinne expecting her first child—and as full of hate as ever. She didn't like the idea of taking in Harrison Summers's half-breed son on a permanent basis. Jake was thirteen that year, and big for his age, dressed in fringed buckskins and moccasins. He never went anywhere without at least one knife strapped at his side, and his eyes were defiant and angry. He was, in fact, a frightful sight.

Harrison Summers had been delighted to have his son on the ranch. It took a while, but eventually they cut Jake's hair and dressed him in denims and cotton shirts and leather boots. For a while he was uncomfortable, but he grew to like the sturdy clothing and the respect he got from the workers on the ranch. Jake was a hard worker himself, but he was also the owner's son—and a child on the threshold of manhood.

He learned to accept and even to enjoy the roof over his head, the varied meals—an abundance of food that would have fed a small tribe for a week—and he no longer thought of himself as Little Wolf. He was Jake Summers, and he had a real home.

That idyllic existence had lasted for two years . . . and then it had come to a crashing end.

Jake rolled over and ignored the pain in his side. The incident that had driven him from his father's house had taught him a valuable lesson. Women would do anything to get what they wanted: lie, cheat, deceive. And they all wanted the same thing: money, power, a rancher husband . . .

He had almost forgotten that lesson when he met Beryl Garrett, but he wouldn't forget it again.

Chapter Six

During the next few days, the women of Silver Valley came to the cabin alone or with friends and daughters, bringing cakes, warm loaves of bread, smoked meats, and fresh vegetables. They arrived, each and every one of them, hoping to find Renata and Jake Wolf rolling in the grass just as Donnie Boyle had. Renata knew that was the reason for their visits, that despite their gifts and their smiles they came looking for gossip, the lifeblood of a small town. And they expected to have nothing but contempt for Mel's Philadelphia cousin.

But she charmed them all, pouring cup after cup of tea, praising every sweet, pastry, and loaf that passed under her nose. She asked for recipes for the vegetables, and admired calico and lace and hats festooned with ribbons. She easily swayed the ladies of Silver Valley, even the preacher's wife and the schoolteacher, a sour and judgmental pair who seemed to stick together on every subject that was discussed, no matter how trivial.

Jake always made brief, but memorable appearances, and as he had discarded his bandage he had also abandoned the simple courtesy of donning a shirt when he left the shelter of the bunkhouse. He stormed about in nothing more than his buckskin trousers and soft moccasins, so she couldn't even hear him approaching. More than once she had turned to find him watching her, that all too familiar scowl on his too perfect face.

Now, as she looked at her guests, she pushed thoughts of Jake away.

"It must be very exciting to be married to the sheriff," Renata said as she poured second cups of tea for the women. "Frightening at times, I would imagine, Mrs. Collins."

"Call me Sylvia, dear." The sheriff's wife leaned forward and took the steaming cup. "Fortunately, Silver Valley is not an exciting town to live in. Walter spends most of his time making sure the town drunks don't break up the saloon. He's forever locking them up for a day or two, and then they're right back at the bottle again. And then there's . . . but forgive me, Miss Parkhurst. What an unpleasant subject."

Renata smiled at the woman. She was already tired of the constant parade of callers. Still, that morning she had put on a lovely yellow day dress with a touch of delicate lace at the throat and a full skirt that seemed to float around her as she walked. "I'm certain the presence of a strong authority figure in Silver Valley is what allows it to remain the quiet little town it is." She turned her attention to Sylvia Collins's daughter, a washed-out looking girl, though she couldn't be more than seventeen. Her hair was light brown and her eyes were the same. The dress she wore was an unsightly yellow-green that made her face look sallow.

"Felicia." Renata didn't acknowledge the fact that the girl nearly jumped out of her skin when her name was called. "I do admire your hat." She nodded to the wide-brimmed straw hat that rested on Felicia's lap. "I imagine if I am to stay here for any length of time I will need something like it to keep the sun off my face. Did you purchase it at the Boyles' general store?"

Felicia nodded, too shy even to answer such a simple question. Being unable to speak was a problem from which Renata had never suffered.

"Perhaps we could go shopping one day," Renata continued, "and you could help me choose a proper bonnet." She liked the quiet young girl better than the mother; Felicia was very close to her own age and looked as if her life could use a little fixing. "You could introduce me to the dressmaker. Melanie tells me she's quite talented."

Felicia smiled, but just a little. "She's very good. And sometimes Mrs. Boyle can order store-made dresses."

"But there's nothing quite like a well-made gown that's been crafted just for you." Renata would never admit to a stranger that all of her clothes had to be specially made, because she was short, and her breasts too large and her waist too small. She'd been told she had a perfect hourglass figure, but she would have much preferred to be tall and slender, like Amalie.

She was about to sigh with relief when Sylvia and Felicia Collins prepared to leave without Jake having made an appearance. Maybe just this once . . .

"What's for dinner, sugar?" He came striding through the front door, shirtless as usual. "Sorry. I didn't realize you had company."

Renata had to bite her lip to keep from shouting, "The devil you didn't!"

Sylvia Collins looked at her feet, finding the tips of her shoes of sudden interest. Felicia stared openly at Jake's bare chest, her face turning pink and her mouth clamped shut. Renata knew all too well how disconcerting the sight of that bare chest could be, especially to a young girl like Felicia, who blinked twice and turned to Renata.

"Come to see me anytime, Miss Parkhurst, and I'll show you around town." Her eyes were still wide, and her face flooded with color as she avoided looking at the man in the doorway.

85

"Call me Renata," she insisted almost flatly, but her eyes were on Jake and not on her guests. Her smile was gone and her eyes narrowed as Jake walked to her and planted a quick kiss on her cheek. Renata tried to pull away, but Jake caught her and held her with one arm—a long, well-muscled arm. Felicia watched them and sighed.

Renata tried to bid her new friends good-bye with decorum, but her face was so warm she knew she was as red as Felicia, and her attempts at explaining away Jake's behavior, claiming that he was just teasing the three of them, were met with the same disbelief with which she had been confronted all week. No one in Silver Valley could accept Jake as a kidder. No one.

Renata knew, from the look on Felicia's face, that Jake had appeared behind her as she waved good-bye from the front porch. She saw, with a turn of her head, that he was leaning nonchalantly in the open doorway, a huge chunk of the loaf of bread the sheriff's wife had baked in his hand. As she watched, he took a big bite, and then laid his hand on her shoulder. She shook it off, but his move had served its purpose: The ladies had seen it.

Renata turned and faced him. "You are beneath contempt," she said coldly. "It's bad enough that you parade yourself around here dressed like a savage, that you continue to insist on perpetuating this . . . this lie. . . ." He stood in the doorway, blocking her path, his blue eyes steady as he glared at her. "But must you stand there and eat like a savage as well?" She snatched the bread from his hand.

"Are my table manners the worst of my offenses?" he asked icily.

"Not by a long shot. It's just a brand-new offense." Renata's eyes fell to Jake's side; she couldn't help it. He was healing well, but there would be a nasty scar. There were other, smaller scars on his arms and his back, so small that she only saw them when he was very close to her. She thought, before she could stop herself, that the scar on his side marred his perfection. Nonsense! Jake Wolf was far from perfect!

"Why are you still here?" she asked, exasperated. "You're certainly well enough to travel."

Jake didn't answer for a few minutes. Why *was* he still there? He couldn't admit to Renata that he couldn't explain even to himself why he was still at the cabin, sleeping in the bunkhouse, when he could have been sleeping in the mountains. He certainly couldn't tell her that he felt a growing attraction to her that was inexplicable. That every day he expected to walk into the cabin, see her, and realize that she was not the vision he had dreamed of the night before . . . and every day he was disappointed. Somehow she looked a little prettier every day, a little brighter.

Which was why he had to get her away from Silver Valley. The arrangements had been made, and she would soon be on her way back to Philadelphia . . . back to where she belonged.

"I'm leaving tomorrow," he said solemnly, still refusing to step aside. His arms were crossed over his chest as he blocked her path.

Renata smiled. It was a real smile, not the stiffening of her lips he'd seen lately as she tried to act as though his charade didn't bother her. A real smile that made her green eyes sparkle and her cheeks flush slightly with a pink glow. "Tomorrow? Really?"

"Really," Jake said, stepping aside for her to brush past him and move into the cabin. "As soon as I put you on the stage."

"I'm not going anywhere." Renata turned to him, spinning around in a graceful motion, all yellow and red-gold and milky white.

"Yes, you are. You're going home."

"I most certainly am not," Renata insisted.

Jake hesitated. They could stand there all day and not finish this argument. "If I have to truss you up and toss you in the back of the buckboard with your trunks, I will." He turned away from her, and she failed to challenge his threat. She believed him, and that was good. He walked out the door, his long strides carrying him away from her quickly.

Renata stood in the middle of the main room, speechless for once in her life. Home. She couldn't go home. Not yet!

Then Jake appeared at the door, stalked into

the room, scowling, pulled her against him with a low curse, and kissed her.

This was not a kiss on the cheek like the ones with which he had favored her when her company came calling. This was a kiss that locked his lips to hers, and he held her so tightly against his chest, she could barely breathe.

Renata dropped the slab of bread and beat her hands against Jake's imprisoning arms. What was he doing to her? His arms were like restraining iron bands. The heat from his body enveloped her, and his heart pounded against hers. His mouth was hard and demanding, his arms as intractable as Jake himself.

And then something changed. He still held her, but not quite so tightly. His lips still pressed against hers, but they too had softened. He moved his mouth gently, parting his lips and flicking his tongue against hers.

Renata stopped pounding. There was an alien and not-at-all-unpleasant feeling in the pit of her stomach, though it felt more like it lodged at the pit of her soul. So this was what it was like to be properly kissed, she thought as she wrapped her arms around Jake's waist and pressed her palms against his back. His skin was warm to her touch, hard yet silky.

She felt as though she were dissolving in his arms, would never be able to stand if he weren't holding her up. He pushed his tongue between her lips and she parted them willingly, taking what he offered: the heat, the fire that blazed within her, the tingling down her spine. One of his large hands moved to cradle the back of her head, and he wrapped his fingers through her hair as a low moan escaped his throat.

They both heard the booted footsteps at the same time, and Renata jumped back as Jake released her. There was the strangest look in his blue eyes, as if he was as unsure of what had happened as she was.

Lester Patton stood in the doorway, his face as red as a fresh strawberry, his hat in his hand. Renata had seen Lester several times since their first encounter, when he had offered to take Jake away, and he had always been respectful and polite. And somehow he managed to maintain his unchanging layer of dust and filth.

"I brung over the buckboard like you asked, Jake," he said, his eyes never leaving the floor. "You sure you don't need me to drive . . ."

"I'll do it," Jake said coldly.

"Sure will hate to see you leave, Miss Parkhurst." Lester's eyes were focused on either the floor or the tips of his dusty boots.

Renata stared at Jake. Another one of his performances! He had seen Lester coming, and that was why he had come back inside and kissed her. Part of her anger, she knew, stemmed from the fact that she had enjoyed the kiss so much. Jake Wolf must be so proud of himself!

Before she had time to think about what she was doing, Renata drew back her hand and slapped him as hard as she could. She had never struck anyone before, had never even been tempted. Her palm stung and turned red, and she saw the evidence of her attack on his cheek.

The crack of the blow caused Lester's head to snap up. He looked almost frightened . . . of her? For her? Renata knew that Jake was considered a dangerous and unpredictable man . . . not one to be trifled with. But she wasn't afraid of him, a man who was capable of making her lose herself in his kiss and then moments later infuriate her: two unknown emotions for Renata.

"I'm not going anywhere, Mr. Patton," she said calmly. "At least, not until I see Melanie." She knew she'd never find a husband in Silver Valley. Jake had seen to that. But she wouldn't allow him to run her out of town! She was nearly twenty years old and she was almighty tired of being told what to do!

"Yes, you are," Jake said in a deep, ominous voice.

"No, I'm not!" Renata snapped.

"Yes, you are . . ."

Renata stamped her foot . . . a childish gesture, she knew, as soon as she had done it.

Jake just glared at her and raised an eyebrow. He looked so blasted smug!

He turned away from her, and Lester Patton quickly moved away from the doorway, evidently relieved that he had not been forced to step into the middle of their little altercation.

Chapter Seven

Renata had packed her trunks because Jake
had threatened to leave everything she owned
behind if she didn't. She was dressed in an
apricot muslin traveling suit that made her
milky skin glow because he had threatened to
dress her himself. She had climbed into the seat
of the buckboard because he had threatened
to toss her in the back with her trunks if she
didn't. It had been a long and tiring morning
for both of them even before they had pulled
away from the Maxwell cabin.

Now silent as they traveled, Jake hid a fire-
storm of emotions behind his calm exterior.
As far as he was concerned, emotions were
a weakness, and he didn't know how to deal
with them. Hate, fear, sadness, happiness . . .
love. Jake had known little love in his life,

but he knew it made a man weak, just like the other emotions he denied. But whenever he looked at Renata Marie Parkhurst he felt those long-buried emotions just beneath the surface.

It made no sense at all. She was everything he hated in a woman: vain, pretty, silly; a city girl who talked too much. The only logical way to handle the situation was to get her away from Silver Valley, as far away as possible.

His unwilling passenger was, remarkably, silent. Jake kept his eyes on the road, never glancing sideways even when he felt her eyes on him. It was a disquieting feeling, but he knew when she was looking at him . . . almost knew what she was thinking.

"Why on earth are you dressed like that?" she asked sharply, as if she'd just realized what he was wearing. Jake was dressed in a skin-tight pair of fringed buckskin pants and a fringed shirt decorated with—she leaned closer to him to make certain she wasn't mistaken, and then leaned away quickly when she realized she was correct—the sharp teeth of some poor animal. Jake wore a beaded belt over his long shirt, and a wicked-looking knife rested at his hip. He had even tied a beaded headband across his forehead and knotted it at the back of his head. He looked every bit the wild Indian.

"I always dress like this when I go to town," he said simply, not looking at her.

"Why?" she pressed.

"Because it's expected of me."

Renata sighed deeply, losing a bit of her anger when she heard the bitterness in his voice. "For goodness sake, Jake. It's expected of you? You feel obligated to play the barbarian because the town expects it of you?" She shook her head. "It's much more fun to give people what they least expect."

"Is that what you do?"

Renata actually seemed to give his question serious thought, even though it was delivered with a cynical bite. "No. Normally I do exactly what's expected of me. Running away was my first act of defiance. Probably my last." She sighed. "It didn't work out exactly as I planned." There was a hint of sadness in her voice. Her plans had gone awry from the moment she'd stepped off the stage and found that Melanie was in Texas.

She could still take the train to Texas. She could go directly to Uncle Richard's ranch. Melanie and Gabriel should still be there, and they could introduce Renata to every eligible rancher in the state, if that was what it took. Surely she wouldn't fail as miserably there as she had in Colorado. How could she? She wouldn't have Jake there to spoil her plans by pretending . . .

Renata frowned at him. Yesterday's kiss had seemed so real . . . not a gambit at all. There was no telling where a kiss like that might lead. But he had been acting for Lester's benefit, and that had angered her for some unfathomable reason. It shouldn't have bothered her any more than his other false caresses and endearments.

But it had.

Jake gave her a quick sidelong glance. Whatever had driven him to go back into the cabin and kiss her? Where had that uncontrollable urge come from? He knew she believed the kiss to be another part of his plot to ruin her reputation, an embrace intended to startle Lester and nothing more. He would allow her to believe that, was grateful, in fact, that she did. He had no explanation for the act otherwise. None at all.

He couldn't shake the memory of that kiss. It had been like being caught up in a storm . . . the lightning coursing through his body, the thunder in his heart, the whirlwind that surrounded them, encompassing them completely. He had never experienced anything like it before, that feeling of losing control. Except for Mel, his past dealings with women had been as cold and calculating as the rest of his life, and as devoid of emotion.

But Renata Marie Parkhurst was all emotion. He had only to look at her face to know what she was feeling. Just now it was clear that she was extremely angry with him, but there was a twinkle in her eye that he didn't like . . . not at all. She hadn't begged him to allow her to stay since they'd left the cabin, and though he'd been relieved initially, that fact had him worried now.

"What are you up to?" he snapped.

"Up to?" Renata raised an eyebrow quizzically. "What makes you think I'm 'up to' something?"

Jake shook his head. "You're going home."

She answered him with complete silence.

"Renata." He rarely used her first name, didn't think of her that way, and when he did address her, he called her Renata Marie Parkhurst, as if it were her title. She gave him a little sideways glance, acknowledging the slip.

"I suppose eventually I will go back to Philadelphia," she conceded.

"That's not what I said," Jake insisted.

"Well, what are you going to do, Jake? Ride with me to the railway station? It's just half a day on the stage. You could put me on the train . . . but who's to say I won't change my route along the way? Will you ride all the way to Philadelphia with me? Will you carry me to my house and hand me over to my father as if I were some sort of criminal? And just to clear the air, what business is it of yours where I go? You are not my keeper. I will go where I choose and . . ."

"All right," Jake conceded in a tight voice. "But you should go home. A woman isn't safe traveling alone, especially out West, where the sight of a pretty woman has been known to drive some female-starved men mad."

Renata leaned forward and gave him a small

grin. "Why, is that a compliment? Do you think I'm pretty, Jake?" There might have been a wry twist in her voice, but there wasn't.

Jake made a noise of disgust. "You know damn well that you are." He didn't care much for false modesty, especially in a woman as beautiful as the one beside him. Of course she knew that he found her pretty. Didn't everyone?

When he risked another quick glance at Renata she had a perfectly serious look on her face. "Thank you," she said. "I think. I do believe that's the strangest compliment I've ever received."

As they rode in silence Jake was more eager than ever to get Renata Marie Parkhurst on the stage and away from Silver Valley, though he couldn't rightly explain why.

Their arrival in town caused a small uproar of which Renata seemed oblivious. But Jake saw every curious move.

The schoolteacher put a piece of penny candy into a student's hand and the boy ran off . . . in the direction of the church. Sylvia Collins all but ran down the boardwalk toward her house. The two old men who regularly sat in front of the general store stopped arguing and watched the arriving buckboard with uncommon interest. And so it went, the entire town in a controlled frenzy.

Jake stashed his rifle under the seat and jumped to the ground, sauntering slowly to

Renata's side to assist her as she attempted to leave the high wagon.

"You should't be jumping around like that," she admonished him gently. "You must be careful of your injury for a while longer."

"Yes, doctor," he answered her coldly.

"Nor should you be lifting me," she said as his hands circled her waist and he lowered her to the ground. Renata didn't touch him but grasped the lacy and delicate parasol that matched her apricot suit.

He released her quickly, not allowing his hands to linger on her for a moment longer than necessary. Then he turned his back to her and strode into the general store.

An unusually large crowd was gathered in and around the Boyles' establishment. He simply ignored the townspeople, who looked with unusual interest at the canned goods, penny candy, and newly arrived notions.

Jake disregarded them all and turned a scowling face to Mrs. Boyle. "A ticket for the stage," he said tersely.

"Never mind, Mrs. Boyle," Renata said sweetly from directly behind him. "I've changed my mind. I believe I'll take a room at the hotel."

Jake looked down at her, barely controlling his fury. "You will be on that stage," he said in a low voice.

"I've decided to wait at the hotel for Melanie's return," she said with a determined set to her mouth. "Do you have a problem with that?"

He looked away from Renata and back to Mrs. Boyle. "Will the stage be on time?"

"Last week he was an hour late, but normally he's pretty good about gettin' here by two." Mrs. Boyle's eyes flitted from Jake to Renata and back again.

"I won't be on it," Renata said in a voice that was so low, only Jake and Mrs. Boyle could hear her, although the room was strangely quiet, for all its occupants. "If you put me on that stage, I will kick and scream, and I'll be back on the street before it's had a chance to move more than ten feet." She was smiling as she delivered her threat.

Jake turned his back on her and placed both hands on the counter that separated him from Mrs. Boyle. "A ticket for the stage and a length of rope."

Suddenly Jake felt her parasol strike him squarely across his back.

"You bully," she hissed. "You'll still be rid of me. I'll stay here in town, far away from the ranch, and you won't ever have to see me again. That's what you want, isn't it? To have me out of your sight?"

As Jake shrugged his shoulders, trying to relieve his stinging back, he knew the people in the store were waiting to see what he would do. They had all seen him flatten men for less . . . several times. He was so fast and accurate that the offender, whether he had insulted Jake, brushed up against him, or, heaven help him, challenged him in any way, often found himself in the dirt, unable to move, before he knew what had happened. It was a reputation Jake had cultivated very carefully.

Now he knew they were wondering if he would hit the girl. If he were truly as savage as he appeared to be . . .

He turned slowly and looked down at the woman who had pelted him across the back. She looked defiant even as he gave her his fiercest glare. There was not a flinch, not even a flicker of regret in her eyes. She knew that he wouldn't hurt her.

"You will be on that stage, Renata Marie Parkhurst, even if I have to truss you up and toss you on the roof with the baggage."

Her frown deepened. "Why? Why is it so important that I leave now? Can't I see Melanie first?"

Jake took his newly purchased rope and turned away from her, with her trusting green eyes and carefully mastered pout. He had hardened his heart against such practiced pleading, but Renata Marie Parkhurst was much too good at that particular maneuver. She was making him feel guilty . . . but just a little.

Renata watched through the open doorway as Jake ignored her and walked away. She kept her eye on the very spot where she had last seen his stubborn and resolutely stiffened back.

"Are you all right?" Felicia Collins appeared and put her hand on Renata's arm.

"As well as can be expected." Renata turned to her new friend with a wistful smile. "It seems Jake is determined to be rid of me."

"Why?" Felicia whispered her question. "I thought . . . I mean . . . I would just die if a man ever looked at me like that. Why is he making you leave?"

"Because he's a pigheaded bully," Renata said sharply. "Who's to say why men do what they do?"

The townspeople who had been loitering on the boardwalk moved away from the door. A shout drew Renata's attention, and she moved to the doorway with Felicia.

The two young women moved with the tide that was flowing to the end of the street, and suddenly Renata knew that something was wrong. Her heart started to beat fast and her head was spinning even before she saw what was happening.

Jake was surrounded by half a dozen men. They circled around him like buzzards, and he turned slowly so that none of them was out of his sight for very long. The knife he'd had strapped to his hip was in his hand, long and thin and deadly looking, but the men who surrounded him were pointing guns—pistols and rifles—at Jake, and that was all Renata could see.

"Stop it," she heard herself saying as she pushed her way to the front of the crowd. Her words sounded distant and unreal to her ears. "What do you think you're doing?" There was panic in her voice, giving it an unnatural pitch that rose to the surface in an uncontrollable wave.

Jake's eyes met hers just for an instant. Then one of the cowboys who stood behind him brought the stock of his rifle down on Jake's wrist. Jake's only weapon fell from his grasp and hit the dirt. Renata heard the crack of the wood against his wrist, saw the sun's sharp reflection in the blade of the knife as it fell, and then the crowd converged on Jake, blocking her view of his rigid face.

Chapter Eight

Renata turned her back on the melee and ran toward the buckboard. She knew how much the people of Silver Valley hated Jake. Melanie had told her that much, and she had seen the reaction Jake caused, both at the cabin and in the general store. As much as she resented Jake for sending her away, she knew without a doubt where her loyalty lay. If Silver Valley was going to take on Jake, then they were going to have to take her on as well.

She leaned into the buckboard, standing on her tiptoes and jumping as high as her skirts would allow, her fingers reaching, straining for the weapon Jake had stashed under the seat. Her efforts came inches short of her goal. Renata looked down the street. No one was watching her; the crowd had moved as one body farther down the street. Muffled shouts and the growing murmur of the crowd drifted her way. She couldn't see Jake, but she knew he was at the center of it all.

Her heart was in her throat and her hands trembled slightly as she remembered Donnie Boyle's words to her that first day. Something about stringing Jake up . . .

With her foot perched precariously on the wheel spoke, Renata boosted herself up. Her hand brushed the barrel of the rifle. She wrapped her fingers around it gratefully and pulled it toward herself, falling back to the ground with the weapon in her hands. She studied it closely as she hurried down the street to join the crowd. It was almost identical to Melanie's rifle, thank goodness.

Renata worked her way through the crowd, shouldering her way past gawkers and keeping her eyes straight ahead. The people gave way, either without thought or when they saw the rifle Renata clasped firmly in both hands. When she finally reached the front of the crowd Renata looked up, and for a moment she couldn't breathe. In fact, she thought she should faint. It would be the ladylike thing to do.

Jake was standing in the back of a wagon, the rope he had bought in a noose around his neck, the other end tied securely around a sturdy limb of the old oak tree that shaded one end of Silver Valley's main street. He was surrounded by the same six men who had circled him earlier;

though his hands were tied and he had a rope around his neck, their weapons were still trained on him.

There was still fear in their eyes, too, Renata noted. Three of them had blood-smeared faces—a split lip, a bloody nose, a rapidly swelling eyelid—and Renata knew Jake had not surrendered to the mob without a fight.

Renata stepped forward and away from the crowd. She felt a lightly restraining hand on her sleeve but brushed it away without ever knowing who had tried to stop her.

"Cut him down," she said in a voice that was surprisingly strong and authoritative. There was no hint of her earlier panic.

Four of the men looked at her, two from the back of the wagon where they stood with Jake, two from the ground just a few feet away from her. The other two kept watchful eyes on Jake.

"Back off, lady," one of them said curtly, a young man with pale hair and sky-blue eyes. "This don't concern you."

Renata lifted the rifle and aimed it at the man who had spoken. "I said cut him down this instant."

Her order brought a smattering of laughter from the six rough men. "Come on, sweetheart. We know you don't know how to use that thing in your hands. You're gonna hurt somebody if you're not careful." It was the same fair-haired young man who had looked at her condescendingly, as if she were a child with a stick in her hand, playing at being a cowboy.

Renata licked her lips, which were suddenly dry, but kept the rifle trained on the arrogant cowboy. "This is a Winchester '73, a most effective center-fire repeating rifle. It's also called the .44-40-.44 caliber, with a cartridge containing 40 grains of powder." Renata dropped the lever and pulled it back up again, readying the rifle for fire. "My cousin Melanie taught me how to shoot last year when she visited my family in Philadelphia. She said I was a quick study. A natural."

Everyone in Silver Valley knew that Melanie Maxwell was a crack shot, the best in town. She had beaten every cocky cowboy who claimed to be a shootist, shooting at cans and bottles and coins tossed into the air.

The young man who had done all the talking lost his air of confidence and lowered his own six-shooter. There was a distinct nervousness in the way he shifted his weight from one foot to the other, and his mouth hung open slightly.

"I believe I know who you are," Renata said, her voice stronger now that she felt a bit of control. "Melanie described you perfectly, Mr. Mails. Kenny, isn't it? She said you were vaguely handsome . . . and not very bright. Now, why don't you cut down Jake as I asked?"

"He burned Harrison Summers's barn." One of the other men responded hotly. "That was the last straw, I tell you. This town will be well rid of this troublemaker." As if to make his point, he swiped roughly at the blood that trickled down his chin.

"I'm certain you're mistaken," Renata said sensibly. "Jake didn't burn down anyone's barn."

"Ben Beechcroft saw him riding away," another of the mob called out. "The barn was on fire, and he saw Jake riding away on that damn black stallion of his. Summers lost four fine horses in that fire."

"Yeah," a previously quiet man called out. "Hell, Ben saved some of the animals and would have gone after Jake right then, but that big storm was brewin' up."

Renata felt her heartbeat slowing and her panic ebbing. Everything was going to be all right after all. "The storm a couple of weeks ago? The night of all that thunder and lightning?"

"Yep," the man answered assuredly.

"In that case I can prove your Mr. Beechcroft was mistaken. Jake didn't go anywhere that night. Perhaps the lightning started the fire . . ."

Kenny Mails stepped forward. "So you're claiming Jake didn't leave the cabin at all that night? Not even while you were sleeping?"

"I didn't sleep at all that night," Renata admitted. "And I swear to you that Jake didn't go anywhere." Her anxiety was coming back. They didn't care if Jake was innocent or not. They wanted to get rid of him, and would do so with no more regret than they might squash a spider with a heavy boot.

"So you're willing to swear in front of the entire town—" Kenny Mails waved an arm to indicate the silent crowd behind her— "that you and Jake have been living up there in sin . . ."

"I never said that," Renata defended herself, but it was no use. Between Jake's antics and her alibi, she knew what everyone was thinking— and they still intended to hang Jake.

Renata risked turning away from Kenny Mails to look at Jake. He was impassive as always, looking straight ahead with a far-off look in his eyes and bitter acceptance on his face, as though he'd known that one day . . . one day this was how it would all end.

With a flourish of her skirts, Renata turned and faced the crowd. This was all a show to them. It seemed not one of them thought of Jake as a human being who was about to die. If only Melanie and Gabriel were here! They would know what to do.

Her eyes scanned the crowd. Even the sheriff stood at the edge of the mob, silent and accepting. Renata gave him a disdainful look, and he pulled his eyes away from her. What a coward.

"Will you allow this to happen?" Renata asked the crowd. She looked at the faces of the people she had come to know. Donnie and Janie Boyle; the women who had visited her at the cabin and brought her food and friendship. It was as though they had been entranced by the lynch mob and would willingly accept whatever punishment the ruffians meted out.

"Don't you realize what will become of this town if you allow this unruly band to hang an innocent man?"

There was passion in her voice, and she made the question she asked seem suddenly important. She paced in front of the crowd, turning to the lynch mob often enough to keep them at bay with her vacillating weapon.

"I won't allow it," she said. "I'll start shooting, and the only way you'll be able to stop me will be to shoot me dead," she said dramatically. "What would that say about Silver Valley? A heartless town where innocent men are hanged on a whim and young girls are gunned down in the street. You may try to keep it a secret, but it will only take one among you to tell the truth." She searched the faces before her and called out the names of every woman who had visited her. She saw the guilt in their faces as she called their names. If she could sway the women, the men would follow.

"The truth will be known, and it will spread like wildfire until there won't be a man, woman, or child in this country who doesn't know the story. Who will want to come here? Who will want to live in such a cruel place? The town will die . . . and every one of you will carry the guilt of what you allowed to happen to your graves."

Renata had always been a good storyteller, mesmerizing even Melanie's boisterous twins with her passionately told tales of princes and dragons and damsels in distress. Soon she had the crowd in the palm of her hand as they listened raptly.

There was only one person who was not swayed: Kenny Mails walked to the front of the wagon and prepared to slap the horse's rump, sending it forward and Jake to his death. Renata swung around to aim the rifle at Kenny. Panic welled up in her again.

"No!" she shouted, searching desperately for an answer. "What about my baby?"

Kenny stopped. The lynch mob stared at her. There was renewed murmuring in the crowd behind her. Even Jake looked down at her with an unreadable fire in his eyes.

"If you hang Jake, what will happen to my baby?" she repeated her question. "A child with no father. An innocent babe without a name . . ."

There was a rumble in the crowd at her back. Renata heard only bits and pieces of what was said.

"What will Mel say when . . ."

"It's just not proper . . ."

" . . . Christian duty . . ."

"Such a sweet girl . . ."

"We all knew what was going on up there . . ."

Two men stepped forward—the sheriff, prodded by his wife, and the minister, his stiff white collar setting him apart.

"Kenny." The sheriff nodded to the leader of the mob. "Let's think about this, now; keep our wits about us. If she swears Jake was home that night . . . I'm going to have to ask you to cut him down."

Kenny swore, but he stepped into the wagon and shoved his cohorts aside with a growl. They quickly jumped to the ground and blended into the crowd. Kenny had picked up Jake's knife out of the dirt and shoved it into his own belt, and now he withdrew it with a flourish. He started to cut Jake down, but hesitated and waved the blade in Jake's face. "Just can't keep your hands off white women, can you? Knock up Mel's cousin, and now we're gonna have to watch you marry the pretty little thing. Don't seem fair."

Renata smiled at Jake as he finally looked down at her. But there was no answering smile on his face, no look of relief.

"You're loco," he said to her, his voice low. "I'd rather hang."

Only Renata and Kenny Mails heard his statement. Renata's smile faded, and Kenny grinned maliciously.

"You know," Kenny said, the knife poised to release Jake, "we would be doing Mel and Gabe a real disservice if we didn't take care of this pronto. Preacher? You available this afternoon?"

The minister nodded, and Renata turned to him with a restrained smile. "That's really not necessary. There's no hurry . . ."

"Nonsense." The minister laid a hand on her shoulder. "There's no reason to delay."

Five guns were trained on Jake once again as Kenny Mails finally cut him down; only this time they were leading him to an altogether different fate. He gave Renata a malevolent scowl, and for once he really did scare her. Still, she merely shrugged her shoulders in response to his glare.

For goodness sake. Married to Jake Wolf.

Chapter Nine

"I'll not get married without my wedding gown," Renata insisted for the third time. "It's in the Saratoga trunk in the buckboard." She was surrounded by women—Felicia and Sylvia Collins, Janie Boyle, the minister's wife, the schoolteacher, and several of the other women who had called on her at the cabin. They were all standing in the minister's parlor, and Renata wore a frown that was, for her, highly unusual. There seemed to be no way out of this, so she stalled. "And flowers. I must have flowers."

Jake was waiting, she knew, in the church next door. In her heart she believed that if she stalled long enough Jake would find a way to escape. In her mind she knew that Jake was guarded by more than a dozen men, and even he couldn't overcome those odds. It seemed the town of Silver Valley was determined to see them married.

Sylvia Collins stepped forward, a stern look on her face. "Felicia, have your father fetch that trunk and bring it here. Alice—" she turned and nodded to the schoolteacher— "cut a few flowers from your garden and set them on the altar." Felicia was already out the front door, and Alice was right behind her.

Renata paced the small room, wringing her hands. "I'd much rather wait until Melanie returns," she said to no one in particular.

"And give that Jake Wolf a chance to disappear?" Janie Boyle spoke up. "That wouldn't be wise, my dear."

Renata stopped pacing. Her frown disappeared and a small smile crossed her face. It would have been best to wait for Melanie and Gabriel; they would have known what to do. But that wasn't going to be allowed, she acknowledged serenely. Might as well make the best of this.

"It appears the entire town will be present for my wedding," she said with more than a trace of amusement. "Wouldn't a reception afterward be appropriate?" She turned questioning eyes to the women around her. "Something out-doors, in that field behind the church? Surely we could put together some kind of party . . . punch and little sandwiches . . . music. Melanie said there were a few local men who played for dances now and again . . ."

"They're not very good," an anonymous voice

from the back of the room observed.

"They're not that bad, either," Janie said, "and I've got a cake settin' on the kitchen table."

Other women started calling out what they could contribute, and plans for the reception were underway. Renata listened, and her smile broadened.

The gown had been made in preparation for her marriage to Lord Edenworth, and while she had detested the idea of marriage to Percival, she had adored the wedding gown. The white satin fit snugly over her arms and torso and the high neck was lined with tiny pearls. The skirt was full and trailed behind her in a shimmering train, so that she seemed to float on a lustrous cloud. A lace overlay, the finest lace Renata had ever seen, covered the satin bodice, and she felt like a princess in a fairy tale.

Her face was covered by a veil, but she could clearly see Jake waiting for her at the end of the aisle. She smiled, knowing that he couldn't see her face. Let him suffer, she decided; served him right.

The church was full, and every man in the room but Jake was armed. The front pew was filled with men, their six-shooters and rifles trained on her groom. A shotgun wedding, with the entire town in attendance. Shops had closed, the stage had been quickly hurried through—even the blacksmith's was silent—as on a weekday afternoon the residents of Silver Valley congregated to witness her marriage to the stubborn man who had plagued them for years.

More than once she'd been told, as she prepared for her wedding, that if anyone could straighten out that heathen Jake Wolf, she was the one to do it.

Even though she felt like a princess, Jake looked very little like Prince Charming at the moment. He stood at the altar, waiting for her like an impatient barbarian warrior, his long hair touching his buckskin-clad shoulders, his feet planted far apart and his arms crossed over his wide chest.

She could feel the anger radiating from him like the heat from a fire as she approached and stood next to him, their arms almost touching as the minister began the ceremony.

Jake leaned over and whispered in Renata's ear. "I'll get you for this, little girl."

The minister faltered a bit but continued even as Renata stood on her tiptoes so she could respond to her groom in a like manner. "This is entirely your fault, Mr. Wolf." She knew Jake couldn't see her face very well, and she tried unsuccessfully to disguise the humor in her voice. "Now be quiet and pay attention to the ceremony."

"I'll strangle you with my bare hands." He breathed the words into her ear as the minister recited haltingly and grasped the Bible in his hands. "If it's the last thing I do . . ."

"No, you won't," Renata answered him confidently.

"Jake?" the minister interrupted. "I do?" he prompted, leaning toward the couple.

Jake glared at the poor minister. "Do I have a choice?" He looked pointedly at the men in the front pew. "I guess I do."

The minister repeated the oath to the bride, and Renata was much more responsive than her groom had been, answering in a timely and appropriate fashion.

And then the minister pronounced them husband and wife. "You may kiss the bride."

Renata turned to face her new husband. "You're supposed to lift the veil and kiss me," she whispered.

Jake stared at her, his face coldly impassive. "I've done all I intend to."

Renata sighed deeply. The room was quiet as everyone waited. "For goodness sake, Jake. If we have to do this, we might as well do it right. A little kiss on the cheek will suffice."

Jake reached out to touch the delicate veil with the tips of his fingers. As Renata watched, his fingers tightened on the fragile fabric, tearing the veil from the wreath of silk flowers on her head. His other hand came up, and he ripped the flimsy mask in two, revealing her face to him in a startlingly violent manner.

He wished she wouldn't look at him like that, her green eyes large and just slightly condemning, her face flushed and all the more beautiful for it. She had been a vision as she'd walked down the aisle to him, but at least he hadn't had to see her face. There was so much hope and laughter there, he didn't think he could stand it. He was supposed to kiss her but he didn't know if he could.

She was waiting for his bloodless, chaste kiss on the cheek, and the men with their weapons trained on his back probably expected him to strangle his bride.

And then her words came back to him. *It's much more interesting to give them what they least expect, Jake.*

And so he did. He gave Renata what she obviously didn't expect. He wrapped his arms around her, lowered his lips to hers, and gave her a searing kiss that rocked her to her very soul.

The guns in the front pew were lowered, and still he kissed her.

The minister cleared his throat loudly, and still Jake kissed her.

Men in the back pew rose to get a better look and were jerked back into their seats by their disapproving wives, and still Jake kissed her.

When he finally released her Renata took in a deep gasp of air, and Jake gave her a devilish grin when he saw that he had indeed surprised her. By the stunned silence in the church, he knew she wasn't alone. Jake decided his new wife had been right; it really was more fun to give people what they least expected.

But Jake knew that wasn't the only reason he had kissed Renata. He had kissed her because he wanted to . . . because he needed to.

In one quick, graceful motion, Jake lifted his bride, sliding one arm behind her back and the other under her thighs. Her face was inches from his, but he kept his eyes on the double doors at the end of the aisle as he walked with long strides away from the minister.

"This part comes later, Jake," Renata whispered. "You're just supposed to walk me . . ."

"Shut up, woman," Jake said gruffly. "You are my wife now, and you will do as I say. And if I say that I'll carry you out of the church, then . . ."

Renata wrapped her arms around his neck for support, locking her hands behind his head. "I haven't had a chance to explain my plan to you . . ."

"Plan? This is all part of a plan?" he asked as he kicked open the massive doors.

"Well, in a way. I'll explain later, after the reception."

Jake stopped in his tracks, and the crowd that was following after them stopped as well. "Reception?" he repeated in disbelief.

Renata nodded. "The whole town's invited. All the women provided food and lemonade and punch, and there's going to be music."

Didn't she realize that he would prefer to be anywhere else on the earth rather than in the company of the people of Silver Valley on a sunny summer afternoon?

"Please, Jake," she whispered softly. "Just for a little while."

She was looking at him with wide, bright eyes, and somehow his anger fell away. "All right. But don't expect me to dance."

"Why not?"

"I don't dance."

Renata frowned slightly. "Perhaps I can teach you."

"No."

His eyes met hers and held them in a silent challenge that had nothing to do with dancing or wedding receptions. He felt a small tingle of warning deep inside.

"Don't worry, Jake," Renata said gently. "I have a plan. I'm going to fix everything."

Jake pulled his eyes away and continued down the path that led to the clearing behind the church. It was there that picnic suppers and occasional dances were held, though Jake had never been to either. There was a large wooden dance floor to one side, and tables had been set up on the other edge of the lawn. The tables were covered with food—meat, cakes, punch, bread, fruit—it looked like the town had been scavenged and the booty piled high. There were vases of flowers everywhere, and a banner hung above the dance floor. It was crudely lettered, obviously the work of a child:

CONgRADulATIOns REnATA AnD JAkE.

Jake stopped suddenly and looked at the sign. "People like you, Renata Marie Parkhurst," he said in a low voice.

Renata smiled. "That's Renata Marie Wolf, if you please. And don't give me that scowl. I'll . . ." She stopped abruptly as the minister appeared at Jake's elbow.

"You should probably put the bride down now, Jake," the minister said, more than a little embarrassed. His pale face was flushed.

Jake lowered Renata to her feet, and the crowd rushed past, parting to flow on either side of them as they made their way to the food and drink. "You'll what?" he asked as he released her.

Renata looked around almost surreptitiously. She looked like a little girl, dying to impart a forbidden secret; then a serene look of acceptance settled over her face.

"I'll tell you later. Hungry?" She grinned at him, and his heart did a sudden flip-flop that surprised and frightened him.

When everyone was fed and had greeted the bride and groom the band began to play. It was a small group, consisting of a fiddler, a banjo player, and a foot-tapping man on the harmonica. He was one of the old men who seemed forever planted in front of the Boyles' store, and he didn't seem as old as he usually did now, as he pranced on the makeshift stage.

The couples danced their quadrilles or did an occasional two-step, and Renata stood aside and watched. It was torture.

Renata loved to dance. When she'd been younger she'd listened to the music wafting upstairs from her mother's parties and danced with an invisible partner. Once she'd been deemed old enough to attend parties and balls herself, she had danced every dance with a smile on her face, never tiring until the music was done for the evening.

Jake stood stoically beside her as she watched the dancers wistfully, his thoughts a mystery to her as he kept a suspicious eye on the rest of the townspeople.

"Can we go now?" he asked tiredly.

"Not yet, Jake," she said, her eyes on the dancers. "We don't want to be rude."

"We don't want to be rude?" Jake's voice was strained. "I was nearly hung, forced to marry at gunpoint, and now you tell me that I shouldn't be rude?" His voice rose slightly, drawing a few stares, though no one dared to approach them.

Renata laughed. "Rather preposterous, isn't it?" Without thinking, she reached for his hand and took it in her own. "The Bible says it's better to marry than to burn. Surely it's better to marry than to hang."

His look told her that he didn't agree, and her smile faded. Reluctantly, she released his hand. "Don't worry, Jake. I told you I'd take care of everything."

Jake obviously wasn't satisfied with her response, but the conversation was brought to a halt when Kenny Mails appeared at Renata's side and placed a hand on her arm.

"May I have a dance with the bride?" Kenny managed to make even that simple request sound lascivious, and Renata shook his hand away.

"No, thank you, Mr. Mails," Renata answered him coldly. "I really would not care to dance. Not at all." She looked up at Jake, into his cold, unreadable face.

Jake looked down at her. She wanted to dance so bad it was driving her crazy, but she had refused Kenny Mails. Thank God. He couldn't have borne it, to have stood there and watched her dance with another man's hands on her . . . Jake shook his head. Stupid thoughts. This wasn't a real marriage. It was a sham, a farce. He couldn't be jealous. Wouldn't be.

And then Kenny Mails touched her again, this time laying both hands on her shoulders. "At least let me kiss the bride."

The fair-haired cowboy lowered his face to Renata's, even as she tried to back away from him. She pursed her lips and turned her head away, but it wasn't necessary. Before he could touch her face with his lips Kenny Mails went flying backward and landed in the dirt on his tailbone. He barely had time to recover and take a deep breath before Jake was lifting him by the front of his shirt and thrusting his face close to Kenny's.

"Touch my wife again and I'll kill you," Jake whispered. He had the attention of everyone once more, and he expected a crowd to come rushing forward at any moment to pull him away from Kenny and to defend their friend. It had happened more times than Jake could count.

But no one came forward. All Jake heard were whispered condemnations . . . of Kenny.

"Tried to kiss Miss Renata . . ."

"That Kenny Mails never did have any manners . . ."

"Jake took care of him, but good . . ."

And then Renata was beside him as he glared at Kenny's terrified face, trying to decide whether he should hit the cowboy again. Kenny wasn't even trying to fight back. He just wiped his hand across his blood-smeared mouth.

"Jake?" Renata placed her hand on his shoulder, her touch tentative, tender and unsure.

He had defended her instinctively, even though he had done his best to run her out of town, even though he swore that he cared nothing for her.

"You can let him go," she continued when he didn't move. "He didn't mean any harm. He's just a . . . a . . . an ill-mannered oaf."

Jake let Kenny go with a shove that sent the cowboy stumbling backward, and then he turned to look at Renata. Her hand was still on his shoulder, warmer and softer than anything he had ever known. With a scowl he stepped away so that Renata's hand fell back to her side.

The sun was setting and the party was breaking up. There were no lanterns lit, so darkness would mean an end to the gathering. Renata stepped away from Jake's side and tapped Donnie Boyle on the shoulder.

"This is very bold of me, I know," she said softly, "but would you dance with me? I love a waltz."

There were only a few people on the dance floor. Jake watched Renata move gracefully in Donnie Boyle's arms, gliding across the crude floor as though she were dancing in a grand ballroom to the strains of a waltz performed by a fine orchestra.

It didn't seem to matter that Boyle was old and growing fat, or that his wife watched with a smile on her face from a few feet away. Jake realized with a rush of disgust that he was jealous. Jealous! Impossible.

But he stood there silently as Renata continued to dance with the man who was old enough to be her father, and her long train followed her, catching the pink rays of the setting sun in her hair and on her shimmering dress. Jake wished that he could hear what she was saying so earnestly to the old man.

"I'm going to ask you a tremendous favor, Mr. Boyle," Renata said as the man swung her around.

Donnie looked down at her and smiled. "What's that Miz . . . Miz . . ." He wouldn't or couldn't call her Mrs. Wolf. "Miz Renata?"

"Be nice to Jake," she said seriously, and her eyes were drawn over her partner's shoulder, to meet her groom's intent gaze.

Donnie made a low noise of disgust. "I don't know what you see in that . . ."

"Don't say it," Renata warned. "Don't condemn a man for the blood that runs in his veins."

"That's got nothing to do with his meanness," Donnie defended himself.

Renata looked into Donnie's face, giving him her full attention. "Jake has known more pain in his life than you or I will ever know." Renata felt tears sting her eyes. "Certainly, he can be difficult."

"Difficult?"

"All right," Renata conceded. "Very difficult. But he needs friends, and he needs . . ." He needs love, Renata thought, but she couldn't say that. She didn't love him; she couldn't. Falling in love with Jake Wolf wasn't part of her plan. "Give him a chance . . . well, give him several chances, because he's likely to bungle the first one or two."

The music ended, and Donnie Boyle came to a halt and looked down at Renata. He was, at least, giving her request some thought. "This is the damndest wedding I ever did see."

"Will you do as I ask?" she implored. "Will you be nice to Jake? As a . . . a wedding gift?"

She stared up at him with pleading in her eyes. He wanted to refuse her, she could tell, but he didn't.

"I'll think about it," Donnie finally agreed, and Renata didn't have time to press for a more definitive answer. Her anxious groom was coming to fetch her.

Chapter Ten

They could have gone back to the cabin, but it would have been long after dark before they arrived. Some industrious wedding guests had carried Renata's trunks to a room on the second floor of the hotel. A band of rowdy wedding guests practically herded the newlyweds into the hotel and up the narrow staircase. Renata half expected her groom to punch and kick the lot of them down the stairs, but he didn't. He wanted to—she could see it in his face—but he didn't.

Renata closed her eyes and leaned against the door when she and Jake were finally alone, taking a deep breath of musty air. She was exhausted, suddenly tired to the very bone. And the ordeal wasn't over yet.

She opened her eyes and was greeted with

a view of Jake, silent and frowning, but with a strange light in his eyes. It was the same unreadable light that had been there when he'd kissed her in the cabin and in the church. That look made her shiver.

"Quite an eventful day," she said, and immediately knew the lighthearted words were a poor choice. Jake's scowl deepened and he looked away from her, obviously disgusted.

"I didn't mean for it to go this far, Jake." Renata took a single step away from the door. "Things just . . . got away from me a bit."

"It was stupid," Jake said flatly.

"Stupid?" Renata's exhaustion lifted and she took another small step toward the center of the room. "I couldn't stand there and watch them hang you."

"Why couldn't you?" he asked coldly.

Renata rolled her eyes and lifted her arms, her palms up. "Jake Wolf, I have no doubt that you will one day come to a violent end, but I have no wish to see it." She tried to snap at him, but of course he didn't know yet about her plan. "Besides . . ." Her voice trailed off. How to explain?

Jake walked to the corner of the hotel room, where someone had propped his rifle. He lifted it and studied every angle carefully, then looked at her with twinkling eyes. "Do you really know how to use this?"

Renata sighed and shrugged her shoulders. "Well, yes and no," she admitted. "Melanie did try to teach me to shoot, and she told me all about the rifle, but she said I couldn't hit a bull's ass with a handful of banjos."

That statement, delivered seriously, elicited a short laugh from Jake, and Renata raised her eyebrows. It was a nice laugh, deep and real, one she had never heard before.

"I never expected it to go this far, Jake. Truly I didn't," Renata said solemnly. "Even the part about the baby just . . . just sort of slipped out. But it did work."

Jake's eyes stayed on her as she began to pace the small room. She wrung her hands and began to chew on her bottom lip. The soft light from a single lamp lit the room, a primitive but clean space with a single bed and one chair, a chest and a mirror, and a nightstand by the bed.

"All we have to do is pretend to be happily married for a few weeks. Something else will come along—it always does, you know—and everyone will forget about us. We can go to Denver and get an annulment." She spoke quickly now. "You can tell everyone whatever you want . . . I don't care. I can't ever come back here, anyway. Tell them that I left you, if you want, or that you kicked me out because I made a terrible wife, or . . ."

"I could always tell them that you left me because you were tired of living with a savage. They'll believe that." Jake's words were bitter, with that hard edge they sometimes had.

"Jake, don't . . ."

Jake spun on his heel and swung open the

door. He had that determined set to his jaw and his back, in a hurry to get away from her.

But he stopped in the doorway, and Renata heard a slightly drunken voice from the hall.

"You need anything, you just let us know." There was a smattering of nervous laughter. "There's no need for you to leave your honeymooooon suite."

Jake slammed the door on their laughter and crossed the room to throw open the window. Voices drifted into the room from beneath their second-story room.

Jake took a deep breath and turned to face her. "It seems the entire population of Silver Valley is determined to see that we spend the night together in this room."

Renata bit her lower lip again and felt the heat rise in her cheeks. "I guess there's nothing to be done for that. It would be a problem if we intended to get the annulment here, but if we go to Denver . . ."

"What if I don't want an annulment?" Jake asked, and Renata spun on him just in time to see him smile wickedly.

"Why, Jake Wolf. You do have a sense of humor." Renata returned his smile. There was something in his grin that made her chest tighten, though she tried to ignore it. He was incredibly handsome when he smiled, and he would make a wonderful husband for someone . . . someday . . . though of course he made it clear that he didn't even like her much. And he certainly wasn't a part of her plans.

She fought the attraction she felt for him, the intrusive thought that she could be the woman to fix his life, to love him . . .

But it was impossible. Jake Wolf wasn't the reason she had come out West. He wasn't a rancher, he had a terrible temper, and as for love at first sight . . . for her it had been terror at first sight. And he had made it clear that he didn't like her at all. Didn't like anybody, if he was to be believed.

"And I suppose after the annulment you'll go down to Texas and find yourself a rancher husband?" Jake's smile had faded, but there was a trace of amusement in his tone.

Renata hesitated. Something about her dream had faded. She could no longer envision her plan to ensnare a rancher husband clearly, could no longer imagine stepping from the stagecoach and seeing the perfect man across the way and falling in love with him at first sight. She closed her eyes and shook her head. She was tired; that was all. Tomorrow everything would be clear again. "Of course," she replied, a frown passing over her face.

"Are you certain you can't get out through the window?" Renata asked, brushing past him to look down on the crowd below.

She'd sat up with Jake many nights when he was injured, watching him sleep, sitting by his side during the storm. But this was different. He was healed. They were married, and it was real. They'd been married in a church with the entire town in attendance. Would he think? . . .

Would he expect? . . . Certainly not . . .

Renata brushed past him once again and opened the door just a crack. The four men sitting on the steps didn't see her, but she saw them . . . blocking the only other way down. Jake could easily bypass those four men, but what would people think?

She closed the door silently and turned around, leaning against it heavily. "Well. It looks as though we're . . . trapped." The way he was looking at her reminded her of the way he had kissed her . . . after the wedding, certainly, but even more she remembered the kiss he had given her when he'd seen Lester coming toward the cabin. That kiss had made her head spin and her knees weak. If he kissed her again like that . . . but she was determined to see that he didn't.

"We'll have quite a story to tell our grand-children," she said, her voice trembling. "Well, not *our* grandchildren," she amended quickly. "I'll tell my grandchildren, and you can tell your grandchildren. It's quite scandalous, I know, but when we're old and gray and wrinkled it will somehow become charming to be scandalous, don't you think?" She was talking fast, as she always did when she was nervous. "I have a friend in Philadelphia, and her grandfather . . ."

"Shut up, Renata," Jake said without anger as Renata held herself flattened against the door.

"I just . . ."

"I'm not going to attack you," Jake assured

her, and she relaxed slightly.

"I never thought . . ."

"Yes, you did. But I think you will agree that it's in my best interest as well as yours to . . . to see that an annulment is possible."

Jake turned his back on her, every bit the gentleman, as she removed her wedding gown, twisting uncomfortably to undo the buttons down the back. She could have asked Jake to help, but she didn't dare. She found her most modest nightdress in one of the smaller trunks, drew it over her head, and climbed into the creaking bed, pulling the coverlet up to her chin.

"You can turn around now," she said, her voice softer than she'd intended.

Jake turned to face her and was stunned by his reaction. She'd been gorgeous in her satin, lace, and pearls; delicate and decidedly feminine.

But she looked even better sitting up in the bed, the covers pulled up so that all he could see was her face. It was her hair, he decided, falling loose around her face and spilling out over the covers.

As if she had read his mind, Renata sighed and reached for the brush she had placed on the bedside table and began to brush her hair. She brushed the red-gold tresses and then braided that long hair over her shoulder. Jake sat on the floor beneath the window, his back against the wall, and watched her blatantly.

"What about the baby?" Jake asked suddenly. "What should I tell everyone about the baby after you . . . leave for Texas?"

Renata sighed deeply, looking not at Jake but over his head. "I suppose we'll have to tell them that I lost the baby."

Her words brought a frown to her face, and the lamplight glistened on the unshed tears in her eyes.

"What's wrong?" he asked softly. Renata was lit by the soft light, but he was in shadows. Still, she stared right at him.

"It's just . . . very sad," she said, a hint of confusion in her voice. "Losing the baby."

"How can it be sad to lose something that never really existed?"

"It makes as much sense as cowering because there's a storm outside my window, but it hurts just the same. I like all my stories to have happy endings."

Jake couldn't take his eyes off her. A single tear rolled down her cheek and she wiped it away hurriedly, as though she were ashamed of it.

"I'm sure the town will be relieved to find that they won't have a Jake Junior to deal with." He tried to say it lightly, to cheer her up, but it didn't work.

"Don't say that," she admonished. "One day you will have children, and . . ."

"No, I won't," Jake said fiercely. "Our brief marriage will be the only one I'll ever have."

"But you need . . ."

"A nag? A keeper? A ball and chain?" he finished for her. This conversation was beginning to hit too close to home.

"That's not true," she said, though she hadn't become angry, as he had expected she would. "Well, sometimes it is true, but it doesn't have to be. Somewhere out there is the perfect woman for you. Someone who will love you and take care of you, someone who lights up when you smile and knows what you're thinking before you say a word. Someone who can read that twinkle in your eyes . . ." Renata stopped abruptly, clamping her mouth shut. A look of indecision crossed her face. "Well, you know what I . . . I mean . . . I suppose you . . ."

"Romantic hogwash," Jake said coldly, saving her as she faltered. He had long ago given up on the concept of love. Suddenly, when he tried to picture the perfect woman all he could see was red-gold hair and green eyes . . . dangerous territory. He knew what she was: an opportunistic fortune hunter who, he had learned that day, was capable of deceit, even though she looked as innocent as an angel.

He waited for her argument, but he didn't get one.

"Good night, Jake," she said simply, a little sadly, and then she turned her back to him and doused the light.

Yes, she was capable of deceit . . . but he knew he would never forget the sight of Renata standing there, holding the entire town at bay as she spun a tale and swung the rifle. He had never known a woman who would do such a thing . . . at least not for him. He still wasn't certain why she had done it . . . why she had saved his skin.

She was just too tenderhearted. She would have done the same for any man . . . Renata Marie Parkhurst and her naive sense of justice.

For a brief time he'd believed that she actually wanted to be married to him, had tricked him somehow, but as she'd paced the room and attempted to explain her scheme, he had realized with a sinking heart that he didn't understand, that she was as reluctant a bride as he was a groom.

He sat in the dark with his back against the wall and listened until he heard her even, deep breathing, and was certain she was sleeping soundly.

And then he whispered, "Good night, Renata Marie Wolf."

Chapter Eleven

They returned to the cabin, and Renata busied herself with anything that kept her eyes and her mind off Jake. She mended . . . her clothes, his clothes, old clothes Melanie and Gabriel had left behind. She cleaned, every corner of the cabin getting a proper and thorough inspection. She would not allow her plans to be ruined by a pretty face that hid a short temper and a difficult manner.

Jake moved his things back into the house and slept in the bedroom across the hall from Renata. She would have preferred that he continue to sleep in the bunkhouse, but they were too close to the new house, and she didn't want any of Gabriel's hands to realize that the marriage was a sham. If that knowledge got back to town, there was no telling what would happen to Jake.

Her reluctant husband seemed as anxious as she to put some distance between them, disappearing early each morning and arriving home late. Renata was especially grateful on those days when he didn't arrive back at the cabin until very late, after she'd gone to bed. She'd hear him enter the cabin quietly, believing her to be asleep, and listen as he rattled his plates and silverware and ate the supper she had left on the table for him. Only then could she manage to sleep.

Some nights he came home while Renata was still awake, often as she sat in the main room and brushed her hair or sat in the rocking chair and concentrated on her mending. He talked little when he was there and, surprisingly, so did Renata. She found she was too often putting her foot in her mouth, her simple statements suddenly taking on double meanings that caused her to blush while Jake tried to ignore her babbling.

And still the callers continued to come. Of course, Jake was never there to scandalize them, as he had been before. Renata entertained alone, with tea and meaningless conversation, and answered all the prying questions with noncommital chatter and attractive blushes. There were times, as she looked into probing and curious eyes, that she wondered if she had been mistaken about the town's interest in her marriage fading anytime soon.

Usually very social, Renata could have done without the callers. Felicia Collins was the only one she truly liked. She was close enough to Renata's age that Renata thought they might become close friends if she stayed, which she wasn't going to do. Unfortunately, Felicia was always accompanied by her mother, and Sylvia Collins dominated her.

One afternoon Renata was enduring another long monologue by Mrs. Collins when, after a while, she ceased listening, as did Felicia. Sylvia's daughter stared blankly around the room, occasionally looking at Renata with an accepting, almost imperceptible shrug. It was no wonder Felicia hadn't had an opportunity to blossom.

"And we've been quite surprised not to see you and Jake at church on Sunday." Sylvia Collins waited for a response.

"Well, Jake's been working awfully hard, with Gabriel and Melanie away."

"Everyone around here works awfully hard, Renata. You really should bring your husband to church if he's going to become an accepted member of this community. We've never been willing to do that before, but with you and the baby . . ." Sylvia pursed her lips. "Perhaps Jake's ways are too heathen after all."

"Not at all." Renata saw in a flash what she had to do. If Jake was happy, accepted by the townspeople, with friends and a sense of belonging that she knew had always eluded him, she could leave Silver Valley with a clear conscience. "I can see that you are right, Mrs. Collins. Thank you so very much for bringing our negligence to my attention."

Mrs. Collins all but preened. She was an overbearing woman who liked nothing better than to be told, again and again, that she was right. "We'll see you this Sunday, then."

Renata nodded. Convincing Jake would not be easy, but neither would it be impossible.

Felicia rose from her chair as her mother did. "You should bring a picnic. Most everybody does, and after church we all visit in the churchyard . . . where you had your wedding reception."

"Thank you, Felicia," Renata said brightly. "What a lovely suggestion." And it was, Renata thought as the wheels of her mind began to turn again.

"Church?" Jake shouted when Renata put the proposal to him at the supper table. He had been surprised to see her still awake when he walked into the cabin, and even more surprised to see that she had waited to eat supper with him. "You're out of your mind if you think I'm going to take you to church."

"Until we become the perfect married couple, as boring and predictable as everyone else in Silver Valley, we can't possibly sneak away for that annulment." Renata looked at his shoulder, then at his chin, avoiding meeting his eyes.

"In order to do that I have to go to the church where I was forced to marry you at gunpoint, listen to a sermon delivered by the man who pronounced us man and wife" —he said the words as if they were bitter— "and sit there on display for a group of people who would just as soon see me dead as sitting in the pew in front of them."

Renata hesitated, apparently searching for a credible argument. Finally she answered, "Basically."

"No."

"Fine. We'll just have to stay married a while longer," Renata said sensibly. "If you're not going to cooperate . . ."

"All right," Jake agreed bitterly.

Renata smiled slightly. "I'll even pack us a picnic."

Jake groaned. "A picnic."

Renata lost her smile and narrowed her eyes as she glared at him across the table. "It's good to see that you'll endure tortures heretofore unknown to man to get your annulment. What an enormous sacrifice, to spend a Sunday with your wife." She clamped her mouth shut and her eyes widened.

Jake watched her bustle around the table, looking everywhere but at him. She had gathered together too many plates in her hands, and they were threatening to topple at any moment, but she was so angry, she didn't seem to notice. It hadn't taken her long to learn to hate him, just as everyone else did. She looked at the floor, looked at the ceiling, looked at the unsteady stack of plates in her hands. She tripped and fell so suddenly that Jake barely had time to rise from his chair before Renata was sitting on the floor, tin plates and bits of food all around her, the scraps from their shared meal in her hair, on her yellow dress . . . There was even a shrunken, overcooked green bean stuck to her face.

She looked so comical, Jake almost laughed, but then he saw the tears welling up in her eyes.

"Are you hurt?" He knelt down beside her, his voice gruff.

With a sniffle and a grimace she lifted her right hand. "I think I sprained my wrist."

Jake took her arm gently and pushed back the lacy yellow sleeve. Her wrist was already swelling a little bit. "It's not too bad," he said in a comforting voice as he reached out and flicked the green bean from her face.

Renata sniffled and started to cry again, but she stopped herself with a deep, calming breath.

Jake lifted her to her feet, his hands on her waist. She frowned at the bits of food that fell off her and hit the floor, examining the clutter and sighing with disgust.

"I'll take care of it later." Jake watched her eyes take in the mess on the floor.

"I don't make a very good wife, do I, Jake?" she asked sadly.

"You better set your sights on a rich rancher, one who has servants for difficult tasks like clearing the table." He said the words lightly, meaning to make her laugh, but his statement had the opposite effect. Renata burst into tears.

He couldn't make her stop, even though he commanded her to stop, begged her to stop. Finally Jake wrapped his arms around her with a curse and held her head against his shoulder while she cried herself out. He felt oddly helpless, a man for whom that feeling had been a foreign one until a few weeks earlier. The ambush, the marriage, and now this . . . He had to admit that Renata made him feel more helpless than he'd ever been.

"I was just teasing you," he said softly. "You'll make some rancher a very good wife."

She muttered something completely unintelligible into his shoulder.

"What?"

"No. I'm a terrible wife."

Jake smoothed her hair with his hand. It was as soft and silky as he had known it would be. When he'd kissed her before his hands had merely brushed against her velvety curls, but now he allowed his fingers to caress her red-gold hair as he had longed to.

He wanted her, had wanted her from the moment he'd allowed himself to kiss her. That had been his first mistake. But his longing had become an obsession on their wedding night, as he'd sat in the dark and listened to her breathe. Even now, he sometimes peeked in on her at night, parting the curtain that shielded her from view and staring at her.

She was a deep sleeper, never sensing that he watched her, never hearing his footsteps stopping outside her room.

She slept like an exhausted child, and he had reminded himself over and over again that she was little more than a child, playing at being married while she searched for her happily ever after. It would have been easy for him to make the marriage real . . . to climb into that bed with her one night and bury himself inside her as he ached to do.

But he didn't, and he wouldn't. She'd saved his life with her spur-of-the-moment story, and he wouldn't ruin hers by making the tale a reality.

"Stop crying," he said into her hair, which smelled of crushed flowers, "and I'll . . . I'll go to church on Sunday."

"And the picnic?" she asked through her tears.

"And the picnic." He had the feeling he'd been had, but it didn't matter. Her sobs were slowing, her breathing returning to normal.

Renata backed away from him, a frown on her face.

Jake wrapped her wrist snugly, using a scrap of the lavender calico with which she had bandaged him. His hands were able and tender as he assured her that purple looked much better on her than it had on him. Renata could only watch silently, her wonder increasing with every minute that passed.

Here was the man Melanie had told her so much about. The man who had helped Melanie once, when she'd needed it most, the man who carried the twins on his shoulders and told them stories, as Renata had when they visited Philadelphia. A man who tried so hard to hide every bit of tenderness with a scowl and a quick temper. How could he be so mean one minute and so tender the next?

Renata's wrist was bandaged tightly; she could barely move her fingers, they were so swollen. She couldn't unbutton her dress, so Jake unfastened it for her, his hands steady and almost chaste. Almost. His fingers brushed against the thin chemise from her breasts to her navel. But he turned her around and gave her a gentle shove toward her room when he was finished.

Renata removed the yellow dress and pulled a nightgown over her head before slipping into a robe. It was a slow process, since her hand was all but useless. She heard Jake in the other room, cleaning up the mess she had made, scraping the tin plates against the floor, dropping the dirty dishes onto the table.

It had been silly of her to cry, and even sillier because her tears had not been caused by pain. One minute she'd been harping like a shrewish wife and the next she'd found herself sitting on the floor with food all over her face and her dress. It was true that her wrist hurt, but she had cried from humiliation.

She felt so incredibly stupid. Melanie and

Amalie never would have tripped over their own feet like that. She was such a clumsy fool.

Renata started to brush her hair awkwardly with her uninjured hand, and she wandered into the hall silently. She knew she should stay in her room and go to sleep, but she couldn't.

Jake turned away from the table the moment she entered the room, and in two long strides he was in front of her. She half expected him to order her to bed, but he didn't.

He had a puzzled look in his deep blue eyes, the same puzzlement she felt. Jake grabbed the loose ends of her robe, brought them together, and tied the sash tightly.

"Completely helpless, I see," he said casually.

"Evidently."

Jake led her easily to the main room, a guiding hand on her arm. On a cooler evening there might have been a fire, but the fireplace was cold now, the lantern hanging on the wall giving off the only light. He sat her down on the rug, his hands firm on her shoulders, and then he sat down behind her and took the hairbrush from her hand.

Renata just sat there. His hands never touched her—he was very careful about that— and he brushed her tresses much more tenderly than she ever did. A hundred strokes. How did he know that? Had he watched her at night as she sat and brushed her hair, while she believed he ignored her as always? And counted?

She didn't ask. At the moment she was afraid

to know. Renata closed her eyes, and Jake started to braid her hair. This time she felt his fingers in her hair, stroking her head and her neck, brushing against her back. Did he know that he was making her heart beat fast? Did he know that he was confusing her terribly?

"There now." He tossed the braid over her shoulder, his voice regaining some of its gruffness. "Get to bed, Renata."

She turned and looked at him, meeting his full glare for the first time in days. There was no tender softening of his features now, as she had seen earlier. "Jake, I . . ." What do you say to a man when you sense that you're falling in love . . . in love with the wrong man? If she could see just a glimmer of warmth in his eyes, could see just a hint of what she'd seen earlier, she would break down and tell him. She wouldn't be able to help herself.

But his eyes were like blue ice, cold and distant, and she made herself remember that he considered a wife to be a burden; a ball and chain, he'd said. In a way it was a relief not to have to confess. She would probably feel differently in the morning.

"Thank you," she finished feebly. "You're . . ." Renata decided to break the spell that bound them. "Where on earth did you learn to braid a woman's hair?" The tone of her voice changed, grew louder and harsher.

Jake raised an eyebrow. He could look so imperious when he put his mind to it. He looked down that perfectly straight nose of his at her and said in a voice that was almost challenging, "I used to braid my own."

Renata gave him a perfectly innocent smile. "Of course; how silly of me to forget."

It would be silly to forget who he was, to throw everything away for a handsome face that made her heart quicken. She couldn't allow a passing physical attraction to ruin her plans for her future.

But she couldn't deny that she felt a certain responsibility toward Jake. If only she could get his life in order before she left . . .

Chapter Twelve

On Sunday they rose early to prepare their picnic before they dressed, and left for church services. As he had in the days since she'd fallen, Jake helped Renata in the kitchen. Together, and with a great deal of flour flying through the air, they made fried chicken, biscuits, and potato salad, and packed the food in a basket, along with a small cake Renata had baked, with Jake's help, the night before. The kitchen was a disaster, but there was no time to clean it.

Renata dressed quickly, her still-bandaged wrist hurting slightly. There was a little more mobility in her wrist and fingers than she'd had in several days, so she didn't need Jake's help in working the tiny buttons of her green muslin dress. It was probably a bit fancy for

Sunday services in Silver Valley, but it was one of her favorites, and she hadn't had an opportunity to wear it since heading west. The color was flattering, and the embroidery was delicate, flawless. She wondered, as she tied her hair with a matching ribbon, what Jake would think of her in her Sunday best.

Jake, she assumed, would be waiting for her impatiently, wearing the same old buckskins he had always worn to town, determined to maintain his image as a savage to be feared and avoided.

She didn't care. This was just the first step, and it was an accomplishment just getting Jake to agree to accompany her to church.

Jake was waiting, and impatiently, as she had imagined he would be. But Renata was not prepared for the sight of him in his city clothes, had not even imagined that he owned any. He wore a white linen shirt, a gray waistcoat under a black jacket, and superbly cut black trousers. He had even pulled his hair back and secured it at his nape with a thin leather strap. Only his scowl was the same.

She stood on the front steps and stared in a very unladylike fashion. Jake was pacing beside the buckboard, his plain black boots kicking up little clouds of dust. Their picnic basket and an old quilt had been tossed into the back. He turned his head and looked at her, the impatience on his face fading momentarily.

The morning sun was on her face, but that

wasn't what warmed her cheeks as Jake stared at her and waited for her to come to him.

She hesitated a moment, then walked to the buckboard. It wasn't far, but it seemed to take her an eternity to reach it.

"You look . . . very nice, Jake," she said, the surprise evident in her voice.

He frowned. "You look . . . nice too." The words seemed to pain him, and Renata smiled lightly.

"What's so funny?"

"I wore my prettiest dress, and no one will even notice." She looked down at him as he helped her onto the seat. "No one will see anything but you. You devil. No woman likes to be outdone by a man."

Jake's scowl deepened. "If you think I look ridiculous, I can change real quick . . ."

"No," she said hastily. "You look . . . magnificent, Jake. Every girl there will be jealous of me." She smiled, but she was half serious. Surely Jake would marry again after the annulment, especially if she saw to it that he was accepted by the town before she left. Who would it be? She made a mental list of every woman in town and found them all lacking. Not one of them was good enough for Jake.

Jake lifted Renata down from the buckboard, her hands on his shoulders, his hands on her waist. He kept his hands on her just a moment longer than was necessary. That was good, she thought. People were watching. With that in mind, she reached up and brushed the dust from Jake's broad shoulders.

And people *were* watching. Renata saw them out of the corner of her eye as she brushed Jake's jacket and straightened the collar. Women stopped and stared . . . and then pulled their eyes away and proceeded toward the church. And no wonder, Renata thought with a rush of what seemed to be jealousy. He was quite easily the handsomest man she had ever seen.

Renata took Jake's arm as they walked away from the buckboard. It was a perfect summer day, with a cloudless sky and a soft breeze offering relief from the warmth of the sun. Renata stopped, forcing Jake to stop with her. She closed her eyes and took a deep breath, holding that delicious sweet air in her lungs. It was as if she could smell the green of the trees around the church, mingled with Jake's pleasant male scent. She could feel the muscle of his forearm beneath her hand, could feel the light, warm breeze on her face.

"Are you all right?" Jake bent his head and whispered in her ear.

"Yes." Renata opened her eyes and smiled at him. She forgot herself for a moment, her reserve gone. "Every now and then I realized that I'm living in a perfect moment. And I make myself stop so I can memorize it. This moment will never come again, and I want to remember

153

the sun and the trees and . . ." *And you, Jake.* But she couldn't tell him that. " . . . and that wonderful breeze."

"A perfect moment," he repeated.

"Um-humm." Renata began to move forward again, leading Jake reluctantly toward the church.

As they walked toward the church, Jake's collar was suddenly tight and uncomfortable. He didn't know if it was Renata's presence at his side, or the smile she had bestowed upon him, or the idea of sitting in church with every eye in town on him and his "bride," that made him edgy. No matter what the reason, he had the urge to run. It had been his way of dealing with difficulty for a long time. Not physical confrontations, no. He was very good at handling those. It was his emotions he had a hard time managing. It was feelings he ran away from, and all he wanted to do now was turn and leave Renata alone in front of the church, run into the mountains and not look back. Instead he leaned over and whispered in her ear, "Can I sleep during the sermon?"

Renata kept her eyes straight ahead. "Only if you promise not to snore."

"I don't snore."

"Yes, you do," she said, her lips twitching at the corners as she suppressed a smile.

She had a way of making his worries disappear, and Jake began to relax as they walked through the open doors of the church. They were being studied, openly by some and surreptitiously by others, and his scowl returned.

"I feel like a monkey on display in a cage," Jake whispered.

Renata led him to a pew in the back of the church. He was grateful for that much, at least. If the townspeople had to gawk, then let them turn their heads to get a good look. Still, his posture relaxed and his anger turned to mere discomfort. As they took their seats, Renata smiled warmly at the people around them, but Jake's face remained impassive. It was an inconvenience, that was all. He would certainly survive an hour or two in the close company of these people.

And then through the open double doors a middle-aged woman entered. Her head high, wearing a fancy blue dress more suitable for a ball than church, she regally glided down the aisle. Her hat was festooned with ribbons and a plume, and a lace fan was clasped in one of her hands. She had aged—he noticed that right away—and it wasn't his father who accompanied her, but their foreman, a rough-looking cowboy as out of place and uncomfortable as Jake was. Behind them were three young women, stair-steps, with the same nondescript brown hair as the woman who was so obviously their mother. They were younger than Renata, but children no longer. They wore solemn faces and frilly pink dresses, and Jake felt every bit of his peace drain away.

*   *   *

Renata turned to Jake and saw his pale face as he stared at the woman. His eyes were hard again, cold and blank, but Renata saw something flicker there. Hate? Fear?

As if sensing that Jake was staring at her, the older woman stopped and turned to look at him from the aisle. She looked a bit surprised but in control as she studied Jake with an air of condescension, and turned her calculating eyes to Renata. Then she turned away with a disinterested wave of her fan and walked with her escort and the trio of young women to sit in the front pew.

"Jake, who . . ." Renata began, but he silenced her with a glare.

The sermon began, and Jake didn't go to sleep as he had threatened. Renata studied his stony face, as he stared straight ahead into nothingness. He was taller than anyone in the room—couldn't have been inconspicuous if he tried—but his icy stare over the heads of the worshippers only called more attention to his presence, and the people around him were squirming before the sermon was done. It had nothing to do with the minister's message. She knew Jake was ready to explode.

They were the first ones to leave once the service was over, Jake fairly bursting through the double doors at the back of the church. Renata had to run, taking short, quick steps to keep up with him as he stalked toward the buckboard. She had never seen Jake so tense, not even when he had been set to hang, not even during their shotgun wedding. She could see the tension in his straight back and his shoulders, could almost feel it radiating from him.

Jake stopped at the buckboard and offered his stiff arms to help her up, but Renata jumped back.

"What about our picnic?"

"Not today," Jake said, his words low and somehow ominous.

"You promised." Renata knew she sounded like a spoiled child, could hear it in her petulant words.

They stared one another down, each supremely stubborn and unyielding in his own way. Jake's face would have frightened most grown men half to death, but Renata met his anger with a determination of her own. Then his eyes flickered and left hers as he stared over her shoulder, and the hard look on his face changed . . . so slightly, Renata didn't think anyone else would have noticed. Moments later a fine carriage passed them, drawn by matching bays. Renata glanced and saw the woman who had stared at Jake earlier, the woman with the three young ladies. The man who had escorted the women drove the carriage, and he looked at Jake, a casual but somehow hateful gleam in his eyes. Renata doubted the driver was related to the women. He seemed more like an employee, a servant. He didn't have that air of confidence the snooty woman emanated.

"Who are they, Jake?" Renata waited until

the carriage had passed, all her earlier determination fading in the light of Jake's unease.

"Nobody," he said brusquely, turning away from her.

Renata stepped up behind him and tentatively laid her palm on his back. He stiffened at her touch but didn't pull away. He seemed to her such a mystery, rough one minute, tender the next. Impervious to the taunts of an entire town, with a hint of pain in his eyes that seemed invisible to everyone else. At that moment she was desperate to understand but terribly afraid to push him.

"If you're really not up to a picnic today, I understand," she said softly. "Sometimes I try to do . . . too much."

Jake turned and looked down at her, all sign of his consternation and pain gone. He was cold and casual. "You'll get your picnic, Renata."

Jake swung the picnic basket and the old quilt out of the back of the buckboard. He appeared to have washed away his anger and doubts, but Renata knew no one could push away his emotions like that. They walked to the grounds at the rear of the church, where their wedding reception had been held, Jake shortening his stride so Renata didn't have to rush to keep up with him.

Jake spread the quilt in the broken shade of an old oak tree. Irregular spots of sunlight fell on the quilt like diamonds, but the air was cool in the shadows provided by the dark green leaves.

Many families were scattered around the large grassy area. Children ran in the sun, women laid out an abundance of food, and men slept . . . or pretended to, until it was time to eat. Renata was not surprised that Jake had chosen a spot far away from the others, nor was she disappointed. They were there to make an appearance, not to socialize. That would come later.

Jake shrugged out of his jacket and sat cross-legged on the quilt, like an Indian. With a jerk he pulled the leather band from his hair and shook his head. Renata could see the defiance rising within him, the flash in his eyes.

Renata tucked her legs beneath her and spread her skirt as she faced Jake. The stark white of his linen shirt was a breathtaking contrast to his dark complexion, and she stared at the little bit of exposed skin at his throat before she shook her head and brought herself to her senses.

"All right." She sighed. "Let's get this over with." Her voice was pragmatic, in perfect control. "I am going to burst if you don't tell me who those people were." She was curious, that was true, but in fact she was afraid Jake was the one who was about to burst.

Raising his eyebrows, showing a spark of cynical amusement, Jake hesitated. It was almost as if he was judging her, trying to decide if he could trust her.

"That woman is married to my father," Jake said coldly.

Renata leaned forward and whispered loudly, "She's your stepmother?"

"She's my father's wife," Jake corrected her sternly.

"And obviously you don't get along with her," Renata said unnecessarily.

"Obviously."

"And the girls? Are they . . ." Renata frowned. "Your sisters?" She couldn't imagine having a sister and watching her pass by in the street, unacknowledged.

"Half sisters," Jake corrected her again, the same ice in his voice.

Renata was momentarily at a loss for words. There were sisters? "Melanie never told me . . ."

"Mel knows that family is a part of my life I don't discuss." It was clear he was sending her a message to leave it alone.

"Who was that man with them?" Renata ignored his wishes and plowed forward.

"Ben Beechcroft. Their foreman."

"That name's familiar." Renata searched her memory, and it didn't take her long. "That's the man who said you burned that barn. That he saw you that night. That liar. I detest a liar."

Jake smiled wickedly. Renata cocked her head and stared at him, realized what he was thinking, and slapped his knee in mild admonishment. "Jake Wolf. I don't lie; I tell stories. There's a big difference."

Jake reached into the basket and passed Renata a chicken leg. She took it, glad to see that the anger in his eyes had faded. Then he reached in and grabbed a biscuit, and passed it to her casually. She took the biscuit with her other hand.

"I did pack plates in there, Jake," she said, laughing as he came up with another piece of chicken and tried to give it to her, still smiling.

Jake rested his hand over her belly. Even through the layers of clothing she felt the warmth of his hand, the strange, electric surge that passed through her body. Her smile faded slowly at her immediate reaction to his touch.

"You're eating for two, remember?" he reminded her with a half smile, not moving his hand.

"Jake, you really shouldn't." Her voice was little more than a whisper. "People are watching."

Jake slowly drew his hand away, letting his long fingers trail lazily across the fine fabric of her dress. Renata felt an uncontrollable shiver. There was something between them, some kind of unchained energy that was getting harder and harder to control.

Chapter Thirteen

Renata put the finishing touches on the apple pie she was preparing, crimping the edges of the crust and trimming off the excess dough with a quick swipe of the kitchen knife. She was turning out to be a good cook, beginning to feel confident enough to improvise on the recipes in Melanie's cookbook. The warm smells of the kitchen, with a touch of herbs and spices in the air, were comforting, and she had the fulfilling experience of creating something for the first time in her life, even if it was just a simple apple pie.

Her wrist had almost healed, but she continued to wear the calico bandage around it and to allow Jake to brush her hair at night and braid it for her. She could easily have done it herself—surely he knew that—but she had come to enjoy the simple ritual and was reluctant to give it up. That was the time she felt closest to Jake, though he was always silent as he sat behind her on the rug and ran his nimble fingers through her hair.

Jake had been more pensive than ever since their near disastrous Sunday visit to Silver Valley and the revelation that Jake's estranged family lived nearby . . . that he had sisters. Melanie had told her Jake's father was a rancher, but not that he lived so near to Silver Valley.

It had been three of the longest, quietest days of her life. Even when Jake was with her in the cabin he said nothing, ignoring her when she chattered. She knew his thoughts were far away, and there was nothing she could do to bring them back to the present.

Sisters; maybe that was the key. If Jake could learn to get along with his family, even if only the girls, he wouldn't be alone, and Renata could leave behind her concerns for Jake and make her way to Texas. Her own sister was such a comfort to her. If only Jake could find that solace in his own family. She had decided that reuniting him with them would be a much easier task than finding him a new wife. That prospect was turning out to be much too difficult.

Renata slid the pie into the oven with a frown on her face. This was getting complicated. Her original plan had been so simple: Find a rancher like Gabriel, fall madly in love at first sight, marry, live happily ever after just like in the fairy tales. The plan had seemed perfectly logical when she'd stepped from the stage and her feet had touched the dusty Silver Valley street. Now, if she thought about it too much, her scheme seemed childish and impractical.

With a heavy sigh, Renata realized that she needed to get away from Silver Valley and start over. In Texas her plans would come alive again, would become real again.

She glanced out the window, half expecting to see Jake approaching on that frighteningly large black stallion. Of course, he was nowhere to be seen. It was almost as if he'd been avoiding her since Sunday. Maybe he regretted telling her that the woman was his stepmother—his father's wife—and the girls were his half sisters. Maybe Jake wanted to keep himself distanced from everyone, even her. She'd felt that gulf between them in the days since then, a cold distancing that she knew was necessary, and yet was somehow hateful.

Jake piled the goods on Donnie Boyle's counter, silent as always, his scowl in place. Janie Boyle was stacking newly arrived bolts of material next to ribbons and laces on a counter in the back of the store. Once or twice Jake's eyes had wandered to that table. He'd never noticed it before, in all the times he'd been in the Boyles' general store. Certainly it had been there all along; he'd just never seen it. He found himself wondering which of those notions Renata would like. What was her favorite color? Did she like the satiny ribbons best, or the frilly laces? He shook his head and returned his attention to the task at hand. There was already a stack of canned goods on the counter, and he added an assortment of penny candy, some store tea and coffee, and dried apples.

Jake paid no attention to the stares he received as he piled goods on the shopkeeper's counter. When he walked down a particular aisle the other patrons moved out of his way. He was accustomed to the frightened stares, the hurried swish of the women's skirts as they moved away from him, the downcast glances when he met a stare.

He knew the moment Kenny Mails sauntered into the store, a rueful half grin on his face, his hat pushed back on his head. Kenny was looking over the tobacco, his eyes drifting now and again to Jake. The cowhand's fair hair and blue eyes had a way of making him look angelic, no matter what he was up to, but the gleam in his eyes hinted at devilish tendencies.

Jake ignored Kenny, as he always tried to do. He signaled Donnie Boyle with a nod of his head that he was finished with his shopping, and Boyle began to add up the purchases.

Jake could hear the slow thud of Kenny Mails's boots. There was a dark foreboding in the sound as Mails seemed to stalk Jake.

"How's married life treatin' you, Wolf?" Kenny talked in a soft voice, his face close to

Jake's shoulder. Too close for Jake's comfort.

Jake ignored the question, but his back stiffened.

"She's a pretty little thing, your wife is," Kenny continued, a taunting tone in his voice. "What does she think about coming to Silver Valley and findin' herself hitched to a goddamn heathen?"

With great effort, Jake kept his back to Mails. The cowhand was looking for a fight, and it wasn't the first time. Jake was not popular, but Kenny seemed to hate him more than most, and didn't mind taking a pounding if it meant he got in a few good licks himself. The end result was always the same: Kenny went back to the Summers ranch with a reprimand from the sheriff, and Jake spent anywhere from a single night to a week in jail. He couldn't afford to let that happen . . . not now, and he realized that that was exactly what Kenny was counting on. Renata would be left alone at the cabin.

Kenny looked over the goods on the counter, noting the penny candy. "Does the missus have a sweet tooth?" Jake was losing his patience. Normally, it didn't take much to get him swinging. "What else does she like, Jake?" he asked, leering. "I'll bet I know exactly what she likes."

Jake felt the rage growing inside him, a rage that was coming dangerously close to the surface. Every muscle in his body was tense. He was aware of each move Kenny made, every breath the man took, of the way Boyle was staring at the two of them, of the suddenly silent general store. Patrons had stopped, listening to Kenny's taunting words.

"If I'd known what a round-heeled tramp she was, I woulda . . ."

Jake's fist flew back so fast that Mails never saw it coming . . . not until the back of Jake's fist pounded into his face, splitting his lip. Before he could recover Jake had spun around, his fists pounding the man's face as Kenny delivered weak punches of his own. Jake was so enraged that Mails's attempts at fighting him were futile.

Then Jake felt the cold steel of a six-shooter barrel against his neck and heard the click of the hammer as it was pulled back.

He and Kenny stopped moving, two bloody forms on the floor of the general store. Kenny's chest was heaving, and he raised a hand to the cut above his eye.

"Stand up, both of you." The sheriff's voice was cold and tired.

Kenny swiped a bloody hand across the front of his pale blue shirt as he stood, a wry smile appearing on his face even though the blood that covered them both was all his. "He jumped me for no reason, Sheriff Collins," Kenny said petulantly. "Goddamn savage ought to be locked up for good."

Jake's eyes were narrowed as he watched his accuser. This had happened so many times in the past that he had learned not to try to defend himself.

Jake turned his head and looked at Donnie Boyle. Renata liked him, and he seemed to have a certain fondness for her. Jake hated to ask anyone for help, but it wasn't for him; it was for Renata.

"Go to the cabin and tell Renata what happened." Jake's face and voice were indifferent as he looked across the counter at Boyle. "Bring her to town. I don't want her up there by herself." He didn't acknowledge the gun that was now pointed at his side. "Please."

Donnie Boyle stepped from behind the counter and looked at the blood on the floor of his usually immaculate establishment. There was a puzzled look in his eyes. Jake waited for Boyle to support Kenny's claim. It wouldn't be the first time.

"Sheriff Collins," Boyle said with a confused frown on his face, "Kenny started it. Insulted Jake's wife. Truth be known, if Jake hadn't hit Kenny, I probably would have myself."

The sheriff looked at Kenny Mails, tired resignation on his face. "Is this true, Kenny?"

"No, sir," Kenny answered defensively.

Jake remained silent. Why had Boyle stepped forward and defended him? The exact same thing had happened before, in one form or another, more times than Jake could count; and no one had ever come to his defense.

"Daddy?" The voice was soft and hesitant as Felicia Collins stepped forward.

"Pumpkin." Sheriff Collins's face softened. "You shouldn't be here . . ."

"Mr. Boyle's telling the truth," Felicia interrupted her father, wringing her hands and looking at the floor. "Mr. Mails insulted my friend Renata Wolf most terribly. I won't repeat . . ."

"That's not necessary," Collins said abruptly.

Janie Boyle spoke up in a loud voice from the back of the store, where she still stood by the notion counter. "You ought to lock up Kenny. If he was my boy, I'd give him a good whippin' and send him to bed without any supper. Jake didn't do nothin' you wouldn't have done."

One by one the remaining customers in the general store agreed. Sheriff Collins had no choice but to release Jake, who had not spoken a single word to justify his actions.

The sheriff led Kenny from the store, but Jake knew that Mails wouldn't be locked up. He would be sent back to the Summers ranch with a mild warning, and the next time he felt like harassing Jake, he wouldn't have a second thought.

The Boyles' general store slowly returned to normal, Donnie wrapping up Jake's purchases and the customers resuming their shopping. Jake knew that he should thank Boyle, but the words stuck in his throat.

Finally Boyle finished bundling Jake's purchases and took payment. Unlike the other residents of Silver Valley, Jake always paid in cash. He knew that the shopkeeper wouldn't consider extending credit to him, even though the old man knew Jake was more capable of paying his debts than most of the other customers.

As he handed over the last package to Jake, Boyle looked into his face. "You know, Kenny's got it in for you. You got more than just yourself to think of now. Watch yourself, son."

Jake almost flinched at the warning. This was all Renata's doing. He knew that. People liked her, and were beginning to see him as an extension of her. He didn't know if he liked that or not. Until now, he'd always known where he stood with these people.

He left without acknowledging Boyle's warning or his assistance, loading up his saddlebags and heading toward the mountains. It would be late before he returned to the cabin. That was good. He needed time to think, and the ride to Yellow Moon Woman's tepee would give him that time.

If the people of Silver Valley knew there was a full-blooded Cheyenne living in the mountains nearby, Yellow Moon Woman's life would be in danger. It made no difference that she was an old woman with no family and no other place to go. She was an Indian, and in their eyes that made her a threat.

He had found her a year earlier. When Mel and Gabe had gone to Philadelphia Jake had traveled to Indian Territory to see what remained of his grandfather's people. What he'd found saddened and sickened him. Most of the tribe was dead, and those who remained were thin and weak, sick with the white man's diseases and suffering from hunger. Yellow Moon Woman had remembered him well, but he had been shocked to find her so weak and thin, wasting away in a filthy lodge. He'd removed her from the reservation and brought her to her old homeland to die. She had been so near death when he carried her from the reservation, he didn't believe she would live to reach her destination.

But she fooled him. Not only did she live, she thrived. Her strength returned, and her vitality. The sparkle reappeared in her black eyes.

She lived in a tepee high in the mountains, and Jake supplied her with meat, canned goods, and her precious candy. She had developed quite a sweet tooth.

No one knew she was there. Jake had kept her presence a secret even from Mel and Gabe. Yellow Moon Woman was a link to the part of Jake's life that had been hard and cruel, but still warmer than any part of the white man's world.

Until now.

Chapter Fourteen

"I think it's time," Jake said in a low voice as he finished braiding Renata's hair.

Renata fidgeted as she sat on the rug in front of the cold fireplace. Jake had been late getting home, but she'd waited up for him, warming his dinner when she'd heard his horse, hoping that tonight he wouldn't be so distant. If anything, he was more troubled than ever . . . silent and dark, brooding even as he had eaten in silence.

"Time for what?" She turned to look at him, knowing what he meant, hoping somehow that she was wrong.

"Time to go to Denver." Jake affirmed her fears.

"It's much too soon." Renata kept her voice calm. "If I disappear now, they'll probably accuse you of doing away with me and disposing of the body in some clever Cheyenne fashion. Cruel Jake, murdering the woman he was forced to marry, and her unborn baby as well. They'll certainly hang you then, and I won't be there to defend you."

"You're spinning a tale again, Renata," Jake said, no expression on his face. "It's been long enough."

Renata pursed her lips and turned her face away from him. Goodness, he was anxious to be rid of her. And could she blame him? Shouldn't she be anxious as well?

"All right. But I insist on just one more . . . one more excursion." With her back to him, he couldn't see the mixed emotions that played across her face. Disappointment, displeasure, and, finally, a dawning smile.

"Not another Sunday picnic," Jake said solemnly.

"No. In fact, we could do this tomorrow and be done with it, if you like." She made her voice sound lighter, filled with anticipation. "After that we can go to Denver. I'll even agree to stop by the Boyles' store and say good-bye, so they won't really believe you've done away with me."

"The sooner the better."

"Fine. Tomorrow it is." Renata stood and turned to look down at Jake. She had the urge to brush the hair away from his face, but she held back.

"Where are we going?"

Renata rolled up on the balls of her feet and rocked back on her heels, excited and unable to contain it. "I want to meet your family . . ."

"No!" Jake shot to his feet. "I have no family."

Renata circled Jake, her steps slow and calculating. "You've let that woman get the best of you."

"You don't know . . ."

"And you're not going to tell me. I've resigned myself to that fact." Renata fairly danced around him. "But I have a plan."

"I'm very sorry to hear that," Jake said cynically.

"Revenge, Jake. Small, but revenge just the same." Her voice held a touch of intrigue, a hint of humor. "You see, I know your step . . . your father's wife."

"You do?"

"Not personally, but I know people like her. Women who feel it necessary to wear their fanciest dress to church, to dress their daughters to look younger than they really are to make themselves look younger. They worry over every wrinkle, over every possession other women have. They must have the best of everything. They are as power hungry as ambitious men, in their own twisted way."

Jake didn't take his eyes from her face, and his mood remained surly. "No."

Renata placed her hands on her hips and faced him defiantly. "Do you want your annulment?" she asked with a challenge in her voice.

"Yes."

"Then cooperate with me just this . . . just one more time. I promise you, you'll see your stepmother boil. She'll turn red in the face and her eyes will bulge. Goodness, she'll want to explode by the time I'm done with her. Wouldn't you like to see her drop that facade she's built around herself?"

"How can you know my father's wife so well?"

Renata smiled and stepped away, ready to retire for the night. "I've known women like her all my life. This should be fun."

"You should have let them hang me," Jake said darkly.

Renata laughed lightly. "Good night, Jake."

Jake watched her disappear, and she took the life that filled the room with her. Yes, they had to get that annulment soon, so Renata could get on with her life.

He had realized as he rode toward Yellow Moon Woman's camp that if it was possible for the townspeople's acceptance of Renata to rub off on him, then it was also possible for their hatred of him to be transferred to her. She couldn't live like that. She needed people around her, their acceptance, love, and friendship. But if she stayed much longer he wouldn't be able to let her go.

It was all he could do now to keep his hands

off her, not to kiss her, not to touch her. Neither of them considered this to be a real marriage, but something was changing . . . and he felt it grow every day. It was like a long gossamer thread that was binding them together, and every day the thread wound tighter and tighter, bringing them closer toward . . . what? He didn't want to find out. There was more danger in that than in the fiercest storm, than in the sharpest blade.

Renata was perched on the edge of the seat of the buckboard, her back straight, a light of excitement in her eyes. She was wearing a dress Jake had never seen, an azure blue day dress that was simple and elegant, showing off Renata's hourglass figure and at the same time projecting an air of elegance. She held a matching parasol above her head, keeping the bright sun from her skin.

Jake had protested Renata's request that he wear the suit he had donned for their morning at church, and they had finally reached a compromise. Jake wore a plain pair of black pants and a white linen shirt with wide sleeves that gave him the look of a dashing pirate. He had even slipped into the black boots Renata had shined for him, and allowed her to pull his hair back.

He was already regretting his decision, dreading the confrontation that was certain to come. Just the thought of coming face to face with Corinne Summers terrified him. God, it had been fourteen years. But she was just a woman. A manipulative, lying woman.

Only Renata could have gotten him into this situation. He should've tossed her over his stallion and taken her to Denver for that annulment weeks ago . . . whether she liked it or not. But he hadn't. And he wouldn't. How the hell did she get him to do things he'd never dreamed of?

"Remember," Renata reminded him for the umpteenth time as they approached the Summers house. "Don't lose your temper. And whatever I say, when I ask you a question, you simply say, 'Yes, dear.' No matter how outrageous, no matter how ridiculous . . ."

"Yes, dear," Jake agreed sullenly, just to shut her up. He didn't want her to see how nervous the prospect of facing his father's wife made him. And his father? Probably out on the range this time of day. Little chance of seeing him, but it wasn't out of the question, either. A part of him wanted to turn the buckboard around and take Renata back to the cabin. But he didn't.

The Summers house was a fancy two-story affair, with a long front porch studded with carefully arranged rocking chairs. Meticulously tended rose bushes dotted both sides of the steps that led to the wide front door. Lace curtains ruffled in the breeze, and Renata knew that though the house looked warm and inviting, it wasn't.

She could feel the tension in Jake's hand as

he helped her down. A muscle in his cheek twitched, and his shoulders were straighter than usual . . . stiffer. He was an imposing figure of a man, and she could see how he might frighten some people. But not her. Never her.

"Jake?" she whispered hesitantly, wondering too late if this wasn't all a mistake.

"Yes, dear?"

His response brought a smile to her lips. "It'll be all right. I promise."

She kept her hand on his arm as Jake led her to the front door, and she somehow felt that they were walking to their doom. It was a fleeting and inexplicable feeling, gone as fast as it had arrived, washing over her like a cold wind that burst forth and then suddenly died.

Corinne Summers strutted into the parlor with all the confidence of a woman who was accustomed to getting what she wanted. She didn't bother to smile, but neither did she lose her composure as she stared at her visitors.

"What are you doing here?" She directed her question to Jake, her coolness complete from her marble stance to her icy timbre.

"Acually, I was the one who insisted on this visit." Renata stepped between Jake and Corinne Summers. Jake was looking at the woman as if he'd just as soon strangle her as take his next breath, and Corinne was looking at him with just as much hate. "It seems such a shame to live so close and not be on friendlier terms. I am especially interested in getting to know your daughters . . . Jake's half sisters . . ."

Corinne cringed at this, as if she'd never considered the fact that Jake and her daughters were related in any way. "No," she said sharply. "That's out of the question."

Renata faced her down, unwilling to give up so easily. "Why?"

Corinne gave Renata a stare meant to frighten her, but she didn't know how tough Renata was. "You have no idea what you're stepping into the middle of . . ."

"And I don't care," Renata shocked Jake and his father's wife by interrupting. "Obviously whatever divided this family happened long ago. It's foolish to cling to hatred . . . to cling to anything from the past or to ponder too much on tomorrow. Jake has sisters, and I'd like to meet them."

"Out of the question," Corinne repeated.

Renata sighed and began to pace slowly, almost lazily. "I'm very disappointed," she said sadly. "I had so hoped to be able to introduce them to an element of society of which they've been deprived thus far." Her sigh was dramatic. "When the house is finished I hope to entertain often, and Mama and Papa have promised to keep us busy entertaining their friends year-round. Lord Edenworth is so looking forward to hunting in the wilds of the West. He has two younger brothers. William is quite handsome, though a bit of a rake, and Derek is a scamp, but quite good-looking, as well."

Corinne was no longer looking at Jake. "You're building a house?"

"Yes." Renata beamed. "We haven't purchased the property yet, but Papa has assured me that he will buy whatever I want. Price is no object. It's a wedding present, you see."

Corinne smirked. It made her look older, revealing her darker side. "I'm sure your mama and papa are thrilled to have Jake as a son-in-law."

"They are," Renata agreed happily. "Mama was disappointed at first that I broke off my engagement to Percival—that's Lord Edenworth—" she explained, "in order to come to Colorado and be with Jake. But I'm certain they will love him as much as I do."

She turned to give Jake a brilliant smile, found him scowling at her, and ignored it. "Isn't that right, darling?"

Jake hesitated. "Yes, dear."

Renata looked around the lavishly furnished room. The parlor could have been one of hundreds in Philadelphia or Boston, but it seemed terribly out of place on a ranch. "What a lovely little house you have. So quaint." Her voice held no sarcasm, no hint that she wasn't sincere.

Corinne's face turned red. Her already cold eyes narrowed at the insult, and her nostrils flared. She had probably handpicked every piece of ostentatious furniture. Corinne opened her mouth to retort, but Renata beat her to it.

180

"I had so hoped that we could make amends before the baby is born." Renata walked around the room, trailing her fingers over the backs of upholstered furniture and over porcelain figurines. "My own parents will be so far away; it would be nice for the children to have their Grandmother Summers close by."

Corinne almost choked, but she quickly recovered. "You plan to have a big family?"

Renata laid a hand over her flat belly. Certainly Corinne had heard of her claim when Jake was set to hang. "I'd like six—three boys and three girls. But Jake wants at least eight." She turned to her husband. "Isn't that right, sweetheart?"

His eyes riveted on her, he hesitated, but only briefly, before he answered, "At least."

She tried to convey a slight admonishment with her eyes. That was not the response he was supposed to make.

The distant tinkling of a small bell interrupted their conversation, and Corinne turned toward the staircase. "Excuse me. Harrison needs me."

At the foot of the staircase she turned to her uninvited guests. "Harrison has been quite ill. It would upset him terribly to know that Jake is in this house. I beg you to stay here, and to keep your voices down." It wasn't a plea but an order, and she turned with a flourish to glide up the stairs.

"Let's go," Jake said, taking Renata's arm and

guiding her toward the front door. "You've had your fun."

Renata broke away from him and quietly slipped up the stairs. Jake stood at the foot of the staircase, his hands balled into fists at his sides. "I'm tired of this game, little girl," he hissed. "Get back down here."

Renata ignored him, and moved down the hall, listening at each door. The thought that she might get caught terrified her, but it didn't stop her. Finally she heard voices behind one door, a man's muffled tone and Corinne's commanding one.

"Just some ladies from the church, Harrison," Renata heard Corinne explain. "Droning on about a bake sale for a new roof or something. I'll get rid of them right away."

Renata didn't wait to hear a response from Jake's father, but stopped at the door next to his, praying that the room would be empty. The door opened without a sound, and Renata closed it again silently.

"Hello."

Renata spun around and was faced with a girl of perhaps twelve who was apparently not a bit surprised to see Renata appear in her room.

"Hello," Renata whispered, placing a finger to her lips.

The young girl sat cross-legged on her bed, holding a book, the look on her face mere curiosity, nothing more. Renata knew that she would have been terrified if a strange woman had appeared in her own room when she was that age.

"I know who you are," the girl whispered, smiling slightly. "You're married to my brother, aren't you?"

"Yes." Renata crossed the room and looked down at the pretty girl. She had Jake's eyes, blue and fathomless. "My name's Renata. You know about Jake?"

Jake's sister shrugged her shoulders. "A little. We're not supposed to talk about him. My mother says he's a killer, a savage, and we're not even to think about him."

"What does your father say?" Renata asked.

"Nothing."

"What's your name?" There was a plan forming in Renata's mind as she spoke to the young girl.

"Selina, but everyone calls me Lina."

Renata gave Lina her brightest smile. "Jake is downstairs." She saw the doubt in Lina's eyes. She was just a child. With what had her mother poisoned her mind?

"Jake's really very sweet," Renata said, believing what came from her heart. "He's really much more . . . kindhearted . . . than he allows the people around him to know. I think he would love to have a little sister like you. Why don't you go downstairs and talk to him? Introduce yourself?" Renata had developed an instant liking for Lina Summers. It would do Jake a world of good to have a bright sister. "If he frowns at you as if he intends to eat you alive . . . just ignore him."

Lina had to think only for a minute before she jumped from the bed. She stopped at the door when Renata showed every intention of staying where she was. "Aren't you coming with me?"

Renata shook her head. "I'd like to see your father, after your mother leaves."

Lina gave Renata a conspiratorial grin and slipped from the room, closing the door soundlessly behind her.

Renata returned to her place by the door and listened. Minutes later she heard the door to Harrison Summers's room open and close, and she listened as Corinne sighed deeply and moved sluggishly down the hall.

Renata held her breath as she opened the door.

The room was dark and musty, the heavy drapes pulled tight, blocking out the sunlight. The window was tightly shut, and not a breath of fresh air stirred in the uncomfortably hot bedroom.

A single candle burned on the bedside table, a table laden with bottled medicines, a tin cup, and a small silver bell. Renata took a deep breath before she stepped forward, trying to fortify herself.

There was a man resting uneasily in the center of the big bed. His breathing was short and ragged, and his hands occasionally twitched slightly. Renata moved silently to the bedside and looked down at the man, realizing with a start that Jake bore a great resemblance to Harrison Summers. There was gray at his temples, but the rest of his hair was dark. Renata saw Jake in the set of the man's jaw, and when he opened his eyes to look up at the intruder in his room she saw Jake's eyes. It somehow made their estrangement sadder.

"Who are you?" he whispered, weakly.

"Renata Marie Wolf." She introduced herself without her usual bright smile. Her father had tried to keep her away from his patients, away from the uglier side of life, but she had not been completely isolated. This man had the look and the smell of death. "Jake's wife," she explained.

A light came into his eyes as he looked up at her. "Jake's here?"

Renata nodded, unable to tell if the glint in his eyes was from excitement or fear. "He won't see you. At least, not today. But I . . ." She had so many questions for this man, but time was short. Corinne could come in at any moment. "What's wrong with you?"

"Gastric fever," Harrison Summers said with disgust. "I've been healthy all my life, and now this . . . but I don't want to talk about that. How's Jake? I'm glad he's married, finally. I . . . I need to see him before it's too late. Will you bring him to me?" There was a hint of desperation in his deep voice, and Renata recognized his need to make things right before he died.

"I'll try." Renata reached out and took

Harrison Summers's hand. It was difficult to tell in the dim candlelight, but it seemed the man's skin was yellow, and as she lifted his hand she saw the rash on his arm and the back of his hand, the skin flaking away. The hand she held was weak, cold and clammy. He was a very sick man. "There's a lot I don't understand," she admitted to her father-in-law. "I'm afraid there's no time."

Harrison squeezed her hand feebly. "Tell Jake that I . . . that I made a mistake . . . a terrible mistake." He was becoming agitated, his eyes working rapidly, his hand squeezing hers convulsively.

Renata leaned closer to the man. "Mistakes can be mended."

She heard footsteps on the stairs, faint but determined footsteps that could only belong to Corinne Summers.

"Are you taking medication?" Renata asked quickly. She received her answer with a faint nod of Summers's head.

Renata bit her bottom lip. What if she was wrong? Gastric fever? "Stop taking it," she said urgently, just before the door burst open and Corinne Summers flew into the room.

"How dare you?" she asked bitterly. "Harrison is very ill. He does not need this sort of aggravation."

"I was wandering around your adorable little house and I just happened to hear Mr. Summers calling, so I stepped in." Renata smiled radiantly.

"Harrison didn't call." Corinne moved to her husband's side. "When he needs anything he rings the bell." She frowned down at her sick husband. "How dare you go snooping . . ."

"It's true, Corinne," Harrison said quietly. "I heard someone moving about in the hall, and I thought it might be one of the girls."

Harrison reached out and took Renata's hand once more. "You must come again, my dear. We should have a nice, long visit, you and I. And Jake . . . if he'll come. Talk to him. Ask him . . ."

"You're not up to company, Harrison." Corinne tried to inject concern into her voice but didn't manage it well. She sounded more annoyed than concerned.

"I'll be back, Mr. Summers." Renata ignored Corinne's protests. "Very soon. And I have a feeling you'll be fit as a fiddle before you know it."

Corinne ushered Renata from the room, crushing her arm and practically dragging her through the door. Renata ignored the fingers biting into her arm and only flinched when Corinne slammed the door.

She was certain then that she was right. There was something going on in the Summers household, something so dastardly Renata had a difficult time trying to come to terms with her conclusions.

One thing was certain: She couldn't leave Silver Valley. Not yet.

Chapter Fifteen

Renata practically floated down the stairs, Corinne directly behind her. Before she reached the bottom of the steps she saw Jake's back as he leaned forward slightly. Lina was talking to him animatedly, her arms waving as she spoke. Two older girls stood a distance apart, watching warily, neither of them as ambitious or as brave as their little sister.

Corinne was livid. "I told you girls to return to your studies," she said sharply, and Lina's smile disappeared as she backed away from Jake.

The girl who appeared to be the oldest spoke up, obviously terrified of her mother. "Lina refused to leave, and I . . . we didn't think we should leave her alone . . . in here."

Renata ignored the exchange and walked

straight to the two older girls. They favored Lina, but lacked the younger girl's spark. Renata had a feeling that Corinne Summers had done everything in her power to squash any spark of life in her daughters.

"It's such a pleasure to meet you," Renata said with a friendly smile. "I'm Renata, Jake's wife."

"My name's Harriet. I'm the oldest and this is Gilda," the girl answered, studying Renata warily.

Renata turned to face Jake. His face was unreadable, but at least he wasn't glowering at her.

In an act of bravado, Lina stepped forward. "My name's Lina," she introduced herself solemnly, as if she and Renata had never met. The excitement of the secret they shared was in her eyes, those eyes just a shade more pale than Jake's.

"The three of you must come to tea some afternoon," Renata said as she joined Jake, laying her hand on his arm. "Mustn't they, darling?"

Her hand on his arm trembled slightly, but she continued to smile. Her voice might have been a touch too bright, but it was too late to change that.

"Yes, dear."

"But right now I'm afraid we must be running along," she said before Corinne could throw them out. "I have quite a busy day planned for tomorrow. It was a pleasure to meet you all."

They left quickly, Renata never taking her hand from Jake's arm, uncertainty building within her. How much should she tell Jake? It was, after all, just a suspicion. He walked her to the buckboard, and she waited for him to help her up. But instead he placed a hand on either side of her, leaning into the buckboard and pinning her in place. She turned to face him and was greeted with stormy eyes. He was close—too close—and his face was so close to hers, she became anxious.

"What have you done, Renata?" he asked in a low voice. "Tea? Have you lost your mind?"

"I'll explain later, Jake. They might be watching."

"They are watching. I can feel it."

Renata couldn't see the house. All she could see was Jake's dark face and wide chest in front of her. "This will look quite strange . . ."

Jake leaned forward and kissed her then, a feathery kiss that should have passed by without affecting her. But she felt it to her very toes, in the pit of her stomach. His easy kiss stole her breath away.

"Why did you do that?" she whispered.

"You said it yourself: People are watching."

Renata pouted. It was obvious their few kisses had meant nothing to him; they certainly didn't affect him the way they did her. Otherwise, he wouldn't be wearing that small but wicked smile.

"Besides," he ignored her discomfort, "a little kiss seems perfectly normal behavior for a married couple who are planning to have eight kids."

"Six," Renata said with a slight frown, "and they're not kids, they're children. Kids are little billy goats."

Jake leaned forward and kissed her again. His hands didn't move to hold her; they remained pressed to the buckboard. Only their lips touched, but that was enough to immobilize Renata.

She made herself remember that he only kissed her when there was an audience, never when they were alone. That simple fact told her more than she wanted to know.

The lace curtain fluttered down, but Corinne and Ben Beechcroft could still see the couple at the buckboard.

They were alone as Corinne had hurriedly ushered the girls from the room, even Lina's confidence gone with Jake and Renata out of the house.

Ben placed his arm around her shoulder, letting his hand drop to brush her breast, a gesture not of affection, but of possession. "I can shoot him right now," Ben offered easily. "With that pretty little wife of his diverting his attention, he'd never know what hit him."

"If you were a decent marksman he would have been dead weeks ago," Corinne snapped, picking up his hand disdainfully and shrugging his arm off her shoulder. "That won't work now. We have the girl to think of."

Ben kept his eyes on Jake as the half-breed helped his wife into her seat. "I shoulda killed that goddamn savage years ago." There was venom in his voice. "That's why I came out West . . . to kill Indians. I won't rest until there's not a drop of Indian blood left in this country. My brother died at Little Bighorn. Did you know that?"

Corinne bit back the sharp retort that came to her lips. She had heard the story a dozen times . . . and was sick to death of it. But the telling fueled Ben's anger, and she needed that anger now.

"The baby that girl carries has Indian blood in its veins. Just an eighth, of course," she said.

"Even that's too much," Ben said heatedly.

Corinne knew full well that there was something not quite right with her husband's foreman. He was prone to obsession . . . with his hatred of the Indians and his love for her. She'd used that particular obsession, taking him to her bed when she needed him and pushing him away when she didn't. He was rather like a slow child who kept coming back to her again and again.

Corinne smiled. "An accident, perhaps. Something that would claim the lives of both of them."

She had her own reasons for wanting Jake Wolf and his wife out of the picture. Permanently. She didn't share all of those reasons with Beechcroft. They were too practical for him to understand. Ben preferred the driving forces of hatred, passion, and revenge. Simple greed would not penetrate through all that.

Even though she had removed his hand from her breast just moments before, she turned and placed her palms against his chest. "A fire, perhaps?"

Ben nodded. "That old cabin should go up pretty fast." There was excitement in his voice. "Like when lightning hit the barn. Damn . . . you shoulda seen it, Corinne. The flames spread so fast." A frown crossed his face. "Too bad that girl stood up for the Indian."

"It's funny," Corinne said, her fingers walking up Ben's chest. "Until today I assumed this marriage was a fraud, a hoax to save Jake's neck. I just couldn't imagine that genteel girl and . . . and Jake, so I wasn't particularly worried."

She stood on her toes and kissed Ben's stubbled jaw. Seeing Jake and Renata together had changed that notion, and she knew her earlier assumptions had been wrong. The way Jake looked at his wife when he thought no one was watching . . . the way Renata had placed her hand on Jake's arm and sidled close to him . . . "I can't stand the thought of the two of them ruining our plans."

Ben smiled, and Corinne saw the sparkle of power she had put in his eyes. "I'll take care of them both," he said. "A fire. A late-night, blazing fire."

Corinne lifted wide eyes to him. "When?"

"Tonight."

She kissed him on the lips, and he renewed his vow to do as she wished. "A fire. Tonight."

Renata was quiet as they approached the cabin. How much should she tell Jake? What if she was wrong?

What if she was right?

Jake helped her down from the buckboard, releasing her as soon as her feet hit the ground. "I'll take care of the horses," he said curtly, his eyes dark and unreadable. "You start packing. Tomorrow we go to Denver."

"Tomorrow?" Renata spun around. She had thought to have at least a few more days. "I can't go tomorrow, Jake. It's too soon."

"You said this one visit. Don't you realize that I would rather face the devil himself than spend an afternoon with Corinne Summers?" There was a hint of exasperation in his voice.

Renata chewed on her bottom lip and wrang her hands gently. "I can't leave just yet, Jake," she said softly.

He spun around to stare at her, his eyes filled with foreboding. "And why not?"

"Because I think someone's poisoning your father." She said the words quickly, before she could change her mind. "Arsenic, if I'm correct. My father told me about a case, a doctor who poisoned his wife and said it was a severe case of gastric fever that killed her . . . but that's not all. There's the flaky skin, and the yellowing, and . . ."

Jake hung his head. "Dammit, Renata Marie Parkhurst. I've had . . ."

"Renata Marie Wolf," she corrected him quietly.

"These stories have got to stop. You can't go through life inventing . . . murder plots and nonexistent babies and . . ."

"I'm not making this up," Renata said solemnly.

Jake jumped into the buckboard to drive it to the stable at the big house. It was clear by the clenching of his jaw and the tenseness in his arms that their conversation was not over, but he left her standing on the front porch of the cabin, feeling desolate.

Chapter Sixteen

Jake sat in the dark, his back against the side of the cabin as he looked up at the silvered moon. Clouds raced across the sky, gray and silver, cloaking the moon and then allowing it to shine again.

Renata was sleeping, finally. She had tried and tried to convince him that someone was poisoning his father. Someone. They both knew that the one person in that household capable of murder was Corinne. Jake knew all too well what she was capable of.

Jake had finally convinced Renata that it was her imagination . . . that Harrison Summers was just a sick old man. He had seen the moment she had begun to doubt her own convictions in her eyes and in her frown. She hadn't taken his insistence that she was wrong and her eventual capitulation well, and she had packed her trunks tearfully, leaving out her gray traveling suit—the one she had been wearing when she arrived in Silver Valley.

In a matter of days she wouldn't be his wife anymore. Not that she had ever been . . . not really. That was the way she lived her life, playing games, imagination more a part of her life than reality. How could he blame her? How could he blame anyone for that? Reality could be brutal; Jake knew that as well as anyone.

The problem was, he was going to miss her. Too much. He had teased Gabe once, years ago, for falling for a prissy city woman. Mel had turned out to be anything but. She was a rancher's daughter who could outride and outshoot most men in Silver Valley . . . and most everywhere else, he imagined. Jake had always thought that if he ever married, it would be to a woman like Mel, the only woman he'd ever considered asking to share his life.

And here he was, growing more and more attached every day to the very sort of woman he despised. It was her smile, he decided, that lit up her whole face and made him want to smile back, no matter what he was feeling. Or it was her eyes. Green eyes that delved into his very soul, looking for answers to questions Jake had buried long ago. Or it was her hair, red-gold, just a touch of curl, heavy and silken to the touch and smelling of crushed flowers . . .

Jake buried his head in his hands. He never should have kissed her. He was no expert on seduction; his physical relationships had been with women who understood who he was and what he wanted. Jake had always managed to distance himself, so he had never kissed a woman and had her place herself so completely in his hands. He could feel it, Renata's trust and her wonder, her confusion at what happened when they touched.

He couldn't tell her that it confused him, too, and that he understood it even less. A simple brush of his lips on hers stirred sensations he had never felt before. Sensations that went deeper than simple desire, though the passion was there.

Once, he had been separate . . . completely isolated . . . and he had convinced himself that was for the best. He knew now that he would never be the same. He would always carry a piece of Renata with him, a memory, an empty place in the heart he had abandoned long ago.

Jake heard the sound of hooves nearing the cabin. They were furtive, cautious sounds, and Jake was instantly alert. He rose slowly, his back still against the cabin, and he moved to the corner just in time to see two riders approaching, masks hiding their faces as they leaned forward in their saddles.

Jake's hand went to his side, reaching for the knife that was always there . . . but not tonight. He had stormed from the cabin in nothing but his buckskin trousers.

Hoping that the darkness would hide him, Jake slipped around the corner, easing himself over the rail and onto the porch. The clouds danced overhead, revealing the moon once again, and Jake was still. The riders had stopped; they whispered in low voices as they looked toward the cabin.

And then they lit the torches, bathing their faces in harsh yellow light as the flames grew. One of the riders broke away, and Jake realized that the man was probably headed to the rear of the cabin. Sweat broke out on Jake's face and he bellowed Renata's name. She had to get out of the cabin now! The old place could go up in minutes.

The rider in front of the cabin recoiled in the saddle, and then tossed the flaming torch through the window to the room where Jake would have been sleeping . . . and he realized with desperation that the other man was probably tossing his torch into Renata's room.

Jake threw open the front door and stepped into the main room. Smoke filled the cabin, drifting from the hallway and the kitchen. He heard the man behind him and turned with an impatient grunt to grab the intruder . . . his only thought to immobilize him so he could get to Renata. He called her name again, but got no response as he wrestled the man to the floor.

Even with the mask, Kenny Mails was easily recognizable. Jake glared into the other man's eyes and saw the spark of fear. Kenny had always been a coward.

But Kenny held on, even as the smoke grew

around them, threatening to blind them both. They rolled across the floor, Kenny's grip on Jake's arms tenacious, reckless. Finally, Jake was able to pin Kenny to the floor, and he brought his fist back to still the squirming cowhand.

All Jake heard was a single footstep before he saw, from the corner of his eye, the stock of a rifle swinging toward his head.

The force of the blow knocked Jake back, off Kenny, and he saw the two men rush from the cabin before everything faded.

Black smoke and flaming walls were all Jake could see when he opened his eyes. The men who had started the blaze were gone, and Jake's only thought was to get Renata out of the cabin. He turned, on his hands and knees, toward the hallway.

The smoke was dense, surrounding Jake like an inpenetrable fog that threatened to distort his senses. The flames climbed the walls as he crawled down the hallway. He could feel the scorching heat . . . on his face, his hands, his back. How long had he remained unconscious? A minute? Five? What if he was too late?

He opened his mouth to call Renata, but his voice was weak and hoarse. The calico curtain to the bedroom, to his bedroom, was burning furiously, and Jake increased his pace.

The fire had just begun to lick at the curtain that separated Renata's bedroom from the hallway, and Jake burst through with dread building in his heart.

She was lying on the bed, miraculously untouched by the flames that crawled up the curtains and danced on the walls, but she was deathly still. It was unnatural to be surrounded by such destruction and to lay so still.

Jake felt a curious catch in his throat. What if he was too late?

"Renata!" He leaned over the bed and screamed into her face as he wrapped the quilt around her body and lifted her into his arms. She was limp and unresponsive; it was impossible to tell if she was breathing.

The doorway's curtain was now engulfed in flames, and Jake knew that the hallway was probably impassible. With one hand he yanked the burning curtains away from the window. The glass was intact, and he realized the second torch must have gone through the kitchen window. A heaven-sent mistake on the arsonist's part—Renata would surely be dead by now if the rapidly spreading fire had started in her bedroom.

He couldn't breathe. It might have been possible to lay Renata down and lift the lower panes—propping the window up and passing Renata safely outside—but that would take precious seconds that Jake didn't have. With a piercing yell, he jumped through the window, shattering the glass as he shielded Renata's body. He rolled away from the house, the cool clean air of the night washing over him, and Jake took a deep breath. The clean air burned his lungs.

He lay Renata in the grass and gently unwrapped her, pulling the quilt away from her face, then her body. There was no sign that she had been touched by the fire, but her eyes were closed and she remained motionless. Jake placed his ear close to her face, holding his own breath so he could hear her breathe. It was there, faint, shallow, so weak he could barely hear it.

He knew as he brushed her hair away from her peaceful face that she had inhaled too much of the black smoke as she slept.

"Wake up," he whispered, cradling her in his arms. She was as limp as a rag doll as he held her head against his chest. "Open your eyes and breathe, dammit." His voice was low, husky, the tearing at his heart painful as he looked down at her face, a quiet face lit by flames that grew, engulfing the cabin.

A ragged breath tore from him, and with what strength he had left he shouted at her, commanded her. "Renata Marie Parkhurst, open your eyes and *breathe!*"

Her eyelids fluttered, and a small frown formed on her brow. Renata coughed hoarsely and opened her eyes to look up at the man who held her so close. "Renata Marie Wolf," she corrected him, her voice no more than a whisper.

Renata lifted her head and stared in awe at the burning cabin. The heat was intense even at this distance, and she was overwhelmed by the power of it. It was like a living thing, a monster devouring its prey.

Jake was still holding her close, and she made no attempt to move away from him. "What happened?" Her voice was raspy, as if it hurt to speak, and she closed her eyes tightly. Then she turned her face into his chest, hiding from the destruction.

"It was deliberate," Jake said, his own voice a harsh whisper. "Kenny Mails and another man . . . tossed torches through the windows."

"Thank goodness you're a lighter sleeper than I am." Renata lifted her head and turned her eyes to the inferno.

Jake didn't tell her that he hadn't been asleep, that he had been wide awake and thinking about her. If he had been asleep they might both be dead now.

Renata dead, because of him.

She looked up at him then, perhaps knowing somewhere deep inside that he was thinking of her, and she gasped. He felt the blood trickling in a steady stream down one side of his face, running from the wound on his head. His right shoulder was cut in several places, sliced by the glass as he'd leapt through her window, and her eyes traveled down his arms as she leaned away from him. There were several nasty-looking burns.

His eyes followed hers, and his hand went to the gash on the side of his head. He had felt nothing . . . nothing at all until that moment, but suddenly everything hurt. His head, his shoulder, his hands and arms were burning with the fire of seared flesh.

"Jake." Renata laid a hand on the side of his face. "We have to get to the big house. You need medical attention right away."

Jake frowned. "No. I don't know who the other man was. It could have been anybody." A sudden, unwelcome thought pierced his brain like lightning. Whoever had tried to kill him wanted Renata dead, too. They could have dragged her out while he was unconscious—they could have ambushed him away from the cabin any time of the day—but they hadn't. The fire had been meant for them both. It was just as he had feared; the town's hatred of him had rubbed off on Renata.

Jake pulled himself to his feet, slowly, painfully, holding Renata's hand and helping her to stand. He continued to support her by holding her at his side, feeling her weakness, her uncertainty.

He was surprised that she hadn't tried to argue with him, to stop him as he headed for the stable. They could hear noise in the distance, riders approaching from the big house: Lester and the other hands.

Jake reluctantly left Renata sitting at the base of a tree, her face and her quilt-wrapped body hidden in the shadows, as he crept toward the stable. He could see Lester Patton and the hands pull up short of the cabin, knowing there was nothing to be done. With a stealth few men possessed, Jake led his big black stallion from the stable, not taking the time to do more than toss a blanket across the animal's back and ease a hackamore over its head.

He led his horse toward Renata, making out her still form in the dark shadows. She hadn't moved, except to draw her knees to her chest. When he offered her his hand she took it silently. There wasn't a word of protest as he drew her to her feet, not until he started to lift her and place her on the stallion's back.

"I can't ride," she said softly.

"I'll hold on to you. Don't worry."

Jake vaulted up behind her, taking the reins in one hand and wrapping his other arm around Renata's waist. He turned away from the blazing heat and the crackling light of the fire, toward the mountains.

Even in the dark, the stallion knew his way; Jake relaxed and kept his word. He held on to Renata as if for dear life, and as she leaned into his chest, he watched as she closed her eyes. He felt her shiver, her nightgown providing little warmth, and he wrapped the quilt around her shoulders. After the heat of the fire he welcomed the chill.

Jake said nothing as they moved farther and farther away from the burning cabin and civilization.

Chapter Seventeen

They climbed steadily and silently for more than an hour, passing through areas of complete darkness and patches of faint moonlight without a single misstep.

Jake finally halted the stallion in a rocky clearing touched by silver moonlight. He slid from the horse's back and lifted his arms to Renata; before he had a chance to grasp her waist she slid from her seat, dropping into his arms trustingly.

Jake felt her complete trust in him, her relaxed muscles as he caught her, her even breathing. He had almost wanted to drop her, to let her know that he wasn't worthy of that trust, but he hadn't. And he knew he never could.

There was a narrow, trickling creek close by,

and Renata didn't hesitate in ripping a long section of cloth from the hem of her nightgown and dipping it in the cold water. Jake squatted next to her as she wrung out the cloth, but he drew away from her when she reached over to bathe his face.

"Not afraid of a little water, are you?" Renata knelt before him, the cool cloth in her hands.

"I'll do it myself."

Renata ignored him and leaned forward, wiping his bloodstained face with the make-shift towel. "Don't be silly, Jake. Actually, I'm becoming quite accustomed to taking care of you." Her tone told him she was teasing him, though she wasn't smiling. "I don't know what you ever did without me."

He remained silent, ignoring that last explosive comment. How had he ever gotten along without Renata in his life? Quite well, he tried to tell himself forcefully as she passed the cold cloth over his face.

"There now," she said, satisfied. "How are your arms?" She took a wrist in each hand and tried to study his burns in the moonlight. It was simply too dark to see much of anything.

"Not too bad," Jake said gruffly. "I'll take care of that tomorrow."

Renata sighed, agreeing that would have to do.

It was a shadowy night, with only a slice of the moon to light their way as Jake led Renata to a secluded spot, a flat rock protected by a jutting edge over their heads. He took the quilt from around her shoulders and laid it on the ground.

"Get some sleep," he ordered quietly. "We won't be going any farther until morning."

Renata lowered herself to the hard ground, made only slightly softer by the thick quilt. She sat cross-legged on the edge closest to the back of the protected area, as she faced Jake.

"Come on." She patted the quilt. "You need rest a lot more than I do."

Jake was standing outside the covered spot, already missing the feel of her touch, her warmth against his now cold skin. "No. I'll keep watch."

"No one followed us, Jake. You would have known if they had." Her confidence in him was apparent in her voice. "I won't be able to sleep if I'm worried about you. If you don't rest, I won't either."

Jake looked at her, or tried to. All was dark under the precipice. In resignation he crawled onto the quilt, lying down at the far edge of the makeshift bed, turning his back to her. He heard her sigh of relief, listened to the rustle of her nightgown as she lay down behind him. It was mere moments before he heard her even breathing; she'd been more exhausted than she knew.

Jake knew he wouldn't sleep, not after what had happened. Not with the pain in his head and his arms and his shoulders. Not with Renata sleeping inches away . . .

*   *   *

Renata rolled up against Jake's bare back, snuggling against him, searching for warmth, relief from the cool night air. She pressed her cheek against his smooth skin, feeling his warmth. Jake, still sleeping soundly, turned to face her, throwing his arm around her and pulling her against his chest. Renata sighed deeply, trying to go back to sleep. She had been having a wonderful dream, but she couldn't quite remember it. Her arm snaked around Jake's waist while her foot searched for warmth between his calves.

As dawn cast its first light, Renata squirmed, pressing herself against Jake from knee to cheek, nuzzling her cheek against his bare chest. Jake's hand trailed mindlessly down her back, over her hip to the thigh that had been exposed as her nightgown rode up while she slept. She was dreamily aware of that strong hand on her thigh, those fingers trailing over her skin.

He lifted her, one hand on her thigh and the other behind her head, pulling her face toward his in a dreamlike daze. Her lips left a burning trail over his chest and throat, and when they met his it was a dizzying collision.

Renata's hands roamed with a will of their own. They danced over his broad chest and down his side, fascinated with every muscle, every silky inch of his skin. Her fingers caressed his neck and face and finally grasped the back of his head, her fingers entwining in his long hair.

Linda Winstead

She opened her mouth to accept the tongue he thrust almost lazily, and the sensation he aroused made her ache for more, for all of him. She pressed her breasts against him and moaned deep in her throat.

Jake held her to him, his hands in her hair and on her arched back. Renata sighed and placed herself completely in his hands. Jake rolled her onto her back, towering over her, never pulling his lips from hers. His hand found her breast and he massaged the firm nipple through the thin fabric of her nightgown. Her lips parted, and another unrestrained moan escaped.

Jake's lips trailed down her throat. His hand slowly pushed her nightgown to her waist and found the tapes that would loosen her fine lawn drawers. "Rennie," he whispered softly. "Is this a dream?"

Renata ran her hands through his hair. Her breathing was coming faster now, as was his, and she was almost breathless when she answered him.

"I don't think so, Jake."

Jake stopped moving then. He was completely still, only his warm breath against her throat reminding her of his passion. With his palms on either side of her head, Jake pushed himself up, creating a space between their bodies as he looked down at her.

Renata wasn't asleep anymore, but she smiled at Jake dreamily.

"Don't stop," she whispered.

"I have to," Jake said, but he didn't move. "You'll be . . . we'll be sorry later."

"I won't." Renata locked her hands behind Jake's neck and drew his lips to hers. She loved the taste of him, and now there was no one watching, no one to pull them apart. There was no one but the two of them, and she wouldn't let him run away. Not this time.

Jake lifted his lips from hers. "I should go," he whispered, even as he kissed her again.

"Don't leave me, Jake."

There were no more words spoken, no more needed. Renata clung to Jake and followed her body's instincts. He was a part of her; she realized that with a stunning clarity that eclipsed everything else she had ever known. All along she had believed that Jake needed her, and now she knew that she needed him just as much. Maybe more.

Jake pulled his lips from hers just long enough to slip the nightgown over her head and toss it aside. He lowered his head and kissed one nipple and then the other, and Renata arched her back and cried out for him.

In the soft light of the new morning sun, Renata watched as Jake slipped off his buckskins and tossed them aside to land in a heap with her nightgown. He was the most magnificent sight she had ever seen, and she drank him in with passion-clouded eyes. She had never seen a man naked before; the sight of Jake's manhood, swollen with his need for her, should have frightened her, but it didn't.

Jake would never hurt her.

Jake's eyes traveled over her body as he eased the lawn drawers from her with slow deliberation. He trailed his hands from her ankles to her waist. "You are beautiful," he whispered.

Jake's lips found her eager ones again, and she met him ardently, hungrily, and when he pressed against the moistness between her legs she lifted her hips to take him, driven toward a pleasure she didn't completely understand.

He entered her slowly, more gently than she had imagined he would. When he shattered her maidenhead Renata couldn't help her sharp intake of breath. Jake covered her mouth with his, showering her with comforting kisses and lying very still.

She let him know when her pain had passed, lifting her hips slightly and moving beneath him. Renata returned his kisses with greater passion, and her hands traveled down his back to clasp his firm buttocks. Every move she made, every rocking of her hips or caress of her fingertips was driven by something deep within her, something that had been locked within her, waiting for Jake to release it. It was passion—the passion he had only hinted at with his kisses.

When the spasms rocked her she clutched at Jake, holding him to her as if she would die if she let him go. And when the convulsions faded she felt the warmest, most wonderful sensation of contentment wash over her, filling her from her toes to the top of her head.

She felt Jake's release as he drove hard into her one more time. He whispered huskily into her ear, calling her name, calling her Rennie. Her childhood nickname had never sounded more right, and she smiled at him and buried her face against his neck, memorizing his smell, the soft light of dawn around them and yet not on them. Love. She loved Jake. He was a part of her, an undeniable part of her forever.

Renata felt him roll away from her, slowly, reluctantly, and she wrapped her arms around his neck and rolled with him. Did he love her as much as she loved him? What would he say when she told him how much she loved him? that he was all the world to her?

She looked into his blue eyes, darker now than they had been moments earlier. They were guarded, no longer open and readable, and she felt a moment of panic deep within her. He didn't love her . . . he didn't love her at all. She could have been any woman . . . a warm body on a cold morning.

As if to confirm her suspicions, Jake placed a stiff hand on the side of her face. "I'm sorry, Rennie. I shouldn't have . . ."

"For goodness sake, Jake." Renata turned away from him and grabbed her nightgown. "You needn't apologize." She pulled the delicate nightgown over her head, suddenly anxious to cover her nakedness, which had seemed so natural moments earlier. "You weren't exactly . . . the only one who got carried away."

Jake frowned at her. She was taking it all so casually. Too casually. "Still, I should have . . ."

Renata skirted him and left the shelter. "Just shut up, Jake." She kept her back to him. Her voice was too bright, too sharp. She wasn't so casual after all.

He watched her rigid back as he pulled on his buckskins. So, she regretted it, as well. She had more to regret than he did . . . giving her virginity to a man who was so anxious to be rid of her.

The annulment.

"Dammit!" He slipped from under the precipice and brought the quilt with him, whipping it around as he rose to his full height. "You've outdone yourself, Renata," he said coldly.

Renata turned to face him. She hugged her arms to her body, her moist eyes wide.

"Not this time. No tears. I'm such a fool. Such a complete and total fool."

Renata stepped back from him.

"What are you talking about?"

"You weren't quite ready to leave—isn't that what you said?" He leaned closer to her.

"Yes," Renata answered, her voice small.

"How the hell are we supposed to get an annulment now?"

She paled visibly. She was either a very good actress or she hadn't thought of that herself. He decided she was a very good actress.

"We can lie," Renata whispered. "No one

needs to know . . . ever . . ."

"And your Texan won't wonder why his bride isn't a virgin?"

Renata held her head high, a defiant chin in the air in spite of her too-bright eyes. "I'll think of something."

Jake grunted and gave her a rueful grin. "I'm sure you will."

His smile faded slowly as he stared at her, and he combed his hair away from his face with agitated fingers. "What if there's—" he felt as if a pit had opened beneath his feet— "a baby. Dammit, I can't believe I fell for this."

Renata's fear and anxiety faded from her face, and anger replaced it. "You think I . . . I did this on purpose?"

"Didn't you?" Jake asked coldly. "You got your extra time. We'll have to wait until we know you're not pregnant."

"And if I am?" Her words were whispered, hesitant.

"Then God help us both," Jake said, turning away from her as if he couldn't bear to look at her any longer.

Chapter Eighteen

Renata expected Jake to head back down the mountain, but he turned west and they continued on a course that took them steadily higher. They traveled over ground that looked as if it were completely wild, untamed and unknown to man, but Jake appeared to be following a path.

Renata was uncommonly quiet as she tried to hold her body away from Jake's. He was as uncomfortable as she; the arm that held her was stiff, the corded muscles in his forearms as hard as rock. Only once had Renata looked at his arm, wincing at the burns. Jake hadn't complained once about the burns, or the cuts on his shoulder or the gash on his head. And twice Renata had started to ask him to stop, to allow her to clean his wounds, to bandage the cuts with a strip of her nightgown . . . but then hadn't. She didn't want him to know that she cared about him. Besides, he wasn't a child who needed to be told how to take care of himself.

But now she finally broke her silence and asked him their destination.

"There's a woman who lives not far from here. We will stay with her until I decide what to do with you." His words were so distant, Renata shivered. *What to do with you.* Those words had an ominous ring.

"A woman?" She looked straight ahead, not willing to look at him yet. "You know a woman who lives so far away from everyone else?"

"No one knows about her except me. She is a full-blooded Cheyenne. Yellow Moon Woman. I brought her here last year, from the reservation in Indian Territory."

Renata felt her face turning hot. He kept a woman in the mountains? Was that where he disappeared to when he was away for so long? And she had been so worried about him being all alone. She had misjudged him . . . with terrible ramifications.

"What will Yellow Moon Woman think about you bringing your 'wife' to her home?" Renata had not meant for there to be so much venom in her voice. She sounded petulant and jealous, not at all as she intended.

Behind her, Jake answered in an emotionless voice. "Yellow Moon Woman is very pleasant.

She will welcome you with warmth and kindness, and it would be well for you to do the same."

"You expect me to be nice to you . . . to your . . ." Renata's fertile imagination produced a startlingly clear picture of Jake and Yellow Moon Woman, a beautiful and graceful Indian woman with long black hair and a seductive smile for Jake. "What exactly is she to you?"

"My friend," Jake said simply.

Friend, my foot, Renata thought. Then she stopped herself. Jealous? Impossible. She was angry with the brutish man, and angry with herself, as well. It had just felt so . . . so wonderful to wake in Jake's arms, and she had been half asleep, after all.

That was just an excuse. She could have stopped what happened. Jake had even tried to pull away, but she hadn't allowed it. She'd wanted him to touch her, to love her, to be a real, true husband to her. What had happened to her plans? Jake had blown them all away, like dust before an approaching storm.

For goodness sake, this was a complication neither of them needed.

When they broke through the trees and Renata saw the tepee, she was stunned. The tepee was situated on a grassy flat that was protected on two sides by a tall bluff, one side sloping gently to a clear spring. It was a beautiful spot, green and isolated.

As Jake helped Renata down from the horse,

she suddenly felt inadequate. Her hair was a mess, she knew, as she tried to tame it with her hands. Her nightgown was dirty and torn in several places and missing several inches from the hem.

Standing in front of the tepee's closed flap, Jake called to Yellow Moon Woman and a low voice gave him permission to enter. He threw back the flap and smiled at the sole occupant, and Renata felt an ugly and unwanted tide of jealousy well up inside her, just as it had when he'd told her of Yellow Moon Woman's existence.

"I've brought you a visitor." Jake continued to look into the tepee, but he held out his hand to Renata, who took it tentatively and allowed herself to be led into the shelter.

It was roomy, roomier than it had appeared from the outside, and Renata blinked as her eyes adjusted to the change in light. The space was dim.

"Yellow Moon Woman," she heard Jake say in a low, calm voice. "This is Renata Marie Parkhurst."

"Renata Marie Wolf," she corrected, almost out of habit, as she looked down at the woman seated in the back of the tepee.

Yellow Moon Woman was of an undetermined age but had probably been considered old when Jake was born. Her skin was weathered, cracked and brown like dried mud, leathery and tough. Her white hair was wiry and seemed to grow with an untended mind of its own, but her black eyes sparkled with life and vigor.

"Have you brought me your wife, Jake?" The old Cheyenne woman smiled, creating even more wrinkles on her face, if that was possible. "Sit . . . sit," she ordered.

Jake obeyed her and pulled a reluctant Renata down beside him. The floor was covered with soft animal skins, the cold remains of a fire in the middle of the open space. Renata looked up and saw the small opening in the peak of the tepee that would allow smoke to escape.

"She's not really my wife . . ." Jake began almost sheepishly.

"Yes, I am," Renata said sharply. "But not for long."

Yellow Moon Woman looked from one to the other, and her smile widened. "It's about time Jake took a wife," she said, ignoring their statements. "Renata Marie Wolf." Her head began to nod slightly. "I don't know what that means. I will have to give you a Cheyenne name . . . something that suits you."

Renata was silent as the woman studied her.

"Perhaps it will come to me in a dream or a vision." She grinned at Renata, a warm, friendly smile that immediately put her at ease. "You have hair like the summer dawn, and eyes like the first leaves of spring." The observation seemed to please the old woman, and she turned to Jake.

"It is a good sign. A sign of new beginnings." Her eyes traveled over Jake's arms, her smile fading as she took in every burn and scratch. "You've been hurt. I'll fix you up."

She reached into a leather parfleche and withdrew a smaller bag that looked to Renata as if it was made of oilskin. Yellow Moon Woman directed Jake to clean himself in the spring, and from the parfleche, she gathered together bandages and herbs, and a dried powder.

Jake seemed reluctant to leave Renata behind, hesitating near the exit. Renata ignored him. She wasn't about to follow him to the spring or anywhere else.

When he left Yellow Moon Woman studied Renata so carefully, she was certain she could feel the Indian's eyes on her, seeing more than any other person would ever see. There were questions in those black eyes, and a judgment yet to be made.

"I must show you how to make this salve, so that when I am gone you can make it. Jake is always getting himself into trouble, and coming to me with his blood drying on his skin. Perhaps with a wife and family he will be more careful." She nodded, seeing the wisdom of her statement. "Yes. It is time Jake took a wife."

Renata felt guilty. She didn't want to lead the woman on. "Jake was right. I'm not really his wife . . . well, I am, but we're going to get an annulment . . . or a divorce. We probably should have done that right away, but at the time, well, I didn't think it was wise."

Renata stopped when she felt rather than heard Jake behind her.

Yellow Moon Woman looked up at Jake as he moved to sit beside the old woman. "Your wife talks very fast."

"Sometimes," Jake agreed, looking across the ashes to stare at Renata. "What has she been telling you?"

Yellow Moon Woman shrugged her shoulders as she began to tend Jake's wounds. "I'm not sure. She said she was not wise. That's all I could understand."

Jake kept his eyes fixed on Renata as Yellow Moon Woman slathered the salve on his burns, then sprinkled them with the dried herbs. The cuts on his shoulder she sprinkled with the powder, but they were not deep, and she left them uncovered also. Jake's unflinching eyes told Renata that he agreed with her: She was not wise.

Renata was amazed. Jake never winced, never made a sound, and Yellow Moon Woman wasn't being gentle with him. She worked quickly, her weathered hands practiced and nimble.

Suddenly Renata had to get out of the small space. The walls were closing in on her, and Jake's eyes were boring holes into her soul. It was his presence in the tepee that made her uncomfortable, those eyes on her.

"I think I'll go to the spring and clean up a bit." Renata stood without waiting for a reply. The idea of plunging herself into a cool spring was more than inviting—it was necessary. She wanted to scrub every place on her body that

Jake had touched. Blast his cold eyes. She had felt, for a short time, so much love—or what she'd thought was love—and then she had looked into his cold eyes and seen the truth. He had simply used her because she was convenient.

She burst from the tepee, escaping before Jake could call her back.

Yellow Moon Woman slapped a palmful of salve over the small blisters on Jake's back, and he turned to her and winced. "What's wrong with you?"

The old woman cackled. "Now it pains you. I thought perhaps you had developed skin like iron since last I saw you. It's not good to pretend with the ones you love, Jake."

"I don't love anyone," Jake said coldly.

Yellow Moon Woman ignored him. "I like your Renata Marie Wolf."

Jake snorted. "Everyone likes Renata."

The old woman studied his face. "And this is a bad thing?"

Jake didn't answer her.

There was something about the spring that soothed Renata's frazzled nerves. The water was pleasantly cool; the trees that lined the bank and dipped their willowy branches were silent and fragrant companions.

She soon forgot her intention to scrub the memory of Jake from her skin, and shivered when she thought of how she had awakened that morning. The shiver was brought on not by the cold but by the vivid memory of Jake's touching her. Was that love? Was it always so . . . powerful when a man and woman came together?

Amalie had spoken little of such personal matters, even after a year of marriage. She'd only said she found the marriage bed not unpleasant. Not unpleasant? That was not how Renata would describe making love with Jake. Powerful, yes. Uncontrollable. Magical. Intoxicating. All of those. Lightning. That was what it was.

But was there love in lightning?

And did it matter? Even if she did love Jake, as she was beginning to suspect she did, he obviously didn't love her. When he looked at her his blue eyes were cold and calculating, not warm and loving. But then, Jake hadn't had much love in his life. Maybe he didn't know what love was. Maybe he was incapable of love.

Renata dried herself in the sun, sitting on a flat rock that jutted over the water. She was lost in thought, her fingers occasionally trailing through the water, the ripples hypnotic. The sun on her bare skin was strangely comforting, and she dreaded the thought of putting her dirty nightgown back on. But it was all she had.

She realized, for the first time, how true that was. All her clothes, the money she had hoarded and saved for months, her comb and brush and mirror, the special shampoo her mother had ordered—the shampoo fragrant with the scent of lilacs—were gone. All of it, gone.

Renata sighed deeply and resigned herself. There had been nothing there that couldn't be replaced, and she was alive. Jake was alive. Jake had saved her life. That simple fact was true, and she hadn't even thanked him.

And she certainly wouldn't. Not now.

Jake sat at the crest of the grassy hill and looked down at the girl sunning herself like a lazy animal on the rock below. The sun shone on her hair, copper and gold, red and yellow. A summer dawn. Her hair fell past her waist, but when she reached into the water he could see the curve of her hip, the tiny waist, the pale skin . . . white skin that had never seen the sun.

He watched as she reluctantly pulled the nightgown over her head and freed her long hair from the collar, standing and turning to climb the hill that led to Yellow Moon Woman's tepee. She lifted her head and saw him, and even from his faraway perch he could see her face turn a bright shade of pink.

"What are you doing? Spying on me?" she called as she hurried up the hill. "Don't you have anything better to do?"

Jake watched her silently as she stormed up the hill, her cheeks reddening with an embarrased blush and her hair dancing around her face and curling over one shoulder, still damp and waving in untamed splendor. He waited until she was almost upon him.

"I was watching for bears," he said simply.

Renata stopped. The color drained from her face as she stood looking into his face. "Bears?"

Jake shrugged. "Bears, wolves, mountain lions . . ."

"You didn't tell me . . ."

"You didn't exactly give me a chance, Renata. Don't run off like that again. Understand? This isn't a Philadelphia park."

"I know that," Renata said, her voice small and unsure.

"I'd like to stay here for a couple of days," Jake said, changing the subject.

"Who . . . who started the fire?" Renata asked. "You told me, but none of it makes any sense."

Jake looked down into the spring, avoiding her eyes again. "Two men. Kenny Mails was one. I don't know who the other one was." He touched his fingers to the lump on the side of his head.

Renata started to reach down and touch the side of his head; she caught herself in time and pulled back abruptly . . . but not before Jake saw her, and knew what she was thinking.

"Whatever you say, Jake. We can stay here as long as you like."

She was oddly accepting; he almost wished she would rail against him and insist on being returned to civilization. Any other woman would . . . any other city woman like Renata, at least.

"I think I'll see if there's anything I can do to help Yellow Moon Woman while we're here." Renata walked past him with her head held high, her embarrasment apparently forgotten, her eyes straight ahead.

Jake watched her go, wondering how it was possible that Renata seemed almost regal as she walked away from him in her nightgown and bare feet.

Chapter Nineteen

Yellow Moon Woman soon had Renata busy beading a pair of soft moccasins. The Cheyenne woman seemed pleased that Renata was a quick study, eager to learn what was taught. Renata's fingers were nimble. She had spent many hours sewing and embroidering, but this was a new challenge. Fortunately, the task required her complete concentration, which made her forget her fears and confusion, though she was never completely able to forget Jake. Sometimes she felt his eyes on her, and even though she tried to ignore him she couldn't. There were moments when he seemed as unsure and confused as she.

He was away from the camp only when he hunted for their dinner, and Renata was grateful that Yellow Moon Woman didn't try to teach her to clean and gut the small animals. The old woman handled that chore with ease and amazing speed.

That evening, as the three of them ate around the small fire in Yellow Moon Woman's tepee, the profound silence grew more and more uncomfortable.

When the meal was finished the old Indian reached into a small bag and withdrew several pieces of candy, offering an assortment to her guests. Renata and Jake both declined. Yellow Moon Woman shrugged and popped a piece of peppermint into her mouth.

"Jake brings me sweets, and canned goods for the days I am tired of dried meat and do not have the energy to fish. Of course, when he is here he always leaves me with more than enough fresh meat." She gave Jake a warm smile, as a mother might a dutiful son.

Renata frowned. Jake took care of the old woman; that much was clear. Did that not prove that he had a tender place in his heart? That he was not completely cold? He'd risked his life to save her from the fire, but his eyes could be so flat when he looked at her. Was it possible that he was as confused as she? That somewhere in his heart there was room for her?

As if Jake could read her mind, he rose abruptly, grabbing a parcel that resembled a bedroll from the back of the tepee. He didn't look at her as he mumbled something that might have been good night, or good-bye, or good riddance, and he was gone before Renata could say a word.

Yellow Moon Woman laid out soft, comfortable beds for each of them, and Renata gratefully lowered herself to the ground. She pulled a deerskin, snug and warm, up to her chin, and drew her knees to her chest. Renata was exhausted, and should have slept quickly, but she didn't. Yellow Moon Woman was watching her intently, those sharp black eyes piercing from across the dying fire.

Renata lifted herself up on one elbow. "Do you have a Cheyenne name for me yet?"

The old woman grinned. "Not yet. Perhaps tonight, as I sleep."

"What's Jake's Cheyenne name?" Renata wasn't certain why she asked. Curiosity? Just something to fill the silence?

"High Wolf. I gave him his adult name, when he returned to us."

"But you call him Jake." Renata seemed confused, wondering if this woman might give her some insight into the man who was her legal husband.

"Because he must walk the white man's road to be truly happy. I have seen this in my dreams, many times." Yellow Moon Woman's voice softened. "When I was a girl it was good to be Cheyenne. There was buffalo plenty, and only a few white men. We hunted . . . moved with the herds . . . our village was large, and the people were happy. But that time is gone. Jake would have been a good warrior, but the day of the

warrior is no more. I think he knows that . . .
that he was born too late . . . that the blood of a
warrior flows through him like a great river."

"Why won't Jake let me love him?" Renata
asked, the question surprising her even as the
words left her lips.

"He is stubborn, but he cares for you as he
has for no other," the old woman said simply.

"He doesn't," Renata insisted. She found
herself telling Yellow Moon Woman everything: the night Jake had stumbled through
the front door of the cabin, that he had
made everyone think they were lovers when
they were not . . . and that she had saved him
from hanging. The Cheyenne woman laughed
when Renata described the wedding ceremony,
but her laughter died slowly when Renata told
her that they planned to go to Denver and get
an annulment. She said nothing of waking
in Jake's arms, and what had happened as
morning dawned.

"I see," Yellow Moon Woman said, nodding
her head wisely. "I see what the problem is."

"I should have found another way to keep
them from hanging Jake. Or we should have
gone directly to Denver and gotten that annulment."

"And why didn't you?"

Renata gnawed her bottom lip as she pondered this simple question. "At the time, there
didn't seem to be any other way."

"So you find yourself married by a white
man's ceremony, but not in your heart."

"Yes," Renata agreed. "Jake was never married in his heart."

Yellow Moon Woman smiled gently. "And you?"

"Sometimes . . ." A low rumble of thunder stopped her, and she turned toward the closed flap. "Oh, no. Not tonight." Maybe the storm would pass them by, but she had a sinking feeling that wasn't going to happen.

"Sometimes?" The old woman prodded.

"Jake confuses me. One minute I think I know him, and the next he is as cold as ice. But there have been times, moments, when I've felt love for him." Her voice was reflective, revealing as much to herself as to Yellow Moon Woman.

"Have you told Jake this?"

"Oh, no!" Renata said quickly, horrified. "He wouldn't . . . he never . . . Jake doesn't want a wife. Not at all. I don't want to try to . . . bind him to me. You can't force someone to care for you, no matter how much you love him."

The thunder was coming closer, and was joined by flashes of lightning that lit the sky and brightened the interior of the tepee.

Renata sat up and placed a hand over her rapidly beating heart. How would she survive a storm here in this small tepee? The storm would be right on her, only the thin skin of the tepee protecting her from it.

"Jake. Where's Jake?" she asked, only a little fear in her voice. There was a bright flash of lightning, followed closely by the crack of thunder. Close. Too close.

"On the bluff," Yellow Moon Woman said calmly.

"On the bluff?" Renata rose to her feet. "On the bluff? He can't stay up there during a storm. It's too dangerous."

Yellow Moon Woman shrugged her shoulders. "He has stayed up there before during much worse storms than this. It is his place to think. He has much thinking to do now, I believe."

Renata left the shelter of the tepee. Clouds masked the moon, and she was in complete darkness. Another flash of lightning lit the night, and she saw him sitting motionless on the edge of the bluff, high in the air, apparently oblivious to the approaching storm.

"Jake!" she called, trying to keep the rising panic from her voice. The first drops of rain fell, but she ignored them, calling to him again until she saw, with another flash of lightning, that he was climbing down the jagged rocks from his perch on the bluff above. She felt relief wash over her.

"What are you doing out here?" He grabbed her shoulders roughly. "Go back to Yellow Moon Woman. You'll be safe with her."

"No." Renata could see him well enough to know that he was angry. His jaw was set, his eyes dark and narrowed. "You can't stay up there. It's too dangerous." The rain was falling harder, soaking them both. Renata seemed not to notice the water that pelted her body, that soaked her hair and ran in rivulets down her face.

"Go!" Jake ordered.

"I'm staying with you!" Renata insisted, her voice growing louder so she could hear herself over the rain that pounded against the rock and the grass-covered clearing. "If you climb that bluff again, I'll follow you, I swear."

Jake grabbed her arm and pulled her, running not toward the tepee but away from it. He was running too fast for her, but she kept up, refusing to fall or to break away. His wet hand was slick as it grasped hers, and the rain ran down his back and soaked his buckskins. She didn't know where he was taking her, but she felt no fear as he pulled her along, not even of the storm that was raging around them.

He came to a sudden stop and shoved Renata into a dark cave, releasing her hand as he did so. The recess was completely dark, disorienting in its blackness. Renata had no way of knowing if the space was large or small, deep or shallow . . . but she did know that Jake was still with her, still close by. She heard him, cursing and muttering just a few feet away from her, and she reached out her hand to touch the cool stone wall of their shelter.

Moments later she heard the striking of a match, smelled the acrid odor, and saw the flash of a flame. Jake built a fire near the entrance, and when it was blazing he turned to look at Renata with fury in his eyes.

Renata watched without a word as the anger

was replaced by something else . . . the same bewilderment that was tearing her apart. It was gone as quickly as it had appeared, and Jake turned away from her to squat by the fire, tending it roughly.

Her thin nightgown was soaked, and as Renata stood away from Jake and the fire she became cold and started to shiver slightly, hugging her arms to her body and wondering why she had run from the tepee. A quick look around the cave assured her that she would be safe from the storm. There was room for even Jake to stand upright. Behind her was a narrowing path into a black chasm . . . a path Renata ignored. Her imagination was much too fertile to allow her to ruminate on the possibilities therein.

"Why did you leave Yellow Moon Woman?" Jake asked tiredly, finally turning to her again.

"She said you were on the bluff, and I was worried. The lightning." Renata remembered her earlier deduction, that what had happened between them was lightning, bright and beautiful and dangerous. She shivered again.

Jake unrolled the buffalo skin she had seen him take from Yellow Moon Woman's tepee. He had stashed it in the cave, planning to spend the night there. Inside was a change of clothes—fringed buckskins—and a long wide knife sheathed in beaded leather.

He pushed the shirt at her, demanding that she change from her wet clothes, and when he turned away from her Renata looked down.

Her wet nightgown was adhering to her body, from the modest neck to the torn hem. Every curve was accentuated, and her skin showed through the clinging fabric. Renata flushed as she quickly pulled the soaked linen over her head and drew on the buckskin shirt.

The warm, dry shirt hung to her knees, and fringe dangled from the sleeves and the hem. "Thank you," she said softly, and only then did he turn to her again.

"I don't understand you, Renata Marie Parkhurst," he said, a gruff wistfulness in his voice.

"Renata Marie Wolf," she corrected him, sitting cross-legged on the buffalo skin and inching toward the fire. She could have reached out and touched his leg, or lifted her hand and touched his. "This morning you called me Rennie. I rather liked it."

"This is dangerous," Jake warned.

Renata turned her head and looked back into the cave. "There aren't bears here, are there?"

"You know what I mean," he said sharply.

Renata sighed. At some time during the day she had decided what she wanted. That was the easy part. For once in her life she didn't know if she was going to have her heart's desire. She reached out a hand and patted the buffalo hide, indicating to Jake that he should sit in front of her. She wanted to see his face, and she was tired of looking up at him.

"Yes, I know what you mean," she said as he joined her. "Lightning."

"What?" Jake sat on the skin, but as far away from Renata as possible.

"Lightning," Renata repeated. "That's what we are, you and I," she said serenely. It was easy. She had thought of little else all day. "You can't capture it, but it's there. And if you try to hold it, it can be deadly."

"You're not making a bit of sense," Jake said, his voice low and threatening.

"Am I not?" Renata asked lightly, and she moved up onto her knees and toward him. Jake had placed himself against a wall and had nowhere to go. Renata chewed her bottom lip, uncertainty beginning to haunt her. "I can't believe that what happened this morning happens between every man and woman."

"No. It doesn't," Jake agreed. "But that . . ."

Renata was on her knees in front of him, and she leaned forward to lay her lips on his. It was a gentle kiss, a tender meeting of their mouths that he tried to resist. She had meant only to brush his lips with hers, but she lingered until she heard a moan low in his throat, and her desire to throw herself into his arms was almost overpowering.

"Tell me that's not lightning," she dared him. "Tell me that's not special. Tell me we wouldn't be fools to let that get away."

Jake pulled her into his arms and kissed her again, a raw, hungry kiss that was almost brutal in its power. She gave herself over to him completely, melting in his embrace, parting her lips and darting her tongue into his mouth.

His hand was holding the back of her head, pressing her to him, holding her possessively as he plundered her mouth.

Jake forced himself to pull his lips away from hers. There was fire in his eyes, hungry and hurting. "Are you sure this is what you want?" His voice was husky, hesitant.

"Yes," she whispered. "I want you, Jake. I . . ." She faltered. What if he didn't want what she offered? "I love you. I don't want to go to Denver . . . ever."

"You don't know what you're saying." Jake's voice was no more than a whisper, the wind through the trees. A flash of lightning lit the night, and a crack of thunder sounded close by. Renata didn't move, didn't jump, barely seemed to be aware of the storm that raged outside the shelter of the cave.

"Yes, I do." Renata kissed his throat, letting her lips linger on the soft skin there. "I want to be your wife. I want us to be married in our hearts . . . as well as lawfully."

"Married in out hearts?" Jake lay her on her back against the buffalo skin. He smoothed the hair away from her face and kissed her cheek with amazing tenderness, and the side of her neck. He held his face above hers, his lips hovering so close to hers, she could almost taste him. She saw it in his eyes, the same hunger she felt. Hunger, and an odd contentment. "Married in our hearts," he said, as if he really understood.

His hands were magic, and soon Renata

and he were naked and lying together on the buffalo skin. Renata's contentment had faded and her hunger for him consumed her. His touch burned every inch of her skin, and she cried out for him—her love, her husband—and as he entered her she felt complete.

It was impossible, but the shattering completion he brought her to was even more powerful now than the first time . . . all-consuming and somehow frightening in its intensity. Because she knew she loved him? Because she knew this was the man she would live with for the rest of her life?

"I love you, Jake," she whispered into his ear as he breathed her name and claimed her as his own in a manner as ancient as the stars. "I love you."

She wanted to hear Jake say that he loved her, though she realized that for Jake the words might be a long time coming. But she believed that it was true, that he did love her. She wouldn't push. She would wait . . . a lifetime, if that was what it took.

"You're mine forever now, Rennie," he whispered, and for the time being that was enough.

That was perfect.

Chapter Twenty

The days that followed were the happiest of Renata's life, and she hoped with all her heart that they were for Jake as well. Their days were spent bathing and swimming in the spring, listening to Yellow Moon Woman's tales of Jake's youth, and exploring the wild countryside. Renata walked the shaded trails dressed in Jake's buckskin shirt and clasped his hand securely as he shared with her the wonders of his mountain retreat.

The nights were spent on the buffalo hide bed in the small cave, a place that had become surprisingly comfortable for Renata. But only because Jake was there. He held her and loved her, and for the first time she felt all his defenses fall. Sometimes, when he looked at her, Renata was certain Jake loved her as much as she loved him . . . but at other times she saw a flicker of the old pain that was so much a part of Jake . . . a part she wanted to erase forever.

Yellow Moon Woman presented Renata with a deerskin dress, beaded across the chest and fringed at the hem, along with the moccasins Renata had helped to bead. Renata protested, not wanting to take the old woman's clothing; she obviously had so little. But Yellow Moon Woman brushed aside Renata's objections and assured her that the dress had been made with Jake's wife in mind. The elaborate beading had taken months. . . .

"How did you know Jake would ever take a wife?" Renata asked, a teasing lilt to her voice. "He can be so ornery."

"I saw you in a dream," Yellow Moon Woman answered seriously. "Not your face, but your essence . . . I saw that you would save Jake from his destructive ways."

Jake frowned, uncomfortable at being the subject of their conversation, as he had been often in the past few days. "Do you have a Cheyenne name for Rennie yet?" he asked impatiently.

"Yes." The old woman smiled, and her face became a mass of deep wrinkles. "Last night I had a vision." She turned and took Renata's hand. "Thunderheart Woman."

Renata clasped the old woman's fingers with her own, finding Yellow Moon Woman's skin surprisingly soft. In a matter of days she had come to have great affection for the Cheyenne woman who was a part of Jake's life. Renata didn't remember her own grandparents—they had died while she was still a baby—and Yellow Moon Woman had filled that void in her life with apparent ease.

"Thank you," Renata said softly. "For the name and the dress and the stories of Jake's childhood." Her grip became more urgent. "Won't you come to Silver Valley with us when we leave here? I'll worry about you, up here all alone."

The old woman shook her head. "No. I belong here. I will die here. I have seen it in my dreams."

"Don't speak of death," Renata said gently.

Yellow Moon Woman smiled. "I do not fear death. I will follow the path to join my family and friends, and live in a great white tepee in the sky, where buffalo are plenty and we will live in peace."

"I still wish you would come with us . . . let us take care of you."

Yellow Moon Woman's refusal was decidedly firm. Jake led Renata from the tepee into the late-morning sun with the deerskin dress and moccasins in her hands, and a slight frown on her face.

Jake laid his arm across her shoulders and pulled her to his side possessively. "Don't worry about Yellow Moon Woman . . . Thunderheart Woman." He grinned at her, and the sight of his smile made her heart turn over. It was such a tender smile.

"But I will worry when we leave." Out of habit they headed down the small slope to the spring. "Maybe we shouldn't leave. Maybe we should just stay here."

"For how long?" Jake sat with his back against a tree and pulled Renata with him. She sat between his legs with her back against his chest, and he wrapped his arms around her.

"Forever."

Jake brushed her hair aside and kissed her neck. He could be so tender with her. "Come winter, I think you'd change your mind."

Renata laid her hands on Jake's forearms. His burns were already healing nicely, thanks to Yellow Moon Woman's salve. "How can we live in Silver Valley? Someone shot you, and tried to kill us both by burning down the cabin. Maybe we should go someplace else."

There was a moment's hesitation before he answered her. "I've been thinking the same thing. I just didn't know what you would think about leaving. You've made friends, and Mel is there. . . ."

"As long as I have you, nothing else matters." The revelation was a startling one, but the surest truth she had ever known. She would be happy anywhere in the world if Jake was at her side.

"But you came to Colorado looking for a rancher. Aren't you . . . just a little bit disappointed?"

Renata laughed brightly and lifted one of his

hands to her lips. "I only thought I came to Colorado looking for a rancher. I came here looking for you, Jake. I just didn't know it." She twined her fingers through his. "So where will we go?"

"West," Jake said with certainty. "Maybe southwest. We could start a horse farm. I've always been good with horses."

Renata craned her head so she could look up at him. She never tired of looking at his face. "A horse farm. For goodness sake, Jake, I don't know a thing about horses." She saw the subtle cloud that passed across his face. "You'll have to teach me everything."

The cloud passed and Jake lowered his head to kiss her lightly on the lips. "I will."

Her eyes widened at a sudden thought. "What about money? Everything I had was burned in the fire."

A gentle breeze rushed over them just then, blowing Jake's hair away from his face. His eyes sparkled, a hint of amusement in his usually solemn eyes. "I have some money saved."

"Enough to get us started?" Renata lowered her head and rested it against his shoulder.

Jake hesitated. He'd never told Renata about the money—the money from the sale of the silver mines, and from the investments Gabe had made for him. In truth, he didn't know exactly how much he had. More than enough to travel West and start a horse farm.

"Enough," he said cryptically.

He'd never thought he would feel as contented as he did at this moment, a loving wife in his arms, a future ahead of him. He'd never thought of the future before . . . had never really believed he had one. He had one now, and she rested in his arms and looked out over the water with a dreamy sigh.

"But what about Yellow Moon Woman?" Renata asked softly. "Do you think she would come with us?"

"No," Jake answered solemnly.

"We can't just leave her here," Renata insisted.

Jake squeezed her lightly. "We'll wait until Gabe and Mel return. That shouldn't be too much longer. I think I can convince Gabe to see to her as I have."

He felt Renata relax in his arms, satisfied with that solution. "Good. That will give us time to find out who is trying to poison your father."

Tension stole over his body, creeping into his arms, his legs, even the breath he took. "Let it go, Rennie," he finally said, his voice soft but still uneasy.

Renata turned in his lap. A loving smile told him that she was willing to forget her suspicions for the moment. "I suppose now that I have my own dress, you'll want your shirt back."

Jake ran his hands over the fringed shirt that had been her only covering for days. "It looks much better on you than it ever did on me."

Her smile was tempting, and there was an invitation in her eyes as she lifted her arms into the air. Jake grabbed the hem of his shirt and slowly pulled it over her head, allowing his fingers to linger against her skin as he undressed Renata and tossed the fringed buckskin aside.

For one who had been so modest, Renata was remarkably relaxed. It apparently didn't bother her at all to sit in front of him completely naked as his eyes devoured her. Or to watch him undress. It seemed as natural to her as it did to him.

"I feel like a swim," Renata said coyly, backing away from Jake an inch at a time.

"Now?" Jake was undressing slowly, his eyes never leaving hers. Already he had memorized every inch of her body, every freckle, every delicate vein pulsing beneath her milky skin. He never tired of watching her, of touching her, and he never would.

Renata jumped up and ran to the water, leaping into the spring from the rock on which she had sunned herself that first day. She was no longer worried about bears or wolves or mountain lions. He had promised to look out for her, and he knew that his word was all she needed.

Jake was right behind her, splashing into the water as she rose to the surface. When Jake broke the water just a few feet away from her she was watching him. She was so beautiful, with that red-gold hair slicked to her head and droplets of water clinging to her nose and her ears and running down her radiant face. She was so guileless, so open, he could see every thought reflected on her face.

She swam the short distance to him and wrapped her arms around his wet shoulders, kissing his wet lips. "I love you so much, Jake," she whispered.

Jake clasped her slick body to his. He still couldn't bring himself to believe that she truly loved him. He wasn't even certain that he knew what love was. If it was this, the way they came together so perfectly, then perhaps it was love. There was still that small seed of doubt, that nagging worry that one day he would wake up and she would be gone . . . that she would come to her senses and see that she deserved better than him. When the fire of passion burned away would she look at him and see a stranger? Would she regret yielding to him so completely—heart and soul—body and spirit?

He'd waited for her to ask him if he loved her. Had expected it for days. A girl like Renata would expect to be loved in return. He needed her. He wanted her. He was afraid to love her.

But she had never asked. She seemed content to take him as he was. That in itself was a miracle, to him. And she asked for nothing in return for all she gave.

She erased his misgivings with her lips against his, with her hands against his skin. He could think of nothing but her as she fondled him under the water and whispered his name in breathy kisses. All his doubts melted away and he lost himself in her perfect body, her passion, her complete surrender.

Neither of them wanted to leave, but the time had come. They had been in the mountains for nearly two weeks, and Jake's burns and cuts were healing well. Renata found herself almost thankful for the fire. If not for the calamity, she and Jake might still be apart, married by ceremony but not in their hearts. The thought that she had been days away from ending their marriage sent chills down Renata's spine.

There were things to be done in Silver Valley before they could go West. She wanted to see Mel, and make sure that Gabe would look out for Yellow Moon Woman. There were friends in Silver Valley to whom she wanted to say good-bye, but there would be no tearful farewells.

If only Jake could make peace with his father. . . . Renata felt that would heal some of the anger in his heart.

She hadn't mentioned Harrison Summers after that one time. Jake was so certain no one was poisoning his father, and she hadn't been willing to sacrifice any of their magic on the mountain to pursue the subject. But now, as they headed down the mountain, she found her thoughts returning more and more often to the Summers household. Haughty Corinne and her ailing husband. That sweet Lina, and her odd sisters. What had happened in that house to make Jake so bitter and cynical? She wanted to heal every hurt, every scar on his heart.

"Jake?" The hesitancy in her voice warned him that he wasn't going to like her question. "Why do you hate your father?"

Jake was silent for several minutes, but at least this time his arm didn't tense . . . the arm that held her securely as they rode slowly down the mountain, the powerful stallion descending at a walk.

"When I was very young he sent me and my mother away. A few years later he married Corinne. He never married my mother. A Cheyenne, an Indian, wasn't good enough to bear the Summers name." Jake's voice was sad, resigned. "I hate him for what he did to my mother."

Renata leaned against him, wanting to assure Jake that she would always love him, that he would never be hurt again. "I can't imagine sending my own child away."

"He tried to lure me back," Jake said reluctantly, "when he saw that I was the only son he would produce. But he never saw my mother again. I always knew that he saw a bit of her in me . . . and wished that I was . . . pure."

"He's a very foolish man if that's true."

"It's true."

"Our children will always know that they're loved. Nothing could ever make me send our child away from me."

A smile crept over Jake's lips. *Our children. Our child.* It sounded so undeniably right.

Perhaps she was carrying his child at that moment. Unconsciously, his hand settled over her belly, much as it had the day of their picnic.

Renata placed her hand over his. "I hope so," she whispered, as if in answer to what he was thinking. "It would be the most wonderful, beautiful thing in the world, to find myself with your baby. A boy, with black hair and sapphire blue eyes. A baby who will scream and cry and grow up on a horse farm with brothers and sisters and parents who will love him so much it hurts.

"I hope you won't find me too unattractive when my stomach sticks out to here." She gestured wildly with her delicate hands.

It washed over Jake then, the sudden certainty. He kissed the top of her head with a tenderness he had never before expressed. "I love you." He mouthed the words she longed to hear, the sentiment lost in his warm breath against her red-gold hair.

Chapter Twenty-one

Jake had caused a stir in Silver Valley before, but nothing like the one he and Renata created as they rode into town that afternoon. Every soul in town came out to gape and stare, gathering on the boardwalk and in the street in silent numbers . . . silent until Janie Boyle raced from the general store.

"You're alive," she whispered loudly, staring at Renata and then at Jake.

"Of course we're alive," Renata said sensibly. Jake dismounted first, and Renata dropped into his arms easily. "I suppose everyone's heard about the fire at the cabin."

None of the townspeople came forward as Jake set Renata on her feet, leaving his hand at her waist. Renata looked to her left and to her right, puzzled by the stony looks on their pale faces.

Janie Boyle grabbed Renata's arm, then reluctantly took one of Jake's and practically pulled the two of them into the general store. She released them and spun around to close the creaking doors, dropping a barricading bar in place. The store was empty, but for the three of them.

"Mrs. Boyle." Renata turned to the storekeeper's wife in surprise. "It's the middle of the day."

Janie looked from one of the newlyweds to the other, indecision and . . . fear? . . . in her eyes. She fidgeted nervously, wiping her hands again and again on her white apron. This was very much unlike the self-assured woman Renata knew.

"All hell's broke loose since that fire," Janie said sharply. "That cabin burned clear to the ground."

"I know," Renata said. "We passed it on the way to town."

"There wasn't enough left for us to . . . well, we figured you for dead." She laid a tentative hand on Renata's arm. Renata thought, for a moment, that there was a tear in tough Mrs. Boyle's eye.

Renata smiled. So that was the reason everyone had stared at them. "We're fine. Jake was burned, and we went into the mountains to think about what had happened. The fire was deliberate. Kenny Mails and some other man started it, and Jake saved me. . . ." She gave her frowning husband a smile.

"We've decided to go to the sheriff," she continued, "and he can deal with Kenny and find out who the other man is."

"Kenny Mails is dead," Janie said sharply, her eyes flitting nervously to Jake. "Murdered. His body was found a couple of days after the fire."

"Oh." Renata's smile faded.

"And that's not all." Janie Boyle turned her attention back to Renata. "Your folks are staying at the hotel. They've been here for a couple of days with some hoity-toity Englishman who claims to be your intended."

Renata paled. "Lord Edenworth is here? My father? My mother?"

There were sharp, quick footsteps on the boardwalk, and then an insistent pounding on the door. Renata grabbed Jake's arm. "They're too late. I'm already married, and I won't be told what to do anymore." Jake's eyes clouded over slightly, masking his emotions.

"Renata?" It was her mother's near hysterical voice calling through the barricaded door. "I know you're in there, young lady."

Janie Boyle looked up at Jake, sending him a silent message Renata didn't understand. "There's a back door," Mrs. Boyle said in a low voice.

Renata ignored her. "It's just my mother, for goodness sake. I'm not going to run away from her."

Mrs. Boyle opened her mouth to protest, but Jake stopped her with an unconcerned wave of his hand. With a shrug of her wide shoulders, Janie Boyle lifted the bar from the iron brackets that were mounted on either side of the door.

Her mother was the first to rush through the doors Mrs. Boyle threw open. She collided with Renata and wrapped her arms around her. "They said you were dead," Cecilia said breathlessly. "I thought we were too late."

Renata comforted her mother. "But I'm fine. I was never in any real danger." She glanced over her mother's shoulder to look at Jake as she delivered this lie. He simply raised his eyebrows.

Her father burst into the room and placed his arms around both her and her mother. Renata was comforting them both, and at the same time wondering why her father seemed to be so . . . small. It was true that he stood barely five foot seven, and compared to Jake that was small indeed. She'd become accustomed to being dwarfed by her husband.

Renata pulled away with an easy smile on her face. "How did you find me? I expected you'd be searching Europe for at least six months."

Her mother pursed her lips at this statement. "You hate the water. I was never fooled by that note."

Renata's eyes met Jake's over her mother's shoulder. Why did he look so . . . so harsh? "I don't really hate the water." But you know that,

Jake, she thought. "I just have a tendency to get seasick."

Her parents turned to look at Jake. Their concerned expressions turned to distaste as they studied the man who had, in their eyes, risked their daughter's life.

Renata recognized the looks, her father's disapproval and her mother's prudish shock.

"Mother, Father" —Renata extricated herself from their embrace— "this is Jake Wolf . . . my husband." She wrapped her arm around his waist, smiling at her parents innocently. There was no reason for them not to love Jake as she did. He was a part of their family now. But they continued to frown, and her mother pursed her lips in contempt.

"Really, Renata." Her mother's eyes traveled over Renata's dress. "What on earth are you wearing?" She was clearly horrified. "You look like . . . like . . ."

"An Indian?" Jake finished the thought for her wryly.

Cecilia ignored him, as well as anyone could ignore the towering, scowling Jake. "Lord Edenworth is with us. He was quite distraught when you disappeared just days before the wedding was to take place."

"I never agreed to marry him," Renata said sharply. "You tried to force me. I came to Colorado and chose my own husband, thank you." She tightened her hold on Jake, looking for strength in his closeness.

"That's not what I heard." Her father spoke

255

up sharply. "I heard a story of a shotgun wedding to a savage half-breed who rightly should have been hanged long ago."

"Daddy! That's not true. Well, some of it is true, but I do love Jake, and we are married, so that's the end of that," Renata insisted, wishing Jake would defend her, just a little. He was stonily silent.

"He disgraced you before you were married!" Her father snapped.

Renata paled. "That's one of the parts that's not true. I wasn't expecting a baby when we were married. I was just . . . desperate to save Jake's life, and that seemed to be the logical solution." Renata heard a low rumbling of surprise and turned to see half the town huddled in the doorway to the general store. They didn't try to come in; they seemed afraid of something, tense and watchful.

"We're leaving soon. Going west," Renata said, hoping to relieve some of the tension. "Jake wants to start a horse farm, and as soon . . ."

"I don't expect Jake's going anywhere." Sheriff Collins broke through the crowd and appeared in front of them. He drew his Colt and, with the barrel, motioned for Renata to move away from Jake. She refused.

"What do you think you're doing?" She wrapped her other arm around Jake's waist and pulled herself even closer to him.

To her dismay, Jake pried her arms away from him and shoved her toward her father.

The resignation on his face made it clear that he knew exactly what was happening—had known it would happen since Janie Boyle told him Kenny Mails was dead.

"Jake Wolf," Sheriff Collins said harshly, "you're under arrest for the murder of Kenny Mails."

"No," Renata whispered, finding it almost impossible to find her voice. "That's impossible. Why won't you leave us alone?"

Jake didn't look at her as Sheriff Collins led him from the general store, the townspeople parting to let them pass. The sheriff seemed relieved that Jake wasn't putting up a fight, hadn't even muttered a word to deny the charges.

"Let me go." Renata wrestled against her father's hold, watching Jake's back as he was led through the throng of onlookers. He wore the buckskin shirt that had been her only covering for days, and the stubborn courage in his straight spine and broad shoulders told her all she needed to know. He wouldn't even try to defend himself to the sheriff and the townspeople who were so eager to convict him.

With an unforeseen energy she burst free and leapt forward. Jake wasn't a killer. The people parted for her as they had parted for Jake and Sheriff Collins, but just as her feet were about to leave the boardwalk and touch the dirt-packed street a strong pair of hands flew forward and caught her, holding her even as she struggled to get free.

"Jake!" Renata cried as she struggled fruit-lessly against the arms that lifted her feet from the ground and pinioned her arms to her sides. She didn't know who held her and didn't care.

There was a desperate quality to her cry that forced Jake to look over his shoulder. His face was so emotionless, his hooded eyes so dark with resignation, that it broke Renata's heart. She couldn't pull her eyes away from his as she struggled and kicked against the man who held her so securely. She cried out his name again, and he turned to come to her, ignoring the sheriff's protests and the pistol that was pointed at his back. He took two steps, and then he ran across the dusty street to her, and as he approached, the man who held Renata loosened his grip, dropping her silently on moccasined feet.

Jake grabbed Renata's hand and pulled her to him and away from the man who had held her against her will. She wanted to hide from it all . . . from her parents and from the false accusations that had been made. They never should have come back to Silver Valley. Panic rose within her, and Renata buried her face against Jake's chest. Jake let his fist fly and knocked the man who had restrained her to the ground.

Renata watched as if it were all a nightmare as Jake's arms were wrested from her and Donnie Boyle and her father held her back. Her father was silent, but Donnie comforted her softly as she struggled to free herself and run to her husband. The sheriff had help now—three armed men joined him to flank Jake on all sides.

"Settle down, Miss Renata," Donnie whispered. "Dry your tears." His voice was so low that only Renata and her father could hear him. "If Jake tries that again, I'm afeared the sheriff might shoot him."

Renata was suddenly still and quiet. What Donnie said was true. It was a lucky thing that no one had fired at Jake as he ran across the street to her.

"He didn't kill anyone, Mr. Boyle," she said softly, heartbreak in her voice. "But I'm afraid no one will believe me. Look at them." She cast her eyes around, touching briefly on the townsfolk before she returned her eyes to her retreating husband. "They're afraid of him. You can see it in their eyes. No one will believe us because they want to see him hang."

Donnie Boyle sighed deeply. Renata took his silence as proof of her allegations. "I believe you, girl," he whispered after that short pause.

Renata lifted her head and looked over her shoulder to catch Donnie's eyes. She searched those eyes and felt a wave of relief as she realized that he was telling the truth.

"You do, don't you?"

The tall, thin man who had held her earlier rose gingerly from the ground, moaning and cradling his jaw in one hand, dignified even in his pain, elegant in the way he cupped his chin.

"Renata," he said, a spark in his voice and in his pale gray eyes. "Always a pleasure."

Renata pinned her eyes on the man who had stopped her from rushing to Jake, the man from whom Jake had rescued her. His pale blond hair had fallen into his eyes, and he swept it away with a graceful wave of his hand.

"What are you doing here?" she rasped.

"I've traveled halfway across this vast country to save you from the clutches of a heathen, and this is the thanks I get." Percival Evelyn Ashby, Earl of Edenworth, spoke with the precise, clipped accent of a well-mannered English lord, which was exactly what he was.

Renata gathered her courage and calmed herself as Donnie and her father slowly released her, afraid that she might try to run again. "I'm terribly sorry that you've wasted your valuable time, Lord Edenworth."

"Percival, please, my dear," he begged, bowing at the waist.

Renata turned away from him. She had no time for this nonsense. She took two determined steps toward the sheriff's office and the jail before her father grabbed her.

"Back to the hotel, young lady, while we decide what to do about this predicament in which you've placed us." He was treating her as if she was a child who had committed some infraction—leaving the house unsupervised, disobeying her father's orders—well, she had done both of those things, but she wasn't a little girl any longer.

"I must speak to the sheriff," she argued, trying to sound sensible and dignified.

"This is none of our concern, Renata," her father said, refusing to release her.

"None of our concern? He's my husband."

Renata ceased her protests. There was no arguing with her father when he got that look on his face. But she would get away and see Jake. She would convince the sheriff that he was innocent. And then they would ride away from this town and never look back. As long as she had Jake, she needed nothing else.

If she didn't have Jake . . . she had nothing.

Chapter Twenty-two

Renata paced, short quick steps that kept her in front of the window. She was in the room she had shared with Jake the night of their wedding. If she stood in the right place, she could see the jail, though there was no outward sign that anything out of the ordinary was happening. Still, her eyes instinctively went to the jail when she passed by the edge of the window that afforded her that view.

"Renata, sit down," her mother ordered from her position near the door, seated rigidly on the single chair, as if to relax and lean back would mean death itself. "Please."

Renata stopped in her tracks and looked at her mother. Cecilia Parkhurst had always been obsessed with appearances and propriety, and their current situation was wearing on her. Her face was drawn and thin, her normally rosy cheeks pale. Renata found herself wondering if her mother had ever been a happy person. If so, she had hidden that happiness well.

With a sad sigh, Renata lowered herself to the floor, seating herself under the window where Jake had spent their wedding night, feeling somehow closer to him as she leaned back against the wall.

"Not on the floor!" Cecilia snapped. "Sit on the bed."

Renata gathered the excess material of her skirt around her. She was wearing one of her mother's dresses, dark blue and not to Renata's tastes. The waist was too big, the bodice snug, and when she walked a good two inches of cloth dragged the floor. But her mother would have none of that Indian garb on her daughter.

"I love him, Mother." Renata looked into her mother's eyes, never leaving her spot on the floor. "Can't you understand that?"

Cecilia tensed. Renata already knew her mother's views on that "fleeting fancy" others called romantic love. Her own marriage had been an arranged one, and what was good enough for Cecilia Parkhurst was good enough for her daughters. Amalie had rebelled and found love, and now Renata.

"He's a murderer."

That brought Renata to her feet in a heartbeat. "He is not!"

Cecilia flinched. She wasn't accustomed to rebellion in Renata.

"The returning stage will be through in five days," Cecilia said calmly. "We will be on it. You and I, your father, and Lord Edenworth."

"No," Renata said calmly, returning to stand at the edge of the window so she could see the jail. The streets were nearly deserted, as though the town were in mourning.

"Lord Edenworth still wants to marry you. Your father can arrange for a quiet divorce . . . if that's necessary."

"What do you mean, if that's necessary?" Renata's voice was cold. She knew exactly what her mother was thinking. "You mean that if I'm conveniently widowed that quiet divorce won't be necessary."

"Yes," Cecilia whispered.

"No matter what happens" —Renata's words were husky as she fought to keep back the tears— "I'll never marry Lord Edenworth."

There was a moment of heavy silence between them before Cecilia answered her. "You must."

"Never."

Cecilia rose from her chair and approached her. She laid a hesitant hand on Renata's shoulder. "I didn't want to tell you . . ." She faltered.

"Tell me what?" Renata prompted.

"Your father has had some financial troubles." Cecilia looked away from Renata and withdrew her hand. "He made some bad investments, and we are . . . we are on the verge of losing . . . everything."

"What does that have to do with . . ."

"Lord Edenworth has offered to . . . . help your father. To loan . . . to give him the money to get us on our feet again. Without his assistance . . . . we'll be left with nothing." Cecilia's voice was almost apologetic. "He's quite smitten with you. He can give you anything you want."

"I'm already married," Renata said stubbornly.

"That can be remedied," Cecilia said smartly. The little bit of color in her face drained away. "You're not . . . you said you weren't . . . in a delicate condition."

Renata laughed, and her normally enticing laugh was harsh and sad. "I hope . . . no, I *pray* that I am going to have a baby. If you and Father and this damn town have your way, it'll be all I have of Jake."

"Renata Marie! Cursing! That Jake Wolf has been a dreadful influence!" She took a deep breath.

"Your father needs you, Renata. He's given you so much. Everything you ever wanted." Cecilia was brazenly preying on Renata's guilt. "Don't turn your back on him now, when he needs you the most."

"Jake needs me." Renata turned back to the window. "Most of all, Jake needs me."

Renata heard her mother's tentative footsteps approaching. Her father had always been the one to lavish his daughters with embraces and kisses. Cecilia Parkhurst had been the practical one, the pragmatic mother. What did she know of love?

"Think about what I said," Cecilia snapped. "I don't see how you can turn your back on your father at a time like this. He's always given you the best of everything, and he never wanted anything less for you."

Renata listened to her mother's footsteps, the opening and closing of the door, the key turning in the lock.

They had her under lock and key, as much a prisoner as Jake. Just a few hours ago her life had been perfect, and now she felt as if she didn't have a life at all.

Renata's meals were brought to her room, and every day Cecilia tried to convince her to cooperate. In the three days she'd been held in the small hotel room, Lord Edenworth and her father had visited her twice. She had nothing to say to either of them. And she never would. Her father seemed nervous, almost ready to jump out of his skin as he watched her, but Lord Edenworth emanated confidence. He was enjoying himself immensely.

Renata had never been anything other than cheerful and poised. There was no dilemma that couldn't be steered around or finessed through.

Until now.

Late in the afternoon, three days almost to the minute since they had led Jake away from her, the door to her prison opened, and her father admitted Felicia Collins into the room.

Renata was surprised. She'd had no visitors

and hadn't expected any. But there stood Felicia before her, wearing that horrid green dress and a hooded cape that flowed behind her. With one hand she pushed the hood away from her face and attempted a weak smile for her troubled friend.

"How is he?" Renata whispered.

"Fine, I guess." Felicia swept across the room and gave Renata a big hug. "I'm so sorry. I wish I could tell you more, but Daddy won't let me near the jail."

"Felicia, I don't know what to do," Renata confessed desperately. "My own father has locked me in this room, and I haven't even been able to talk to Jake once."

"I know. Donnie Boyle went to Daddy and said that it wasn't fitting, and that he should make your folks let you out of here, but Daddy said that they have the right." She obviously didn't agree, contempt apparent in her mild face. "Your folks have been trying to hire a carriage or a wagon to get the four of you to the railroad, so they won't have to wait for the stagecoach."

Renata's eyes widened. She'd thought she had a few more days.

"Don't worry. Nobody'll take the job, and your pa's offering big money, too. Donnie told him that two of his horses needed to be shod, and that the blacksmith had the . . . the" —Felicia blushed— "the runs. And Lester Patton said the front wheel of the buckboard was just about busted and wouldn't make it half a mile. Everybody else, too. The same stories. Nobody wants them to take you away."

"And Jake?"

Felicia flushed. "They're beginning to have doubts about that, too. If you say he didn't do it, then I believe you, and Donnie Boyle believes you, too. He's been asking a lot of questions, like if Jake was going to kill Kenny, why didn't he do it years ago? Why now?"

"I have to talk to my father, and I must see Jake," Renata said urgently.

Felicia smiled. "I know. I've waited three days for enough clouds to appear in the sky so I wouldn't look like a complete fool in this cape. I wouldn't want to get my hair wet." She giggled, and her cheeks glowed prettily.

"What are you . . ." Renata began, and then she realized what Felicia was up to as the younger girl removed the cloak and tossed it on the bed.

Dr. Parkhurst heard his daughter tell her friend good-bye and turned the key in the door. He felt another pang of guilt. Holding his daughter captive! But what choice did he have? He barely looked at the girl as she left the room, her hooded cloak wrapped around her as it had been when she'd arrived, a skirt of the ugliest green he'd ever seen swirling around her legs.

"Renata?" he called softly as the hooded girl slipped down the staircase. "Can I come in?"

He wanted nothing more than to make peace with his daughter and to go home to Philadelphia, his life magically returned to normal. Edenworth was a good man, a kind man who would take care of Renata and calm her flighty ways.

The only answer to his plea was a muffled and tearful "No!" before he locked the door once again. His baby, his little girl. What if she never forgave him?

What if he never forgave himself?

Renata stepped as quickly as she dared down the stairs and through the lobby to the street. She keep the hood about her face, disguising her features as she all but ran across the street. It wasn't a matter of *if* she got caught, it was *when.* She hoped not before she'd had a chance to see Jake and talk to Sheriff Collins.

She chanced a glance back up to her window and saw Felicia standing there, waving shyly, wearing Cecilia Parkhurst's burgundy silk gown. What a brave act it had been for shy Felicia to defy her father and everyone else and come to Renata's aid. She would never forget it. Never.

Renata didn't knock. She threw open the door to the sheriff's office and stepped inside before she shook back the hood.

Sheriff Collins was at his desk, his boots propped up on the polished wood, a well-worn stack of "wanted" posters in his hands. He looked up in surprise, but Renata barely looked at him. Her eyes went all the way to the back of the room.

The jail cell was part of one large room, the bars and a few feet all that separated Jake and the sheriff. Jake had been sitting on the edge of a narrow cot, and he rose as Renata walked toward the cell, ignoring the sheriff's weak protests.

"Oh, Jake." The tears she had kept at bay for days filled her eyes, but she wouldn't allow herself to break down. Not now. Jake wrapped his fingers around the bars that separated them, and she reached out and covered them with her own, threading her delicate fingers through his. "Are you all right?"

Jake nodded and laid his forehead against the bars. "You should have stayed away from this place, away from me." In spite of his words, his eyes told her that he was happy to see her.

Renata's eyes swept over the clean but tiny cell. The thin, narrow cot had no pillow or blanket, and there was a chamber pot in one corner. She had never been one to rail against injustice, but now Renata felt indignation rising within her.

"I would have come sooner, but they locked me up in the hotel."

"You shouldn't have come," Jake whispered. Renata saw and ached for the pain and resignation in his eyes.

Sheriff Collins put a hand on Renata's shoulder, but withdrew it when Jake glared at him.

"That's Felicia's cloak," he said with amazement. "And Felicia's dress."

Renata turned her head and glared at the sheriff. "Felicia is locked up in my hotel room, wearing my mother's dress," she said coolly. "Perhaps now you will agree that it is an uncivilized act to lock one's daughter away."

"Let's go." Sheriff Collins grabbed Renata's arm, but she pulled away from him and held fast. Her fingers were wrapped around Jake's and the bars that kept him from her.

"Not until you hear what I have to say," Renata insisted. "Jake didn't kill Kenny Mails, or anyone else. You have to let him go."

"Mrs. Wolf . . ." Sheriff Collins began.

"I can prove he didn't. He was with me, from the time Kenny and his accomplice burned the cabin . . . He couldn't have done it."

Sheriff Collins stepped back. "The judge will be here in nine days. If you want to plead your case . . ."

"I may not be here in nine days." She felt Jake's fingers stiffen and begin to pull away from her. "My father has tried to hire every carriage and buckboard in town to take me away from Silver Valley . . . against my will, I might add. Doesn't it fall under your jurisdiction to see that the people of this town are not . . . kidnapped and hauled away? In two days the stage will be coming through, and I have a feeling I'll be on it. I may be stuffed in a Saratoga trunk, or I may be bound and gagged, but I doubt that I will be here nine days from now if you don't let Jake out of here!" Her voice grew more and more hysterical.

Collins sighed and leaned back to sit on the corner of his desk. "All right. Let's hear it."

Renata took a deep, calming breath. "When Kenny was killed we were in the mountains. Together. There was no way Jake could have come down here and killed Kenny and then returned without my knowledge."

Sheriff Collins looked at her confidently. "Kenny was killed the night of the fire or the night after, we figure. Throat was slit. Knife's Jake's weapon; everybody knows that."

"That's flimsy evidence, Sheriff," Renata said confidently. "You can't convict a man on such . . ."

"Did you know that Jake and Kenny had a fight in town just days before the fire?"

Renata looked briefly to Jake. "No."

"Over some insensitive comments about you." The sheriff was as certain of Jake's guilt as Renata was of his innocence.

"That doesn't mean . . ."

"Did you see Kenny Mails the night of the fire, Mrs. Wolf?" Sheriff Collins pressed.

"No. Jake . . ."

"Mrs. Wolf, what we have is a damn good case. Throat cut, a history of hatred between the two, even a bit of buckskin fringe clutched in the victim's hand. The body wasn't far from the cabin . . ."

"I swear . . ." Renata whispered.

"Just like you swore Jake was with you the

night of the fire at the Summers ranch? I heard you confessed that you weren't in the family way after all ... that it was all a trick to get Jake off."

"That's not ..."

"Who's to say you wouldn't lie for him again? You would, wouldn't you? And let me ask you one more question, Mrs. Wolf." His tone was derisive. "How do you know it was Kenny Mails who started the fire that night? Have you ever stopped to consider that Jake might have torched the cabin himself? That he just told you Kenny was responsible? That it was all a scheme to cover up the murder?"

Renata hesitated. She remembered something Yellow Moon Woman had said about Jake. That he had the blood of a warrior in his veins, that he had been born in the wrong time. She turned away from the sheriff and looked into her husband's face and knew he was not capable of the crimes of which he had been accused.

"No. It's not possible."

Renata felt Jake's fingers slip away from hers, and she searched his eyes. They were dark and unreadable, and as his hands left hers she saw his spirit withdraw as well. The Jake she had first met, distant and hard-hearted, was staring her down. Why had he suddenly grown so cold?

"I'll get a lawyer," Renata promised as Jake backed away from her, stopping only when the back of his legs met the cot. "I'll borrow some money from Melanie . . . or wire Amalie if Melanie doesn't get back in time . . ."

Sheriff Collins's laugh was harsh. "Hell, Jake can damn well afford to hire himself a lawyer, if he wants one."

Renata spun around angrily. "I'm not talking about some two-bit country lawyer who can be had for a couple of chickens. I'm talking about a good attorney, and that's going to cost . . ."

Collins continued to laugh. "Hell, you don't know? Jake could hire every lawyer in Philadelphia, if he had a mind to. He's got more money than anybody else in this little town. Could probably buy everyone of us out ten times over and still have money left."

Renata looked to her husband, but his face was impassive, from his eyes to the set of his mouth to his firm jaw.

"But . . ." she began.

"You never told her, Jake?" Collins was enjoying himself much too much.

When Jake answered his voice was cold and harsh. "She came here looking for a rich husband. I didn't particularly feel like handing myself to her on a silver platter. Playing with the little fortune hunter was a lot more fun than telling her the truth. She likes games. She likes stories. That's all it was."

Renata's body had grown rigid as she watched and listened to the stranger who looked like her Jake, but couldn't be. "You don't mean that."

Jake grinned, and it chilled her to the bone.

It was a vicious smile, directed at her. "Don't I?" In a swift move, Jake pulled the buckskin shirt over his head and stepped to the bars that separated him from Renata. "Take this as a memento of this particular story," he said as he slipped the shirt through the bars. "Something to remember this fable by, Renata Marie Parkhurst."

He waited for her to correct him: Renata Marie Wolf. But she didn't. She continued to stare at him with saucerlike eyes, filled not with fear but with anguish.

"I can't wear it anymore," he whispered. "It reeks of you."

She spun away from him with the crumpled shirt clutched in her hands and ran out of the door, cutting off the words with which he'd tried to hurt her. How could he have been so stupid? He had seen it, that brief flash of doubt in her eyes, and in that moment she had become like all the others. The hesitation had been bad enough, but the hint of fear in her eyes as she wondered if he had killed Kenny Mails and set the cabin on fire himself . . . that had killed every tender feeling he had inside.

"Hell." Collins gathered the keys and stuffed them in his pocket. "I've got to go fetch my little girl. She's got a whippin' comin'."

Jake said nothing. He just lay on the cot with his eyes boring holes into the ceiling as his world fell apart. He would have been better

off if he'd never loved her, if he'd never suc-
cumbed to the temptation she'd offered since
the moment he first saw her. There could be
nothing worse than the pain of knowing love,
and then having it ripped away.

Chapter Twenty-three

Renata paced in the lobby of the small Silver Valley Hotel. She heard the commotion upstairs as Sheriff Collins confronted his daughter, and her father discovered she was missing. Her father came tearing down the stairs, his eyes on the open entrance, then stopped when he spotted her standing in the middle of the lobby. She was aware that the cloak covered most of the awful green dress, and she had thrown the hood back. She waited almost serenely for him to approach her, trying to ignore the fact that she felt dead inside.

"I'll do it," she said in a low voice, speaking before her father could confront her with her deceit. "I'll marry Edenworth. But I have a condition." She was not his little girl; she was an adult reasoning with him as an equal. "We will not leave Silver Valley until Jake is cleared. I'll not have his death on my head. The judge will be here in nine days. After that we can return to Philadelphia and obtain that quiet divorce mother suggested. I'll marry Edenworth, he can pay your debts, and I'll go to England with him. Is that satisfactory?"

"Renata." He started to reach out to her but pulled away at the last moment. "It's for your own good, sweetheart. In time you'll forget . . . all this."

Forget? She would never forget a minute of her time with Jake. And she didn't want to. Not even the pain she felt at that very moment.

"Do you agree to my stipulation?"

"If that's what you want," he said softly.

Renata pushed back the tears that threatened to fill her eyes. What she wanted? She would never have what she wanted. The least she could do was see Jake's name cleared and save her father from financial ruin. It was all she could do. But it wasn't what she wanted. Unconsciously, she rubbed her thumb across the soft buckskin in her hand.

"I refuse to remain a prisoner for the next nine days," she said coldly. "I have friends in this town, and I'd like to spend some of that time saying good-bye. I give you my word I won't run away."

Her father tried unsuccessfully to cheer her with a soft smile. "That's good enough for me, sweetheart."

His smile and his endearment did nothing to

soften her stance or the frown on her face. "I'm very tired," she said, turning away from him. "I think I'll retire early this evening, so don't bother to bring me any dinner. Felicia will be wanting her clothes back, I imagine," she said as she mounted the stairs slowly.

Parkhurst watched his youngest daughter's retreating back with a heavy heart. Renata had always been the life in their house, in their lives. She saw good in everyone and everything. It had been Renata who cheered him at the end of a hectic and heart-wrenching day. Renata who, from the age of four, had charmed everyone she met. He couldn't blame himself for the change in her . . . He had only done what was right for Renata. It was that damn Jake Wolf who had ruined her life, had ruined his Renata.

All that would change when they were away from Silver Valley and Jake Wolf. Edenworth was quite a catch, a man any woman would be proud to have as a husband. Renata would see that . . . and soon. She had to.

Lord Edenworth sat back and studied the rough interior of Silver Valley's only saloon. He was seated in the corner, his back to the wall, a position he felt was safe. Never in all his sheltered life had he felt so openly disliked, and he had needed a drink or two . . . or three.

The establishment left a lot to be desired as the only concession to entertainment in this inconsequential town. The furnishings looked more suited to providing firewood than decoration; the chairs wobbled dangerously and the rough-hewn tables rocked with a life of their own. Of course, the decor suited the patrons. Unwashed and unmannered cowhands and townspeople.

But he had needed a drink badly.

And another.

Something in his plan had gone terribly wrong. In the three days since Renata had agreed to marry him, to divorce her heathen husband and become his lady, he had begun to doubt his plans. And they had become so elaborate.

He wasn't certain he wanted her anymore.

The light in her eyes had dimmed, if not gone out altogether, and the smile . . . the smile that had captured his heart was nowhere to be seen. If he'd desired a sulky and difficult wife, he could have had any one of dozens of suitable brides in England. But Renata had been different, so lively and untamed, so bright and daring. She was bright where he was pale. She saw every day as something new and wondrous, where he had long ago lost his zest for life. He had imagined showing her London, his vast estates, and seeing her eyes light up. He had wanted to show her the world, and to see it himself anew through her eyes.

Other men might have balked at taking a bride who was not a virgin, one who had lain with another man, but that was not of great concern to him. He was not a particularly passionate man, but he was expected to produce an heir, and sharing carnal pleasures with Renata would certainly not be unpleasant. But that was not the reason for his attraction to her. Not at all.

Yet the pale creature who had haunted the hotel for three days was not the Renata he wanted. Perhaps, in time, he would be able to bring that light back into her eyes. But what if he couldn't?

Still, he was a man of his word. He would marry the girl and save her father from financial ruin. If she didn't regain her exuberant spirit, he would simply leave her on the Edenworth estates while he continued to travel the world.

He grimaced as he signaled for another shot of whiskey, finally instructing the bartender to leave the bottle. The look of disgust he received from the barkeep was as venomous as the glares he had received from the rest of the town. What had he done? Nothing. Nothing at all.

"You're really gonna marry that prissy Englishman?" Donnie Boyle asked Renata again.

"Yes," Renata answered simply, emotionlessly. "Will you help me? I won't rest if I think Jake might hang for something he didn't do. No matter what else . . . he isn't capable of murder."

In spite of his recent defense of Jake, Boyle

looked skeptical. "He and Kenny have been goin' at it for years."

"And it's never gone this far," Renata snapped. "Why now? You're all so certain Jake is capable of such senseless violence . . . have you ever seen any sign of it? Anything other than that . . . that scowl of his?"

"Jake's always been quick with his fists. But he never killed anybody, that I know of," Donnie admitted.

Janie Boyle laid a hand on Renata's arm. "What happened?" she asked softly, more warm and maternal than Renata's own mother had ever been. "Let us help you."

Renata attempted to smile, but it was weak. "I know I look just awful, but I'm very tired." She couldn't tell anyone that she had discarded her mother's nightgowns for Jake's buckskin shirt every night, and still her sleep was restless, broken. "All this with Jake, and the fire, and my parents and Lord Edenworth . . . Once Jake is cleared I'll be able to get on with my life. Edenworth has a castle, you know." She tried to make it sound exciting and romantic. "It's huge, and is three or four hundred years old— quite a historic landmark—and I'll have hundreds of servants, and he's promised me that we'll travel all over the world. Doesn't that sound just wonderful?" She looked to the Boyles for confirmation. It was wonderful, wasn't it?

Janie Boyle gave her a small smile. "Sounds

like a dream come true." There was little enthusiasm in her voice, and Renata knew she hadn't fooled the woman.

Or anyone else for that matter. Her own mirror told her that her eyes were a dull gray-green, and her cheeks weren't rosy, as they usually were. Jake had taken that away from her, just as he'd taken everything else she'd taken for granted. Love. Hope. Faith that she would always have what she wanted most dearly.

"We'll do what we can." It was Janie Boyle who reassured Renata. "I don't know if the judge will listen to us or not, but . . ."

"He will," Renata said confidently. "Along with me and my father, and Sylvia and Felicia Collins . . ."

"What?" Donnie Boyle exclaimed.

Renata smiled briefly. "Don't tell anyone. Sheriff Collins doesn't know . . ."

"We won't. Who else?"

"The preacher. His wife. The schoolteacher, Alice Clark." Renata recited her short list. The most respected citizens of Silver Valley had agreed to be character witnesses for Jake. That in itself was amazing, and it was all Renata's doing. Since the evidence was circumstantial, their testimony would be critical.

"And after the trial?" Janie Boyle asked. "You'll be leaving directly?"

"As soon as Jake is cleared," Renata said, her words clipped and cool.

Renata turned her back to the Boyles and left the general store with her head held high and her back straight. She was as calm as the surface of a pond on a still day, as poised as the gentlest city-bred woman might hope to be. But there was no spring in her step . . . no bright smile on her face.

His prisoner paced the small cell all day and half the night, a caged animal ready to pounce. In spite of the bars between them, he scared Sheriff Collins. Jake's fury was just beneath the surface, almost tangible, it was so strong. Of course, he had always been a little afraid of Jake. He was too unpredictable, too damn savage.

"Sit down," he ordered for the sixth time in half an hour.

Usually Jake didn't bother to respond, but this time Jake looked up, his eyes locked on him, challenging. "Come in here and make me sit down." His voice was menacing, and Collins looked away, letting it drop. Jake resumed his pacing.

His untouched dinner sat on the floor, the tin plate filled with beans and bacon and biscuits. Collins had held Jake at gunpoint while he placed the meal inside the cell, as he did twice a day.

But Jake didn't eat.

When the door opened and the well-dressed gentleman walked in Jake stopped his frantic pacing. Collins looked up from his desk, and the man gave him a half smile, placid and full of disdain.

"Can I help you, mister?" he asked coldly.

The man showed his disapproval with the arch of a fine eyebrow. "Certainly." He stepped into the room and closed the door behind him. "I'd like to speak privately with your prisoner, if I may." His voice was clipped and precise, his accent indicating his gentle birth.

Collins didn't move. The fop who stood just inside the doorway brushed an invisible speck of dust from his pale gray jacket and smoothed the waistcoat that was a shade darker. His boots were polished to a high shine, and just a hint of Silver Valley dust marred that luster.

"Sorry," he snapped. "Talk all you want, but I stay here."

The man never lost his cool smile, and his gray eyes remained on Collins. "I assure you, I am unarmed." He held open his jacket, as if to prove the point. "And even if I were carrying a weapon, I have no intention of snatching your prisoner from this delightful jail. If anyone wants to see him remain here, it is I."

Collins gave Jake a quick glance, but Jake's eyes remained on the visitor, transfixed.

"All right," he said ungraciously. He grabbed the ring of keys, just to be safe, and with a slow gait left the two men alone.

"Doesn't put up much of a fight, does he?" the man observed when the sheriff had closed the door.

"What do you want?" Jake asked. He stood in the middle of the cell, his arms crossed over his bare chest, his feet planted far apart.

"Right to the point. I like that." The gentleman pulled the sheriff's chair aside and placed it directly in front of the jail cell, and then he sat down gracefully, crossing his legs and pushing an errant lock of fair hair from his forehead. "What the bloody hell have you done to my fiancée?"

Jake stared the man down, the man who had grabbed Renata the day they had arrested him for Kenny's murder. The man Jake had punched in the jaw. He'd never forget the way Renata had called to him, the panic in her voice.

"You must be Lord what's-his-name." Jake's voice was cold, but his gut churned.

"Edenworth." The name was provided with a grim smile. "And you still haven't answered my question."

"Why are you still here?" Jake asked. "You and your . . . fiancée should have been on a train to Philadelphia by now."

Edenworth sighed tiredly. "I was told that you were a difficult fellow," he said under his breath. "I agree. We should be well on our way. However, my bride-to-be has made some rather unusual demands, and it's put quite a damper on my plans." His voice remained light, almost nonchalant.

"What kind of demands?"

"We're not to leave until you're cleared of this murder charge." He was obviously not pleased with the delay. "Renata seems to have taken you on as a . . . cause of the moment, if you will."

Jake's eyes bored into the man. "What the hell does that mean?"

"It means that Renata is running all over town trying to mount a defense for you." He studied Jake through hooded eyes. "Did you do it? Did you kill the man? I promise you, this is just between us."

"No."

Edenworth nodded. "I thought not. Renata's usually such an excellent judge of character . . ."

"She doesn't like you much," Jake snapped.

Edenworth found this barb particularly funny and surprised Jake by laughing out loud. "Touché, old man. But you still haven't answered my initial question. What have you done to Renata? She's absolutely . . . drab."

Jake barely raised an eyebrow. "I didn't do anything."

"You bloody well did," Edenworth insisted, losing his temper and rising from the chair in a shot. Standing face-to-face with Jake, he was forced to look up slightly, even though he was tall.

"Ever since her daring escape from the hotel room she's not been the same. I don't like it. I don't like it at all."

Jake resumed his pacing before he answered. "I only told her the truth, and Renata doesn't like that much." He met Edenworth's pale eyes in an almost primal challenge. "Renata and the truth often part company."

"Well, I can only hope that when this is all

over, and the divorce is final, and Renata is my wife at last . . ."

"Divorce . . ." The word that escaped from Jake's lips was little more than a biting breath.

"Yes." Edenworth's head snapped up sharply. "I don't mind telling you, I'd much rather see you hang. It would be less scandalous for me to return to England with an American widow than an American divorcée. We're likely to create quite an uproar, in any case." He smiled. "But if you are truly innocent . . . I suppose that wouldn't be quite proper."

Jake was barely listening. Divorce. Naturally. What else should he have expected? But why wasn't she on her way back home, instead of wasting her time trying to prove that he was innocent? It was a lost cause. The people of Silver Valley would finally get what they had always wanted—his broken neck at the end of a rope.

Collins walked back in, startling them both. "That's enough. Anything else you have to say, you can say in front of me."

Edenworth bowed formally to the sheriff. "I'm quite finished with your prisoner, I assure you. An unpleasant character, isn't he?"

Edenworth's eyes lit on Jake for a moment, and his smile faded, just a little. With an almost imperceptible nod of his head, he was gone.

Chapter Twenty-four

Jake paced, unable to lie on the narrow cot or sit with his back against the brick wall for very long. He had always known that it would come to this, sooner or later. Sheriff Collins had long been itching to get rid of him, and so had the rest of the residents of Silver Valley. He'd been an outcast here for as long as he could remember. And it didn't bother him. It was the natural order of things.

But Renata . . . How could he have been so stupid as to believe that she was any different? She had managed to fool herself with one of her own stories, one of her elaborate lies, that he was something he was not. And the truth had frightened her.

The flash of doubt had been fleeting—he'd give her that—but it had been there. A moment of fear in her green eyes, a second of tension on her face as she actually pondered the possibility that he had murdered Kenny Mails and set fire to the cabin.

He had trusted her as he had never trusted another human being in his life. Jake had always held something of himself back, but Renata had seen it all. The quiet fears he had denied to himself, the hope he had been afraid to feel. And the love. Yes, he had loved her . . . and believed that she loved him as well.

But she was just a little girl, playing at being married to the town bad boy, pretending that they might have a life together.

Jake hadn't been pretending. He had offered everything he had to her . . . but it wasn't enough. Even if he built her a castle in the mountains, it would never be enough. Because she was Renata Marie Parkhurst, spoiled and pampered, living in a world of her own imaginings. And he was Jake Wolf, a loner who would soon find himself at the end of a hangman's rope for a crime he didn't commit.

That was reality, and Renata Marie Parkhurst didn't like reality. It was much too harsh.

"You gonna eat?" Sheriff Collins asked abrasively, and Jake lifted his eyes to the anxious lawman.

"What's the matter? Afraid I won't be healthy when you hang me?" Jake's eyes bored into Collins's, and the sheriff looked down. His eyes fell on the untouched plate he had carefully placed just inside the cell door.

"Makes no never mind to me," Collins snapped.

Jake wondered what the sheriff would do if he told the lawman the truth, that he was innocent . . . that he hadn't killed Kenny Mails. But he didn't say a word, because he knew the answer to that question.

Collins would do nothing. In the lawman's eyes, Jake had already been tried and convicted.

Jake resumed the pacing that seemed to drive Walter Collins mad. The sheriff watched him with wary eyes, day and night, keeping his distance from the bars as if Jake might reach through and grab the cowardly man.

"Keep this up," Collins said halfheartedly, "and we won't have to hang you."

Jake finally gave in and grabbed a biscuit off the tin plate. The sheriff's wife delivered meals twice a day, though she very deliberately avoided looking at her husband's prisoner.

He sat on the cot and leaned against the wall, breaking off a piece of the biscuit and popping it into his mouth. Not bad. Nothing like the rocks Mel had prepared on occasion when he'd first brought her to Colorado.

Mel was the only woman he had ever trusted . . . before he'd met her cousin Renata. He tried to remember everything Mel had said about her Philadelphia relations, and wished he'd payed closer attention to her observations.

Renata had been the object of those observations more often than her sister or her parents. What exactly had Mel said? Pretty. Energetic. Optimistic to a fault. A bit flighty.

A bit? She was married to him, engaged to an English fop, and apparently trying to see him cleared before she left this diversion behind. And she probably saw nothing unusual in the situation.

Did she really believe he was innocent? Would anyone believe it?

He rose from the cot and placed his hands on the bars, staring at Collins. The sheriff lifted his head and looked up at Jake, apprehension in his eyes.

"I didn't do it," Jake said in a low voice. "I didn't kill Kenny Mails."

Collins was speechless for a moment, as Jake stared at him, awaiting a response.

"Hell, Jake. You've never defended yourself before. Of course, you've never been charged with a hangin' offense before, either."

Jake didn't respond. He just waited.

"You'll have your day in front of the judge," Collins said uncertainly.

"But you don't believe me, do you?" Jake gave the sheriff a biting, crooked smile.

Collins waited a moment before he answered. "No. You killed Kenny, all right."

Jake wasn't disappointed. He'd received exactly the answer he'd expected.

Collins and everyone else in this town believed he had killed Kenny. Even Renata doubted him. He didn't have a chance.

He was going to hang.

Two days remained before Jake's trial, and no one was happier than Percival. It had been quite an adventure, of course, but he was tiring of the Silver Valley charm, nominal as it was, and anxious to get his Renata away from this place and its memories.

She had done all that she could to see that her husband was cleared of all charges, and now there was nothing to do but wait. She was clearly nervous, he saw on the few occasions he was able to catch a glimpse of her. Renata seemed to be avoiding him quite neatly.

So he was surprised when she cornered him in the hotel lobby and, with her mother watching, invited him to walk with her to the general store. Cecilia was left behind, a smug smile on her face as she watched them stroll from the lobby.

Percival was delighted. There was a hint of the old gleam in Renata's eyes, and a bit of color in her cheeks. She was silent, strangely pensive, as they walked down the boardwalk side by side. Percival ignored the baleful stares he received from the people in the street and those looking out the windows as he and Renata passed. He was becoming accustomed to them.

As they entered the general store, Renata took his arm. She wrapped her fingers tightly around the fabric of his sleeve and practically dragged him toward the back of the store. "Mrs. Boyle?" she called to the woman who was straightening shelves of canned goods. "Might I borrow your storeroom?" Percival realized that she was headed straight for a closed door and would probably continue no matter what reply she received from the shopkeeper's wife.

"Sit down," Renata said in a forceful voice as soon as the door was closed behind them. The storeroom was piled high on all sides with goods, and Renata motioned to a dangerously rickety bench against the wall. Percival took one look at the bench and declined with quiet dignity.

Renata paced frantically, looking at the floor and chewing her lower lip. Finally she looked up at him, her face pleasantly flushed with color.

"I'll be nothing but honest with you, Edenworth," she said, her voice softer than it had been in days past.

"I do wish you would call me Percival, or Percy, if you prefer."

Renata shook off his request with a wave of her hand. "I think I may be . . . I suspect I might be carrying a child." She spoke quickly, as though she was afraid she would change her mind if she didn't just come out with it. "I'm not positive, but I'm almost . . . It could be anxiety, I suppose, though I've never suffered from a nervous constitution before." Her eyes dropped to the floor. "It's too soon to be certain, but I can't possibly marry you without telling you all of the truth."

Percival sighed and almost fell onto the bench, balancing its unsteady base with his feet planted firmly on the floor. "I admire your honesty, Renata." That was true, though he felt she was holding something back from him. A baby? Babies cried and required much more care than he was ready to . . . but there would be nursemaids. He and his bride need not be bothered with the less attractive aspects of childcare.

"Any child you carry will be given my name and raised as if it were my own." He pushed aside his own misgivings. If a boy, that child would be the next Earl of Edenworth. "There's no reason for anyone to suspect that the child isn't mine, as long as we're married quickly."

Renata gave him a long, puzzled stare. Had she expected him to run like a frightened rabbit when he heard the news? "You're more noble than I've given you credit for." There was genuine surprise in her soft voice.

Percival responded with an unconcerned wave of his hand. "I am willing to accept anything that puts that sparkle back into your eyes. If a child does that, then so be it. We'll have a dozen more, if that's what you desire." He wasn't blind. He saw the cloud that passed over her face. The prospect of bearing his children obviously had not occurred to her.

"I don't . . . I don't know if I should tell Jake or not," Renata stammered. "He has a right to know, but . . . it might be difficult for him, knowing he has a child so far away whom he will never see." She was looking to Edenworth for answers, true confusion on her face.

Percival's eyes narrowed slightly. How much did he really want to know? Bloody hell. "Renata, dear." His voice was a kind caress. "Are you in love with this . . . with this Wolf character?"

It was the last question Renata had expected from him, and her head jerked up so she could meet his eyes. "I . . . I . . . no." Her face turned crimson. "I thought I did, but it was just a childish infatuation. I hope you won't think too badly of me."

Percival watched the emotions fleeting across her face, the blaze in her eyes, the set of her soft mouth. Jake had been right: Renata and the truth did part company on occasion.

"Then I shouldn't tell him, if I were you," he said evenly. "Best to make a clean break . . . best for everyone."

Renata nodded, but he could see she had her doubts. She kneaded her hands unconsciously. Even in such a state, wearing her mother's ill-fitting gown, which was too dark for her, she was enchanting. Beautiful, yes, but more than that. Alive. Bright as a shooting star.

"Perhaps you're right," she finally agreed. "It would be best if we told no one, not even my mother and father. At least, not until I'm certain, and we're away from Silver Valley."

Janie Boyle frowned at the couple as they slipped from the storeroom. "Not fittin'. Not

fittin' at all," she muttered. Renata seemed not
to hear, but it wasn't she who was the recipient
of the woman's venomous glare. "Poor Jake,"
the woman mumbled. "Can't hardly do a thing,
all locked up like he is. Well, maybe he's not
perfect" —she was talking to herself— "but he's
one of us, at least.

"Not fittin'. Not fittin' at all."

Renata had paced the boardwalk for almost
an hour, carefully staying away from the window of the sheriff's office. How could she face
Jake? It was only right that she tell him she
was leaving—not that he would care—and it
was important that he not know how painful
it was for her. What would she have done if
her father hadn't been in such a predicament?
Would she have tried to stay in Silver Valley
and convince Jake that she was not the shallow
fortune hunter he believed her to be?

That thought caused her anger to rise to the
surface. How could he believe that of her? She
wanted to maintain that it was all a lie—that he
never really believed she was so superficial—
but why else would he not tell her that he had
money? That he was the richest man in town?
Because he believed her to be a man hunter
looking for a rich husband . . . and, in a way,
that was true. She had come to Colorado looking for a husband, a rancher husband, but not
at the expense of love. Love always came first,
even in her wildest daydreams.

She had managed to convince herself that

Jake loved her, but that was foolish. She had made a simpleminded mistake. She had given Jake everything, had loved him completely, and she meant nothing to him. Nothing at all.

Renata opened the door to the sheriff's office and walked in with a smile on her face. She still had her pride, bruised as it was. He would never know how much he'd hurt her.

Renata was wearing one of her mother's dresses, a simple dark brown frock. She had brushed aside her mother's suggestions that they have a few things altered for her for the remainder of their stay and the trip to Philadelphia. The last thing Renata wanted was to stand still for fittings and measurements. That could wait.

The dress dragged across the floor and, like the other dresses she had borrowed from her mother, it was snug in the bodice and loose in the waist. Renata, who had always been so meticulous about her wardrobe, was unconcerned that she didn't look her best, that she looked much better in springlike colors—pale peach, green, and yellow—than she ever would in her mother's dark gowns.

Her hair was brushed back, held with a white ribbon, the soft curls waving down her back. One wayward tendril had escaped and brushed her cheek, and she pushed it back, only to have it fall again.

When she glanced up Jake was staring at her, his eyes blank, his hands on the iron bars.

"Good morning, Sheriff Collins." Renata

swiftly pulled her eyes away from Jake and smiled at the lawman who was seated at his desk. Collins was clearly agitated.

Renata looked up, forcing her eyes to the jail cell. "Jake." She had wanted to appear so calm, so indifferent, but the sight of him undid her. He was thinner—much too thin—and his eyes looked almost hollow. Her heart ached for him. She couldn't help it. She'd never been good at hiding her feelings . . . and her resolve to appear calm and unaffected disappeared.

"Aren't you feeding him?" She looked at the sheriff angrily. "For goodness sake, I thought at the very least you would . . ."

"It ain't my fault he won't eat." Collins pushed his chair back, loudly scraping the legs against the floor. He snatched the keys to Jake's cell off the edge of his desk, rattling them gratingly. "I'll give you a few minutes, Mrs. Wolf," he said, no measure of kindness in his voice. "But just a few."

Renata turned to her husband as Collins left the room. All her plans had flown out the window when she'd seen him. He still needed her, perhaps more than anyone. But her father needed her too.

"You're much too thin," Renata said in a soft voice. "You should eat . . ." She took a step toward the cell.

Jake hadn't said a word to her, but the fury that had been in his eyes the last time she'd seen him was gone.

"You shouldn't be here," he said gruffly.

"I had to come. The judge will be here tomorrow. I . . ." Renata reached out and tentatively touched his fingers. She waited for him to pull away from her touch, but he didn't. "After you're released I'm returning to Philadelphia with my parents, and Edenworth." She couldn't look into his eyes as she told him, but she kept her fingers over his, drawing strength and warmth and hope from that simple touch. "I'll take care of . . . the divorce from there, and if there's any . . . paperwork or anything for you . . . I don't really know what's involved . . . I'll send it to Melanie. I imagine she can get in touch with you if it's necessary."

"Probably."

Renata looked up then, and there were unshed tears in her eyes. "You don't even sound surprised."

"Your . . . Edenworth paid me a visit."

"What for?" Renata snapped. Edenworth had said nothing to her about a visit with Jake.

Jake shrugged his shoulders. "Curious, I think. I'm sure he'll make you a wonderful husband."

Renata pulled her fingers away from the bars. How could he be so calm? "Yes? Well, there's a castle, you know. Very romantic. And servants. More than I can count. Nice catch for a fortune hunter like myself." Her words were uncharacteristically bitter.

"I'm sorry I said that," Jake said without his usual casual scorn. "I was . . . angry."

"Well." Renata looked at the floor again.

"We've both made mistakes. I guess my father was right all along. I'm undisciplined and much too impulsive. I try to make my life the way I want it to be, and reality sometimes gets lost in the process. My imagination is much too . . . fertile for my own good."

She made herself look up and smiled weakly. "After the divorce is final you can go back to playing the savage, trying to scare the wits out of small children and defenseless women." She tried to sound jaunty, but the attempt was lost in her indecision and sorrow over what was gone.

"Maybe you'll get lucky and they'll hang me. No messy divorce, and you can marry Edenworth right away." Jake's voice was fierce, harsher than he'd intended. He wanted, more than anything, for Renata to place her hands back on the bars, wanted to touch her one more time.

Renata's smile widened. "That won't happen." This was a real smile, one that warmed Jake's heart in spite of it all. She came closer and lowered her voice. "The preacher, the Boyles, the schoolmarm, even the sheriff's wife and daughter, have agreed to testify that you couldn't have murdered Kenny Mails."

Jake frowned. "Why?"

"I convinced them that you couldn't possibly have killed a man in cold blood, and they agreed. They'll be character witnesses." She granted his silent wish and wrapped her fingers around his again. "I couldn't stand to see you hanged . . . and it really didn't take much to convince the others that you aren't a killer."

Jake laced his fingers through hers, twining them loosely. She was more beautiful than he had remembered, more breathtaking than the vision he dreamed of every night. Edenworth had said that she was drab, but Jake saw no evidence of that. She was more pale than usual, but her green eyes were like fire, bright, and looking into him as though she was seeing into his very soul.

He couldn't forget the flash of doubt he had seen in those eyes, but it was gone now. He wondered if he hadn't imagined it in the first place.

Whatever had been between them from the moment they'd met was still there. There would never be another woman for him, ever. Was he going to let her go because of one brief moment of doubt? Because he was so bitter, his pride so deeply entrenched, that he couldn't admit that he needed someone in his life? That he needed her? Should he even try to mend the break he had created? Renata was wasting no time getting on with her life. She had her Lord Edenworth waiting anxiously.

They stood silently, neither one able to pull away from the iron bars. The sun shone through the two windows that flanked the door, and dust danced in the rays that pierced the cell. His eyes held hers in a silent quest . . . probing, questioning, searching her soul.

"Rennie . . ." he whispered, the name torn from somewhere deep inside. Could he trust her with his heart?

Sheriff Collins burst into his office, impatient and irascible. "That's long enough, Mrs. Wolf." He sat back down at his desk and propped up his booted feet, making himself comfortable.

Renata pulled her fingers free . . . slowly, reluctantly. There were tears in her eyes, bright and unshed as she looked up at him.

"Good-bye, Jake," she whispered, and he heard the terrible finality in those words.

Chapter Twenty-five

Renata borrowed a buggy from Janie Boyle, a one-horse contraption she felt confident she could manage herself. She avoided the woman's questions about her destination and left the Boyles' general store through the back door. Renata didn't want anyone to know where she was headed for the afternoon.

Maybe the marriage between herself and Jake hadn't worked out. It had never been a normal marriage in the first place, and Jake was so independent. So stubborn. Hardheaded might have been a better word. But Renata remained convinced that Jake led a life that was much too solitary, that whether he admitted it or not, he needed love. Everyone did.

She had heard gossip that Harrison Summers was better, though still ill. Renata didn't know if her theory about the poison had been correct, or if Jake's father had truly been suffering from gastric fever. In any event, it seemed he was the man to see about Jake.

As soon as Renata approached the Summers house, a young man advanced to help her down and see to the horse and buggy. Such a courtesy had not been extended when she had visited with Jake, but she smiled at the young man and accepted his assistance graciously. Her arms ached slightly from leading the horse, but it had not been difficult. Still, she was grateful for the man's help.

Fortunately, it was Gilda who opened the front door; though the young girl protested mildly, Renata had no problem talking her way around Corinne's middle daughter, and as she talked she made her way to and ascended the staircase. Gilda surrendered easily, stopping at the foot of the stairs and watching Renata climb resolutely.

Renata knocked on Harrison Summers's bedroom door, opening it without waiting for a response, and crossed the room to Jake's father. The room was much improved from her last visit. The window was open, the drapes parted to let in the sun, and Harrison Summers was sitting up in bed, his back supported by a number of pillows. And he was alone.

"Good afternoon, Mr. Summers," she greeted him cheerfully, but there was a hesitancy in her step. Now that she was here, what would she say? "You're looking much better than when we first met."

He gave her a small smile. "I quit taking my medicine, much to Corinne's dismay. It's been a slow process, but I've been improving ever since."

"Good." Renata stood over the man. "I could have been wrong, you know. I suspected that you might have been suffering from arsenic poisoning, and that's why I suggested you stop taking that medicine. But I have a dreadful imagination, and I might have been mistaken."

"No. You were right; I'm sure of it. So certain that I won't eat anything unless one of the girls sneaks it up to me. I'm grateful to you." He said the words with a grudging gruffness that told Renata he was not accustomed to expressing his thanks, especially to a slip of a girl. Another way he was like Jake.

"Well, I'm glad you're feeling so much better," Renata said as cheerfully as she could.

Harrison looked up at her. "Is Jake with you?" There was guarded hope in those eyes that were so much like Jake's.

"No. Hasn't anyone told you?" Renata perched on the edge of the bed. It was clear that Harrison Summers knew nothing of what had happened to Jake. "Jake's in jail. He was accused of murdering Kenny Mails. The trial's tomorrow."

"Damn." Summers's face was pained. "I can't believe no one told me. Mails was one of my own men. I didn't even know he was dead. I've got to get out of this bed . . ."

"Jake will be fine," Renata assured the older man. "There are several people who are going to testify on his behalf, and he'll be cleared. He is innocent," Renata insisted.

"I believe that's true," Summers said, and there was a deeper meaning there that Renata didn't understand.

"The reason I'm here," Renata plowed forward, "is that I . . . I think it's important for you and Jake to make amends. He needs you. He needs his sisters. He has been so alone . . . I don't know why this has gone on for so long, but . . ."

Summers smiled. "But he has you now. As much as I would like to have Jake in my life, I don't believe it will ever happen. There's been too much . . . he won't allow it. But it soothes me to know that he has you."

"I'm . . . I'm leaving," Renata said simply. It would serve no purpose to explain it all to Harrison Summers. "After the trial."

"Why?" Summers was distressed. "I thought that finally . . . that Jake would have . . . Is it because of the accusation?"

"Oh, no," Renata assured the agitated man. "I never doubted that Jake was innocent. My reason for leaving is rather complicated."

"I can give you a reason to stay," Summers urged. "My will. I've left this ranch to my firstborn grandson. I've always hoped that would be Jake's child. Jake's and yours."

Renata frowned and fidgeted. Something was nagging at her brain. "What about your wife? Your daughters?"

"There's a provision for the girls, until their marriages, and a small provision for Corinne." He sighed and shook his head. "I should have thrown that woman out long ago. If I had recognized her sooner for the schemer she really was, Jake might . . . Jake might not have left."

The palpable hate between Jake and Corinne . . . his fear of the woman. "What happened?" Renata whispered.

Summers leaned back against the pillows and sighed, a deep sigh that spoke of his regret. Renata could read his expression almost as effortlessly as she read Jake's, when his guard was down, and she saw a heart-wrenching mixture of longing and remorse.

"When Jake was thirteen his grandfather died. His mother had passed on four years earlier, and so he came here to live. He was always quiet, reserved, and a bit uncomfortable, but I thought that would pass with time. It didn't. He was here for two years, and he never felt . . . like this was his home." Harrison Summers looked past Renata as if he were reliving those years.

"One night . . . I heard a scream from the kitchen. It was Corinne. She was pregnant with Gilda, pretty far along, and I . . . I was still fooled by her. I thought she cared for me . . . but she only cared for money, and the security this ranch offered. When I got to the kitchen Jake was crouched on the floor holding his hands under his jaw, blood dripping through his fingers. Corinne was backed against the stove, a knife in one hand, the other hand holding the torn bodice of her dress to cover herself. She was hysterical. Said Jake had attacked her, that she had defended herself with the only weapon at hand, that she wouldn't live under the same roof with a savage."

Summers took a deep and ragged breath. "God help me, I believed her. I dragged Jake to his feet and hit him. He never said a word. He just ran from this house and disappeared. I didn't see him until years later . . . on the street in Silver Valley. He was a man by then, and I . . . I was afraid to approach him. He simply ignored me. By then I knew what a schemer Corinne was, that she had probably lied that night . . ."

"Probably?" Renata snapped. "How could you believe that Jake would do such a thing?"

Summers searched her eyes and Renata saw the suffering there, the indecision. "He'd spent more than half his life with the Cheyenne. When he was with me, even while his mother was living and he was only here for a few months out of the year, I tried to see to his education. There were tutors . . . but I always felt guilty that I hadn't been there to see that he was raised right."

"But Jake . . ." Renata took a deep breath and calmed herself. "No wonder Jake won't trust anyone."

"Not even you?"

"Especially not me," Renata snapped. "Tell him, for goodness sake. Tell him the truth. Tell him that you know . . . and that you love him. He will never admit it, but he needs you." The more she thought about it, the more disgusted she became with Corinne—the woman who had given Jake that scar on his jaw.

"Why do you continue to allow that woman to live in this house? How can you stand to look at her day after day, knowing what she's done?"

Summers gave Renata a disgusted grimace. "I made a commitment. She's the mother of my daughters."

A flicker of dawning knowledge passed over Renata's face. "When did you change the will leaving this ranch to your firstborn grandson?"

"Six months ago."

Renata leaned closer to Harrison Summers. "Do you know that someone shot Jake and then tried to frame him for burning down your barn? A few weeks ago someone tried to kill Jake and me in a fire. Kenny Mails and another man set fire to the cabin. Do you suppose all of that happened because Corinne found out you changed your will?"

"Very good, my dear." Corinne stepped into the room, followed closely by Ben Beechcroft. "And very unfortunate."

"Corinne . . ." The color had drained from Harrison's face as the magnitude of what his wife had done hit him.

"Shut up, Harrison." Corinne never took her

eyes off Renata as Beechcroft moved to the bed and began to bind Summers hand and foot. Summers protested weakly, trying to fight back, but even if he hadn't been so ill, he would have had a hard time fighting the younger Beechcroft. His struggles were futile. When he was tightly bound Beechcroft shoved a handkerchief into Harrison's mouth and gagged the ailing man.

"You should have left well enough alone, missy." Corinne grabbed Renata's arm, digging her fingers into Renata's tender flesh. "What am I going to do with you?" The question seemed to be one of annoyance, not morality. Corinne would have her killed without a second thought. And her baby . . . she couldn't let them know about the baby.

"I'm sure you know by now that I'm leaving Silver Valley tomorrow," Renata said as haughtily as she could. "With my parents and Lord Edenworth. Jake and I are going to be divorced, and I don't care a whit . . ."

"I don't believe you," Corinne said, moving her face close to Renata's. "You've been nothing but trouble since you came here . . . stirring everyone up and barging into my house. Dressing up that damned heathen to look like a civilized human being and presenting him to my daughters as though . . . as though . . ."

Beechcroft had turned his attention to Renata, now that Summers had been taken care of. "What are we going to do with her?" His voice was not completely cold, but neither was his question causing him any distress. He was without emotion, and that frightened Renata. "You want me to take care of her?"

Renata was pinned between Corinne and her foreman, and a chill ran up her spine. Out of the corner of her eye she saw Harrison Summers struggling fruitlessly on the bed. Beechcroft, perhaps sensing her growing panic, took her delicate wrist in his bruising grasp, and Corinne loosened her hold.

"Well, I can hardly have you take her out and cut her throat or shoot her. Not yet, anyway." There was an evil light in Corinne's eyes. "Take her up to the north line shack. If, by some miracle, Jake is found innocent tomorrow, we'll make it look like he killed her . . . and do it right this time. If Jake hangs . . . she can meet with some sort of accident—a fall from a cliff, or an accident under some spirited horse's hooves." She smiled, pleased with her scheme.

"I'll meet you up there later, after I've sent the girls to my sister's house in Denver." She deigned to look at her husband then. "Don't think someone might come in and find you here. You'll be all alone. And when Jake is dead, and his wife, as well, I'll come back and take care of you myself. Your death would have been much quicker, and much less painful, if you hadn't ruined everything by changing your will. But with Jake gone and little Miss Renata here taken care of, I'll have complete control of this ranch . . . forever. God, I'm sick of looking at you," she said as she turned away.

Renata lurched forward, straining against Beechcroft's arm as she kicked back at him and attempted to free herself. Then she remembered the groom who had taken her buggy, and Gilda . . . Gilda was in the house, and there were probably others in the ranch house, as well.

Renata couldn't free herself, but she screamed loudly, a piercing scream that strained her voice. Someone would hear her. Someone would come.

Summers's eyes widened, and out of the corner of her eye Renata saw Ben Beechcroft's pistol poised threateningly above her head. The world was suddenly dark for Renata, a complete void with no images, no thoughts, just a nothingness that enveloped her.

Corinne looked with open disgust at the woman slumped in Ben's arms. A small trickle of blood ran through Renata's strawberry-blond hair. With luck, Ben's blow to the head would be enough to do the trick. But luck hadn't been with Corinne lately.

She heard the commotion she'd expected and stepped into the hallway, intercepting two of her daughters. The cook was right behind them.

"Sorry. I saw a mouse in your father's room." She gave them a sheepish smile. "The little pest didn't seem to bother your father nearly as much as it did me.

"Now, find Lina and pack your bags. You're going to Denver for a visit."

Harriet and Gilda were so excited about a surprise visit to their aunt's house, they dismissed the ear-splitting scream that had brought them upstairs in the first place. As Harriet bounded down the stairs, Gilda turned an inquisitive face to her mother.

"Is Renata Wolf still here?"

Corinne smiled. "Oh, no, dear. I sent her on her way. Thank you for informing me that she had burst in."

Gilda returned her mother's smile and blushed at receiving Corinne's approval.

Chapter Twenty-six

Sheriff Collins grudgingly made the bed in the corner of his office. "Maybe tomorrow night I'll be able to sleep in my own bed."

The implications in his statement were clear: Jake would either be free or dead. They'd waste no time carrying out the sentence if he was found guilty.

Collins obviously hated sleeping on the narrow cot that was almost identical to the one in Jake's cell, but he refused to leave Jake alone for more than a few minutes. They'd both been up since before dawn, and it had been dark for a couple of hours. The sheriff barely glanced at Jake as he pulled off his boots and removed his shirt. He would sleep in his long underwear and twill pants, his holstered pistol close at hand, prepared for whatever might occur during the night. Maybe he expected the ghosts of long-dead dog soldiers to burst into his jail and free Jake.

"Yep," he said, settling himself comfortably on the cot. "Tomorrow will be a busy day, with the trial and all. And I'll be rid of you . . . one way or the other."

He reached out to put out the light, but stopped and looked right at Jake. Collins yawned, resting his head on his hands and continuing to stare at Jake.

"You know, my little girl hasn't said a civil word to me since I dragged her out of your wife's hotel room. Says Renata Wolf is her friend. 'Yes, sir.' 'No, sir.' That's about all I can get out of her."

Jake knew Collins had to be bored to actually pursue a conversation with him. "Are you looking for an apology?" Jake offered dryly.

"Even Sylvia . . ." Collins shook his head, ignoring Jake's comment. "She'd think different if it was Felicia who brought home . . ." He hesitated and doused the light at his bedside.

The door burst open, and Collins reached for his pistol. But the moonlight outlined only the refined Englishman, and he let his hand fall. With a groan, Collins lit the lamp that rested on the floor by his narrow cot.

"What the devil do you want?" the sheriff asked Renata's fiancé.

"Renata's missing," Edenworth snapped, and

he turned from Collins to Jake. "Do you know where she is?"

Jake walked slowly to the bars and grasped them in his hands. "No. What do you mean she's missing?"

Edenworth sighed. "Then you had nothing to do with her disappearance?"

Jake shook his head, unable to dismiss his rising panic.

"She borrowed a one-horse conveyance from the shopkeeper's wife this afternoon, and she's not been seen since."

Jake's knuckles turned white as he tightened his grip on the iron bars. "She's never driven a rig before. She might have had an accident." He had a sudden, unbidden image of Renata, lying unconscious in the road. There was a sharp pain in his chest as he turned to Collins.

Jake and Edenworth were staring at the sheriff, waiting for him to make a move. Collins dismissed their concerns with a wave of his hand. "She's probably fine. It's too late to look for her tonight, anyway. If she doesn't show up by morning . . ."

"You can't wait," Jake insisted. "Put together a search party and look for her . . . now."

Collins shook his head. "Dammit, Jake, don't fly off the handle. She's been missing a few hours. If she doesn't show up by morning, I'll see if I can get together a few folks to look for her."

Edenworth faced the sheriff with a grimace. "I was afraid you'd say something to that effect." He reached under his coat, snaking back a long arm. With a flourish, he drew the weapon he'd had concealed in the waistband of his powder-blue trousers and waved it in the sheriff's direction.

"I must ask that you release your prisoner," he ordered calmly.

Sheriff Collins shot to his feet. "What? . . . I can't . . . You wouldn't dare!"

"I wouldn't kill you, that's true. But I would put a bullet in one or both of your knees." There was a hint of despair in the earl's face. "That results in such a repulsive wound. Not life-threatening, but it can leave one with a nasty limp. Not a desirable trait in a lawman, I wouldn't think. That would definitely hinder your ability to apprehend criminals, would it not?"

The sheriff was rendered speechless, and Edenworth studied the weapon in his hand admiringly. "A Colt six-shooter. The very best, wouldn't you say? I've always been fascinated by the American West. Cowboys and Indians. The vast, open plains. I never dreamed that I might one day be a participant in such an adventure." His eyes turned deadly serious. "You needn't worry that I might miss my target and wound a more vital part of your anatomy. I'm quite a good shot." He gave Collins a smile that never reached his eyes.

The sheriff moved slowly to his desk and picked up the keys to Jake's cell. His eyes never left the Englishman, the cool man who threatened to cripple him. There was no doubt in Jake's mind, and evidently none in the sheriff's either, that Edenworth would do exactly as he said.

"This doesn't end it, Jake," Collins warned as he unlocked the jail cell.

"I know." Nothing would end it—nothing but his death.

Edenworth held the pistol expertly. "You won't strike me again, will you?" he asked as Jake left the jail cell.

"Probably will," Jake promised. "But not until we find Renata."

Jake bound the sheriff's wrists and ankles snugly, but not as tightly as he could have. Then he stuffed one of Collins's own handkerchiefs in his mouth and tied a blue bandanna over that to fashion a secure gag.

"Where do you suggest we look?" With the sheriff locked safely behind bars Edenworth shoved the Colt into his waistband.

Jake studied the man, dressed in his well-cut powder-blue suit, who had released him from prison. Perhaps Edenworth really did care for Renata. Maybe he could give her the kind of life she deserved . . . when they found her.

"I don't know. Did you talk to Janie Boyle? Did she know where Renata was going?" Jake doused the lamp and they left a still and silent Sheriff Collins in darkness.

"I don't think the woman would tell me if my backside was on fire," Edenworth barked. "Like everyone else in this hamlet, she dislikes me with an inexplicable intensity."

"So we do have something in common," Jake said as they crossed the deserted street.

Janie Boyle gave a cry of relief when she saw Jake enter through the back door of the general store. The doors that normally opened to the boardwalk were closed and barricaded, and the store would appear to be deserted to any late-night passersby. Donnie and Janie huddled together, their faces grim.

"Oh, dear. Where could she be, Jake?" Janie laid a hand on his arm before her normal reticence could stop her. "She said she had an errand to run, and that she didn't want her folks to know where she was goin', so I let her borry my buggy. She never came back."

Jake looked at Edenworth. "Where is Renata's father? Are you certain he doesn't know where she is?"

"Dr. Parkhurst is, as we speak, pacing in his room. He's wringing his hands and blaming everyone but himself for his plight," Edenworth said haughtily. "He's all but worthless, and he won't be of any use to us."

The Boyles saddled two of Donnie's finest horses, a pair of sorrel mares. Jake would have preferred his own black stallion, but that would have meant letting the blacksmith who was boarding the stallion in on the knowledge that Jake had escaped. At this point the fewer who knew, the better off they were.

They rode toward the Maxwell ranch. Jake could think of no other place Renata would go.

Maybe she had gone there to have some quiet time to think . . . to leave a note for Mel. Maybe she had fallen asleep or forgotten the time, and now it was too dark for her to ride back to town . . . but he didn't think so. Something was wrong; he could feel it in his gut.

Edenworth kept pace with him on the dark road, never falling back, though Jake cut him no slack. Renata's fiancé—Jake could imagine the two of them living in a castle, like a prince and princess in a storybook. It was what Renata deserved . . . to have what every woman wanted. But did Edenworth love her? Jake decided that he must, to travel so far, and to be so concerned for her well-being that he'd release a condemned man from jail. She deserved someone who would love her.

Love—Jake knew he had tasted love with Renata, but like everything else in his life he had let it slip away. He wasn't meant for the kind of life Renata wanted. And he damn well didn't want this . . . this tearing at his insides when he didn't know if she was safe and well . . . this gnawing pain where his heart should have been when he thought of her and Edenworth together . . . he didn't need it or want it, but damned if he knew how to rid himself of it.

There were lamps lit at the Maxwells' new house, and a wagon was standing out front. For a moment Jake relaxed. All his worries had been for nothing; she was safe. But it wasn't the Boyles' buggy, he noted, as he drew closer to the house. This was a buckboard that was still piled high with luggage, and two horses were still hitched to the wagon.

Gabe and Mel were home.

Jake slid from the sorrel and hitched it to the post near the wide steps that led to the double doors, a grand entrance compared to the cabin Gabe and Mel had lived in when they started their married life. Jake stormed up the steps and threw open the doors, surprising the Maxwells as they opened a trunk, beginning to unpack. Their heads snapped up, their surprised looks turning quickly into smiles when they saw Jake in the doorway.

"Is she here?" Jake asked gruffly.

Mel's smile faded, and Gabe approached his friend. "Is who here? What's wrong?"

Jake's hopes were dashed. If Renata had been here, they would have known who he was asking for. They had just arrived and obviously didn't know anything about what was going on. Their faces were placid as they awaited Jake's explanation.

Edenworth appeared beside Jake, composed as always, offering Gabe and Mel a sardonic tilt of his fair head. Gabe looked at Edenworth with a worried frown before he turned back to Jake.

"My wife is missing," Jake finally said, his voice as emotionless as he could make it.

"Your wife?" Gabe and Mel asked at the same time, exchanging disbelieving looks.

"I'm afraid she's in trouble," Jake admitted.

"Edenworth, here, broke me out of jail so we could look for her."

Edenworth nodded when his name was mentioned. "I have the pleasure of being his wife's fiancé."

To their credit, neither Mel nor Gabe said a word. Mel brushed her blond hair away from her face with both hands, and Jake watched in brief amusement as Edenworth looked at Melanie. His eyes widened, and he leaned forward slightly, as if to get a better view. She was wearing trousers, tight as the dickens, and an oversized man's shirt. Mel was outlandish, shocking, and strikingly lovely, all at the same time.

"What were you in jail for this time, Jake?" Gabe asked.

"This time?" Edenworth asked softly, and was ignored.

"Murder," Jake said. "Trial's tomorrow. Look," he snapped impatiently, "I don't have time to explain. I . . . I need your help, Gabe."

Jake had never asked for help before, but tonight he would beg if he had to.

Gabe calmly stared at him. "We were gone less than three months and you got married. Who is this woman, anyway?"

Jake looked from Gabe to Mel and back again. What would they say when they discovered that he had placed Mel's favorite cousin in danger? What would Mel think of her beautiful cousin . . . married to him?

"Red Rennie," he said crisply.

Mel and Gabe exchanged a stunned and silent glance. Then Mel turned to Jake. "My cousin Renata? Renata Parkhurst?"

"Renata Wolf," Jake corrected her automatically, as Renata had corrected him so many times. "There's no time to explain. She's missing, and I have a feeling something's wrong."

"Damn," Mel breathed. "Those hunches of yours have never been wrong before."

"Let me grab a rifle," Gabe said, all business now. "And saddle the roan."

"I'm going with you," Mel insisted, turning away from her husband to arm herself.

"No!" Gabe grabbed her arm with a forcefulness Jake had rarely seen him use with his wife. "You're staying here with the girls."

"Mary can watch the girls . . ."

"Mel!" Gabe turned a pleading face to Jake. "We finally got her pregnant again, and I'll not have her endangering herself."

"He's right," Jake said, crossing the room and looking down at Gabe's stunning wife. "I know how he feels." The truth of his statement was in his quiet voice. "If he's worried about you, he won't be any good to me. And I need him. I've got to find Rennie."

Mel smiled up at him. "You and Renata. Goddamn, I never woulda . . ."

Edenworth stepped forward. "Before you get too carried away with your congratulations, kindly remember that Renata is divorcing him and will be marrying me in the near future."

Mel gave the English dandy a derisive glance

that made him step back, her eyes traveling up and down his well-cut suit with obvious loathing.

"I'd like to hear that from Renata herself," Mel stated.

She turned away from the Englishman and laid a hand on Jake's arm. "You know, except for Gabriel, you're the best friend I've ever had. I always knew that one day some lucky woman would see the man I see and ignore that damn temper of yours." She gave him a bright grin, showing her dimples. Behind him, Edenworth sighed deeply. "You know I love Renata, even though she's sometimes unbearably cheerful, but I never knew she was so damn smart."

"I don't know about that. This is . . . a real mess, Mel. If Renata was really so smart, she would have run like hell the first time she set eyes on me."

"I'll insist on the entire story after you find her," Mel said. "Every detail."

"You'll have it," Jake promised, though he knew there were details of his short time with Renata that he would never share with anyone.

Mel helped Jake prepare for the night that was still ahead. She handed him a buckskin boot that he slipped over his head and a Winchester with a shortened barrel that he expertly slid into the boot at his back. He dropped a long, thin knife into a recess sewn into his tall moccasin and fastened an ammunition belt across his chest.

Edenworth paced quick, short steps in front of the open door. He glanced at Jake and Mel occasionally, but they ignored him. Obviously, he was a man unaccustomed to a lack of attention.

Jake, fully armed, looked down at Mel and placed a finger under her chin. He was, amazingly, able to smile.

"She is everything you said," he whispered. "Beautiful, smart, sometimes silly. She smiles and laughs at everything . . . and lies with the face of an angel when it suits her purpose." His smile faded. "I won't let anyone hurt her."

"You love her, don't you?" Mel's voice was as soft as his, a breathy whisper.

Jake hesitated. He should deny it, but the smile on Mel's face told him it was too late for that. "It doesn't matter."

Mel placed her arms around Jake's neck and gave him a quick squeeze—no easy task with the weaponry he wore.

"Don't give up," she whispered in his ear. "I speak from experience, remember?"

"Get your damn hands off my wife," Gabriel said casually as he rushed back into the room with a six-shooter at his left hip and a Winchester in his hand.

"I could help," Mel insisted, releasing Jake. "I'm a better shot than either of you."

Gabe kissed his stubborn wife. "No," he said firmly. "I'll not have you endangering yourself and this baby for your addle-brained cousin."

He received a sinister glare from Jake and

smiled repentantly. "Sorry. This will take some getting used to. I can't imagine Renata anywhere but in the city."

Edenworth groaned loudly. "I wouldn't worry if I were you. She won't be here much longer."

Jake and the Englishman stared at one another and, amazingly, Edenworth didn't back down.

Gabe stepped between the two of them, his rifle in the air. "Seems to me we have to find the girl before you two can fight over her."

The statement brought Jake back to his senses, and Gabe led the way down the steps of his house, muttering under his breath.

"Red Rennie . . . and Jake? Goddamn . . ."

Chapter Twenty-seven

There was a single lantern burning in the line shack, casting long shadows and leaving the four corners in darkness. It had been dark for hours, but neither Renata nor her two captors had slept. Corinne stood near the window, glancing out into the night even when it became much too dark to see beyond the sagging porch. She hugged her arms to her body as if she was chilled, and when she deigned to look at Renata or the foreman it was with a condescending glower.

Ben Beechcroft kept his distance. Apparently, he knew better than to get close to Corinne when she was in a surly mood. He sat silently in a ladder-back chair, his back against the wall. His eyes flitted from Renata to Corinne.

Renata sat in a hard-backed chair in the center of the room, her hands tied behind her back, her ankles bound to the chair legs with a rough length of rope. They had threatened to gag her if she made any noise, so she had been silent throughout the afternoon and evening, as Ben and Corinne calmly discussed their plans for her.

Her head still throbbed, the pain shooting through her temples and behind her eyes. When she'd come to she'd found herself bound and gagged and covered with a filthy blanket as she bounced along in the bed of a buckboard. She'd managed to remain motionless and quiet, trying to be calm and rational as she assessed her situation.

Corinne Summers was behind it all. Beechcroft might have done all the dirty work, but Corinne was the mastermind who had put the plan into motion. Beechcroft had shot Jake. Renata realized that if she hadn't been at the cabin, it might have ended there. Jake could very well have bled to death that night.

And, of course, it had been Beechcroft who accused Jake of burning down his own father's barn. Again, if Renata hadn't interfered, Jake might have died. Beechcroft and Kenny Mails had burned down the cabin. She was supposed to have died that night, and Jake as well. All because of Harrison Summers's new will . . . all for a piece of land.

Had Beechcroft killed Kenny because Jake saw Kenny's face? Was he afraid Kenny would talk if he was pressured? Renata turned her head slightly and looked at the Summerses' foreman. He lifted a cold cup of coffee to his lips, a far-off look in his eye. He was wearing a buckskin jacket, fringed down the length of the sleeve and at the hem. There were several strands missing from the arm that was raised as he lifted the tin cup, and Renata could almost see Kenny Mails grasping at those strands as Beechcroft slit his throat. Her face paled and she turned away from him. The picture was too vivid, too real.

None of that mattered at the moment. How was she going to get out of this predicament? She couldn't rely on Jake to save her; he was locked up in jail and couldn't possibly have any idea what had happened to her. The trial was tomorrow. Would all the people she had convinced to testify go through with it if she wasn't there to provide Jake with an alibi? They could only act as character witnesses. She was the only one who had been with Jake at the time of the murder. What would Jake think? Jake would think she had deserted him when he needed her most. She had to find a way to escape.

So far there had been no chance. Her hands and feet were bound. Beechcroft had removed the gag with which she'd awakened, but he promised to replace it if she made so much as a sound. Anyway, she could have screamed her head off and no one would have heard her. The shack was on an isolated hill, far from the main house. It would have been a miracle if any of the hands happened to be passing by.

Ben Beechcroft was the one she should have feared. He was, after all, a man who had acted violently . . . shooting Jake, setting fire to the cabin, killing Kenny . . .

But it was Corinne who scared Renata the most. Her eyes were so cold, so calculating. She wouldn't be the one to kill Renata, but she would order her death without a qualm. Perhaps it was because she was a woman that Renata was frightened of her. All the women Renata had ever known were softhearted. Even Melanie, for all her rebelliousness, was caring and warm to those she loved. Renata doubted that Corinne Summers loved anyone. She certainly didn't love her husband. She hadn't been able to love Jake when he'd come to them as a child. She probably didn't even love her own daughters. Renata found that difficult to fathom, but Corinne was living proof that such a woman could exist.

No matter what, Renata knew she couldn't let them know that she was pregnant. Her child, if a son, would be the rightful heir to Harrison Summers's ranch. Allowing Corinne to know that would mean certain death for Renata and her unborn child.

Of course, it was clear that Corinne meant to kill her anyway. For once in her life Renata couldn't think of a way to talk herself out of the situation she'd gotten herself into.

"You know," Renata said softly, afraid to

tempt Beechcroft with the gag, "Jake has no interest in his father's ranch. He doesn't want it. All your worries have been for nothing." She tried to smile, but it was difficult. "I certainly don't want it. Lord Edenworth and I are going to be married. He has a castle in England."

Corinne sneered at her. "I can't rest knowing that Jake is out there, knowing that he might father a child who could take this ranch away from me. I've lost everything once before." Corinne lifted a finely arched brow. "Have you ever lost everything, Renata? It puts a whole different perspective on life."

Renata kept her eyes on Corinne as color flooded the woman's face and a desperate fire lit her eyes. Harrison Summers's wife was not insane, but she walked a fine line.

"I grew up as you did ... privileged and pampered. My sisters and I wore the best and newest fashions, lived in a fine house, never wanted for food or warmth or ... acceptance. And then my father lost everything. Gambled it away." Corinne spoke harshly. Obviously time, Renata realized, had not lessened Corinne's pain. "I had to marry Harrison to secure my future. And I'll do whatever I must to protect it."

Renata tried to be sympathetic, or at least to appear so. "That's terrible. How tragic for you. But you must realize that neither Jake nor I intend to take your home away from you. I'm leaving, and Jake ..."

"If Jake isn't dead, he'll never let you leave,"

Corinne snapped. "You lie so well, Renata. So convincingly."

"I am leaving," Renata said determinedly.

Corinne stepped away from the window and toward Renata. The way the light struck her face made her look suddenly old . . . as wrinkled as Yellow Moon Woman. "I saw the way Jake looked at you that day, when you had the audacity to bring him into my home," Corinne almost growled. "As if you were some precious angel. He'll soon find out that you're simply a flesh-and-blood twit." The threat in those words chilled Renata so she felt gooseflesh rise on her arms and a tingle of terror race down her spine.

The way Jake had looked at her. Had he looked at her when she wasn't watching him, the way Gabriel had looked at Melanie? Had he loved her that much, the feelings evident on his face? That was what she'd come to Silver Valley looking for—that kind of love. Had she found it, only to lose it?

"You're mistaken," Renata said coolly. "Jake married me at gunpoint, if you'll remember. He won't be sorry to see me leave; he'll be relieved. If you simply tell him what the problem is, he'll probably be happy to sign away all rights to his father's ranch."

Corinne shook her head. "It's too late for that. You know too much, and I don't think even Jake will sit by and say nothing while I finish off his father."

Renata said no more. Corinne wasn't going

to change her mind, and it was clear that Beechcroft would do whatever Corinne told him to. Renata closed her eyes and thought of Jake. What could she have done differently? What could she have done to keep it from coming to this?

They should have stayed in the mountains with Yellow Moon Woman. They would have been happy there, for a very long time. Renata was discovering that what she actually needed and what she'd always believed she needed were entirely different. She could live without dances and fancy dresses and jewelry. She couldn't live without Jake. Unfortunately, it looked as if she wouldn't have to worry about that much longer.

The house was dark, lifeless. It was late, so it wouldn't be unusual to find everyone asleep. But there was something different, a deep silence that went beyond a slumbering household, an ominous dreariness that Jake could almost reach out and touch.

If Edenworth and Gabe felt the same palpable darkness from the Summers house, they didn't show it. Gabe slunk off in the direction of the barn, and Edenworth stayed at Jake's heels. Jake didn't know if the Englishman was frightened, or just worried that Jake might find Renata first.

It was the only place Jake could think of, once they'd left Gabe's house, that Renata might have gone. She had liked the girls and had seemed determined that Jake should forge a bond with his sisters. And then, there was her imaginative supposition that his father was being poisoned, slowly and maliciously.

Jake stepped onto the porch, his moccasins silent against the wood. When he heard Edenworth's heavy footfalls on the steps behind him he turned to glare at the Englishman. Edenworth's face remained in the moonlight, while Jake's face was in shadowed darkness. Still, Edenworth seemed to sense Jake's disapproval and sheepishly lightened his step.

Gabe came up behind them, as silent as Jake, startling Edenworth. The Englishman gave a hushed gasp that made Jake and Gabe cringe.

"There's a buggy in the barn," Gabriel whispered. "Looks like the Boyles'."

Jake opened the front door slowly, noiselessly. It was as if the house were dead, the silence was so complete. Jake stopped in the foyer and closed his eyes . . . listening.

With a wave of his hand he directed Gabe to the kitchen and Edenworth to the library, and then mounted the stairs silently.

He placed an ear to the door of the first bedroom. Silence. No sound of steady breathing or restless turns in the bed. To be certain, he opened the door and looked inside. The moonlight illuminated an empty room. The bed was made, with frilly pillows and a rag doll arranged almost artfully against the headboard. Jake frowned.

Lina's room—he could smell her there. She should have been in the soft bed, sleeping soundly.

Edenworth came up the stairs behind Jake, loud enough to wake a man who was sleeping lightly. Gabe was behind the Englishman, shaking his head and looking puzzled.

There had been no one downstairs, not even servants in the rooms off the kitchen.

Jake hesitated at the next door. This was the room he remembered as his father's. He sent Gabe and Edenworth down the hall to search the other rooms, but he was certain they would be as empty as the first room he had searched.

Jake pressed his ear against the door. This room was occupied. There was the faint sound of ragged breathing, of movement against a sheet.

Without a warning, Jake threw the door open.

Whatever he had been expecting, it had not been to find his father . . . bound and gagged and struggling weakly to free himself. Soft moonlight streaming through the open window lit the room, and the old man's eyes cut to Jake. The relief in those eyes was jarring.

Jake lit the bedside lamp and reached down to remove his father's gag. Summers's wrists were raw and bloody from his efforts to free himself, and Jake removed the bonds as gently as he could.

"Where's my wife?" Jake asked in a low voice. Even now, with his father in such pitiful shape, Jake could muster no warmth for the man. It had been too long, and the scars were much too deep.

"They've taken her, Jake." Summers's voice was little more than a whisper. "Corinne and Beechcroft. The north line shack. That's . . ."

"I know where it is," Jake said sharply. He looked down at the man he remembered as being so strong and robust. Harrison Summers was a shadow of the man he had been . . . pale and thin. Jake turned to walk away, but Summers stopped him with a weak hand on his arm.

"They're going to kill her, son," Summers said weakly. "Be careful . . . they'll kill you both if they get the chance."

Jake looked down into the face of the man who was his father—a man he had turned away from years earlier—a man who had pushed him away. Was it fear that he saw in his father's eyes?

Summers's fingers retained their tenuous grip on Jake's arm. "Lord, you look like the devil himself," he murmured.

"I don't have time . . ."

"You must promise me that you will be careful," Summers insisted, as though he had a right to ask for any pledge from the son he had renounced. "Promise me, Jake."

If he hadn't known better, Jake would have sworn that the fear in his father's eyes was not for himself, but for Jake. But that wasn't possible.

"I promise you this," Jake said darkly. "They won't hurt Renata."

Summers nodded and released Jake's arm, then quickly told Jake everything he knew.

Chapter Twenty-eight

They left their horses at the bottom of the rise, ignoring the well-worn path to the shack and forging their own trail through the cottonwoods, over lush grass and jagged rocks. Jake and Gabriel moved silently, as gracefully as stalking animals.

Edenworth suffered occasional slips and managed to step on every dry twig in his path. Jake was so frustrated by the man's incompetence, he was tempted to toss Edenworth over his shoulder and carry the Englishman to the top of the hill. Either that or throw him to the bottom to wait with the horses.

When they reached the crest of the hill and the line shack was in plain view the three of them crouched to the ground. Even though it was hours past midnight, a lantern burned in the shack, the soft light shining through the single window. Jake had to hold himself back. He wanted to rush into the shack and take his wife, but that could get her killed.

His father had told them everything he'd heard . . . and Jake knew Corinne and Beechcroft wouldn't hurt Renata until after the trial. Of course, if they learned of his escape, that would change.

Soon the black sky would turn gray, and with morning would come fresh danger for Renata. The news that he had escaped from jail would spread like wildfire, but he would see that no one reached the line shack with that information.

Jake whispered to Gabriel, and Gabriel nodded and slipped away, disappearing into the inky black night.

"Where is he going?" Edenworth asked, his whisper harsh and too loud.

Jake glared at the man who squatted uneasily next to him. All of this would have been much easier without the Englishman, though the third man would come in handy when it came time to rescue Renata. Even if he was a tenderfoot who crashed through the countryside like a wandering bull. Still, if Beechcroft and Corinne had not heard Edenworth tramping up the hill, they were unlikely to hear him now.

"He's going to a crop of boulders to our right. From there he can see the back of the shack and will have a clear shot at anyone who comes out the front door." Jake didn't tell Edenworth that he had told his friend that if Jake went into the shack, and Corinne and Beechcroft came out, Gabriel was to kill them. Jake would already be dead as that would be only way the two people who had taken Renata would still be alive.

Edenworth searched the black sky to his right and saw nothing. He told Jake, much too loudly, as much.

"Trust me," Jake breathed. "The boulders are there."

Edenworth fidgeted, making nearly as much noise as he had climbing the hill. "How do you remain so bloody still? Squatting on the ground, indeed. A man isn't built for such awkward positioning."

Jake ignored him, swallowing the urge to break the man's neck.

"What will we do?" Edenworth lowered his voice. Even his whisper seemed loud in the stillness under the trees.

"You watch the front door." Jake glared at him, trying to forget that this was the man Renata wanted. Right now he needed the Englishman . . . like it or not. "I'll go in after her, and if I get the chance, I'm going to get her out of there. Throw her out the front door, if necessary. I want you to grab her and get her out of here. No matter what, don't let her go back into that shack."

"Where will you be?"

Jake looked toward the yellow cast in the window. "Inside. I'm the one they want. You take Renata as far away from here as possible. She said you have a castle in England."

Edenworth nodded.

"Good. She should be safe once she's away from Silver Valley." Even if it all went wrong, if he was killed, and Gabe somehow missed his targets, Jake was convinced that even Corinne wouldn't pursue Renata all the way to England.

Edenworth swallowed convulsively. "That's suicide."

Jake shrugged. "Probably."

The Englishman shook his head. "You Americans—you never cease to amaze me. Such passion for life, such dedication to your concept of justice and righteousness. You're often willing to sacrifice your lives for an ideal. . . ." He stopped when he realized Jake was staring at him as if he was mad.

"It was Renata's passion for life that drew me to her," Edenworth continued, lowering his voice to an acceptable level. "That, and the fact that she's a remarkable woman, beautiful and spirited. Most remarkable women are very aware of that fact, but Renata always seems innocently unaware of her effect on the opposite sex. She doesn't realize how marvelous she is, and that makes her all the more amazing."

Jake felt a knot forming in his chest. He didn't need anyone—especially not this man—to tell him that Renata was special. He knew that was true. "At least you and I can agree on that, Edenworth." When all this was over, whether he lived or died, Renata was going to end up with this lord in his castle. He could envision it too clearly: Edenworth and Renata living their fairy tale.

"Learn to dance," Jake snapped.

"What?" Edenworth leaned closer to Jake. "I don't think I heard you correctly."

"Learn to dance," Jake said slowly. "Renata likes to dance, and she said you don't know how."

Edenworth shifted, making more racket than a bear would have made approaching through the brush. "I'm clumsy," he defended himself. "Not in all things, of course, but I have a tendency to trip over my own feet on the dance floor."

Jake dismissed his admission. "Learn to dance, and treat her right," he insisted. "If I ever hear . . ." He stopped. Even if he survived, he would never see her again . . . never hear anything . . . not from England. That was so far away. So damn far.

"Of course I'll treat her right," Edenworth assured him indignantly. "Renata is a true treasure . . ." He stopped when Jake turned his coldest glare on the man.

Edenworth was silent for a few long moments. When he spoke again he seemed to be speaking to himself.

"Women adore me," he said wistfully. "All women, or so I thought. My charm seems to be lacking here in Silver Valley. A quiet English girl . . . that's what I need . . ." He returned Jake's intense glare, no fear in his eyes, no evidence that he had any intention of backing away.

The man did have guts, Jake conceded.

"The first time Renata smiled at me, she stole my heart," Edenworth said wistfully.

Did the man want to die right there? It took every ounce of control Jake had not to throttle him where he sat. But he understood what the Englishman meant.

They waited in silence as the sun lightened the sky.

Edenworth laid a hand on Jake's arm. "I have a better plan."

Jake jerked his arm away. In minutes it would be light enough for Gabe to get a good look at the people who might come through that door. Jake's heart was pounding, his palms wet with sweat. He practically caressed the knife that was concealed in his moccasin. "No changes now."

"You're more likely to survive if we go with my plan," Edenworth insisted.

Jake shook his head. Whether he survived was of little importance.

"Bloody nobility," Edenworth muttered. There was a frown on his pale face, and resignation in his eyes. "It will be my downfall yet. You should know, before you burst in there and get yourself killed, that Renata suspects that she might be *enciente*."

Jake looked in annoyance at the tenderfoot beside him. "She's what?"

"Preggers, old man," Edenworth said, his agitation coming through in his clipped words.

Jake was startled, disbelief coursing through him; then a half-smile crossed his lips. A baby. A baby conceived in the mountains. His smile slowly changed, and he frowned.

"Why didn't she tell me?" He knew the answer to that question. She knew he would never let her leave if there was a child. Renata didn't want him to know.

Edenworth backed away slightly. "She wanted to. I advised against it."

Jake focused on the man, hoping his desire to choke Edenworth was readable in his eyes.

"It was selfish of me, I know. She believes that you will consider yourself well rid of her. Blast it all, she thinks she's doing you a favor by leaving with me." The man sighed with resignation. "You can't blame me . . ."

Jake continued to stare at Edenworth. He did, indeed, blame him. "What's this plan of yours?" Suddenly, surviving the hours to come seemed important.

A sharp rap on the door caused all three of them to jump. They had all dozed on and off, but no one had really slept. Renata's arms and legs were numb, as she had been released from the chair only once, when she insisted that she had to attend to a personal matter. Corinne had accompanied her to the outhouse, gun in hand, never leaving Renata's side during the short trek and standing right outside the outhouse door impatiently.

Renata had not had the opportunity to break away, as she had thought she might; they bound her again when she was back in the shack.

Corinne opened the door. Beechcroft stood to the side, where he couldn't be seen by the person who had surprised them by knocking so early in the morning. He held a six-shooter comfortably in his hand.

From where she sat Renata couldn't see who stood on the dilapidated porch, and whoever it was couldn't see her. But the sound of the cultured voice startled Renata. Lord Edenworth? How had he found her?

"Good morning." He stepped into the room, past Corinne and Beechcroft. His eyes lit on her, and she saw in them a brief flash of concern. It was soon gone, and he turned to the kidnappers. "Thank heavens the girl hasn't been harmed. I've come to take her off your hands."

He ignored the fact that Beechcroft held a gun trained steadily at his head with a condescending indifference and dismissed Corinne's satisfied smirk.

"You shouldn't have come here, Lord Edenworth," Corinne said smugly.

Edenworth sighed idly. "Don't be tiresome. All I want is the girl. I don't care for your petty schemes and dramatic lives."

"How did you find us?" Beechcroft asked, lowering the pistol slightly.

Percival smiled at Corinne. "I was searching

for my bride-to-be and stumbled across your unfortunate husband. He was quite cooperative."

"So, she really was planning to go away with you," Corinne said thoughtfully. "What a shame she chanced onto Harrison as she did." It was clear to Renata that Corinne felt no remorse, not an inkling of regret, for all she'd done.

Percival began to pace the room slowly, his lean body graceful in a feline way, his bearing regal in spite of the dirt that marred his usually impeccable attire. "I was afraid you might be difficult. You have something I want." He stopped pacing and turned to face Corinne. "I have something you want."

"What is that?"

"Jake Wolf."

"No," Renata whispered, but he ignored her.

"I removed the savage from the jail last night and locked poor Sheriff Collins, bound and gagged, in his own jail. Humiliating for him, I know." He maintained his cool exterior as Corinne looked at him in disbelief. "Send your lackey to town to check my story, if you like. I assure you, it's true."

Corinne frowned. "Where is Jake?"

Percival sighed dramatically. "First things first. I take Renata away from here. Very far away. We'll leave immediately. I must go, as the sheriff will be quite peeved with me. I'll take you to Jake before we depart. He's already trussed up for you. As I said, your petty lives are of no consequence to me. I'll ensconce Renata on my country estate, half a continent and an ocean away from this place. Do we have an agreement?"

"If she's carrying Jake Wolf's son, that child will be rightful heir to my ranch. I can't allow . . ."

Percival laughed, a chilling and distant sound. "Madam, if Renata is carrying another man's child when we marry, it will be taken care of. There's an old woman who lives on my estate, a midwife who is as adept at ridding a woman of an unwanted child as she is at delivering a healthy one." He shuddered. "My firstborn son will be the next Earl of Edenworth. It is inconceivable that that child will not be mine."

"You bastard," Renata seethed, disbelief flooding through her. "I'll never go with you."

For a moment their eyes met, and Renata saw a glimmer of fear there. He was up to something. Then he smiled coldly again. "You will go with me, darling."

Corinne smiled when Percival's confident statement made Renata clamp her mouth closed. But Renata recovered quickly.

"And if I don't agree?" Corinne asked.

Percival shrugged, a movement so like Jake's that Renata was instantly certain that he had copied it from her husband. On purpose? To assure her?

"In that case there might be some difficulties for you. Jake will eventually escape his bonds. He'll go to the authorities and tell them all he knows." Percival looked meaningfully at Corinne. "And he knows everything I do. I made certain of that."

Corinne and Beechcroft held a short conference, their whispers indiscernible even in the small shack. Renata stared at Percival. He seemed unconcerned with the possible outcome of their discussion, cleaning dirt from beneath his fingernails and avoiding Renata's gaze completely.

"All right," Corinne said sharply. "You take us to Jake, and we'll give you the girl."

Renata knew Corinne well enough to realize that she would never agree to such a compromise. She would try to kill them all once she had Jake.

Beechcroft released Renata, harshly untying the ropes that bound her wrists and ankles. She would have run, if she'd been able, even knowing that she might get shot. As it was, they were all going to die.

But she could barely move. Her legs tingled and then began to hurt as the blood started to circulate again. Beechcroft had to lend his support as she stumbled toward the front door. Corinne stood beside Percival, her own small pistol visible from where Renata stood. Renata wondered if Percival had any idea how close he was to death.

Renata stumbled again, and Beechcroft caught her. It was a terrible, helpless feeling, to have so little control over her own legs.

The sun was rising, and Renata had to strain

her eyes against the bright light as she stood in the doorway. Somewhere out there Jake was waiting, not safe in the jail cell as she had believed all night, but bound as she had been. She closed her eyes against the blinding light and said a prayer . . . for her baby, her husband, and herself.

Chapter Twenty-nine

Renata faltered as she stepped out of the line shack that had been her prison for more than twelve hours. Was that all? It seemed like so much longer to her, the hours of waiting and wondering. Ben Beechcroft had a firm grip on her upper arm and seemed to be satisfied to lag behind, but Renata pressed forward, trying to keep close to Edenworth and Corinne. She practically dragged Beechcroft behind her as the life slowly returned to her limbs.

It was warm, and a fragrant breeze washed over Renata's face. Her nostrils were filled with the odors she had come to associate with Silver Valley, the smells of greenery and wildflowers, of unspoiled air, somehow imbued with a life of its own.

Percival and Corinne stopped at the crest

of the hill and looked down the slope. Renata slipped between them and followed their gaze.

Jake was on the ground, surrounded by tall blades of grass and shaded by the canopy of leaves that partially hid him from her. His back was to the trunk of a tree, and ropes were visible at his ankles. Through a gap in the leaves she could see that his head was slumped forward, as if he was asleep or unconscious. Or dead. For a moment Renata couldn't breathe.

"We can hang him right here," Corinne said coldly, "and save the town the trouble."

Renata broke away from Beechcroft. She had been so cooperative to that point, he was caught off guard when she jerked her arm away from him and pushed past Percival and Corinne. Corinne reached out to grab her, but Renata twisted, and Corinne's hand found only air as Renata rushed by her and down the gentle slope.

"Jake!" The hill wasn't very steep, but it was steep enough to be difficult for Renata in her mother's too-long gown and with her legs still weak from confinement. She was traveling faster and faster, and as she reached Jake, she realized that she would not be able to stop. Her foot caught against a protruding rock and she started to fall.

Jake hadn't moved a muscle, but out of the corner of his eye he saw Renata lose her balance and start to tumble forward. He jumped to his feet, the loose bonds at his ankles and his wrists falling away as he reached out to catch her. He caught her with his steady arms and lifted her so that her toes barely brushed the ground.

Jake lifted his head and looked to the top of the hill as Corinne's pistol fired aimlessly. Renata was in his arms, her head against his chest. Beechcroft and Corinne took aim again, and Jake spun around. There was no time to reach for the knife that was concealed in his moccasin, and his rifle and ammunition were on the other side of the tree, hidden under carefully arranged brush. There was nothing he could do but hold Renata and lean over her protectively, bracing himself for what was to come. The barrage of bullets that flew filled the air with deafening blasts, and Jake whispered into Renata's red-gold hair.

"I love you, Rennie."

She couldn't hear him. He couldn't hear himself for the explosion of gunfire around them. He waited for the bullets to pierce his back, but there was nothing but the roar of guns. Too many guns.

And then all was silent. Jake turned to glance at the crest of the hill. Lord Edenworth was sitting on the ground, his hand covering a wound to his upper arm. Corinne and Beechcroft were on the ground, apparently dead.

Jake saw them then, as he turned his eyes to the east. Mel was in the front, her Colt in her hand. Behind her was Harrison Summers, frail and slumped but clutching his own pistol.

Donnie Boyle brandished a Spenser rifle in his hands, and he had turned to say a word to the sheriff, who was slowly reholstering his weapon. They were almost invisible, lost in the rising sun and the smoke from their repeated firing.

He lifted his eyes to the crop of boulders where Gabe should have been and saw his old friend raise his own rifle into the air. Gabe was nothing more than a silhouette with the sun behind him, but there was a triumphant message in his stance.

"Jake." Renata pulled away from him slightly and looked up into his face. She kept her body pressed to his as she searched his eyes.

Jake knew he should let her go, now that the danger had passed, but he couldn't stand the thought of releasing her. He had been so frightened for her. That was a new feeling for him, one he didn't like and didn't care to repeat. "Are you all right?"

As an answer, Renata burst into tears, burying her head against Jake's chest and letting the tears fall unchecked. Her body shuddered against his, and he held her close, his hands in her hair and against her back. Jake whispered soft, comforting words into her hair.

He knew that she needed his strength, and he needed hers—more than he'd ever needed anything.

As suddenly as the storm of tears had started, it stopped. Renata looked up at Jake with a frown on her face.

"We have to get you ready for the trial," she said seriously. "You can't go before the judge looking like this." She wiped a streak of dirt from his cheek and frowned at his bare chest. "For goodness sake, Jake. I hope we'll have time to get you cleaned up and dressed . . . in some of Gabriel's clothes, perhaps?"

"It doesn't matter . . ."

"But it does," Renata said assuredly. "It should be a short trial, with all I know now. It was Beechcroft who killed Kenny; I can testify to that. And he was the one who tried to kill both of us in that fire. Corinne was behind it." She imparted the news softly.

Jake tangled his fingers in her hair. "I know." His voice was low. Renata no longer needed his support, but he was reluctant to let her go. She was so soft and warm, and she was where she belonged. With him.

"Renata!" Mel shouted as she ran down the hill to her cousin. Jake was forced to release Renata as Mel pulled her cousin into her arms and gave her a ferocious hug. "I was so worried!" Mel drew back and smiled. She was a beautiful woman, all big blue eyes and dimples and silky blond hair. Until he'd met Renata, Jake had believed Mel was the most beautiful woman in the world. Now . . . he couldn't take his eyes off his wife.

"Gabriel wouldn't let me ride with him last night, and when I hadn't heard anything in a few hours I put together my own search party.

I got to Silver Valley about the same time as Summers did."

"Where . . . where is Gabriel?" Renata asked shakily. Jake wanted to pull her back into his arms, but she stood close to her cousin and made no move to return to him.

Before Mel could answer Renata's question Gabe came sprinting down the slope. "What in the hell are you doing here?" he shouted. "I told you to stay put." He gathered Mel into his embrace gently, in spite of his harsh words.

"Looked to me like you needed some help," Mel said, a bite of challenge in her voice even as she wrapped her arm around Gabe's waist.

Gabe looked to Jake and shook his head. "Sorry I couldn't get off a clean shot any sooner. I was afraid I'd hit Red Rennie or English."

The rest of the rescuers came down the hill, even Lord Edenworth. His wound was no more than a scratch . . . a scratch he was loudly attributing to the sheriff, a man Edenworth claimed had to be the worst shot in town.

The sheriff was openly displeased with Jake and Edenworth, but he couldn't deny that they'd been right. He didn't even mention Jake's escape, or Edenworth's part in it. In fact, he was a little chagrined.

Renata sidled away from Mel and closer to Jake. Jake waited for Edenworth to insist that she move away, but he didn't, and Renata pressed against Jake's side as she answered the sheriff's questions. Jake kept his arm around her shoulders, and she burrowed into his side.

The men kept their distance, though Jake saw the puzzled glances that came his way. Donnie Boyle seemed satisfied with the turn of events, and Harrison Summers searched Jake's face. Jake ignored them all, silent as his wife answered the sheriff's questions almost breathlessly.

His wife.

She had said nothing about the baby. Jake had waited, as he'd held her, before Mel came darting down the slope to take Renata from his arms. Maybe it wasn't true. Surely Edenworth wouldn't lie about that. The Englishman had nothing to gain from such a lie . . . and everything to lose.

How could Jake let her go if it was true?

How could he let her go, even if it wasn't?

Because it was best for her, he told himself as she raised her palm in emphasis in telling her tale to the sheriff. Because if she stayed with him sooner or later she would learn the truth—that he couldn't give her what she deserved—that eventually everyone would see Renata as an extension of Jake Wolf . . . and the friendships that she loved, the acceptance she needed, would disappear.

And still he couldn't imagine giving her up.

Renata voiced her concerns about facing the judge, in spite of the new evidence. "Corinne and Beechcroft are both dead. Mr. Summers and I are the only ones who know what happened—Jake's wife and his father. What judge will believe that?"

357

The sheriff raised his eyebrows and sighed in surrender. "It's within my power to drop the charges. Hell, I'm not even going to charge these two with Jake's escape from jail. I don't much like having Jake in my jail. Disrupts my quiet days." He grinned. "I can't imagine what it would be like having Jake *and* that mouthy Englishman in that cell at the same time. A nightmare, that's what it would be. A damn nightmare."

Renata smiled up at Jake, and he realized that what the Englishman had said was true. A smile like that could steal a man's heart away . . . or break it into a million pieces.

It seemed forever before Jake and Renata were alone again. Mel had wanted to take her home, to their new house, and the sheriff had wanted to take her back to town, to her father. Renata shook her head to all suggestions and squeezed ever closer to Jake, until the others drifted away.

Finally she lifted her face to him again and smiled, looking deep into his eyes. Her eyes were soft and yielding, and green as summer grass, as he cupped her chin in his hands.

"It's over, Jake," Renata whispered. "You're free."

Free. Didn't she know that he would never again be free? She had his heart, had captured his soul, and no matter what happened, no matter where in the world her life took her . . . Jake knew he would never be free.

"You and Edenworth." Renata smiled mischievously. "I never would have imagined the two of you in cahoots. Deception and trickery, Jake. You never struck me as the sly type." She had to crane her neck to look up at him, but she didn't move away.

"I'm not," Jake said gruffly. "It was Edenworth's idea. I just played along." The Englishman could have the credit. If Jake had had his way, he and Renata might've both been killed. For the first time he realized the recklessness of his original plan.

Jake was silent as he led Renata the rest of the way down the slope. Edenworth and Gabriel had taken their mounts and gone, leaving only the sorrel Janie Boyle had lent Jake. Jake placed both hands on Renata's waist and lifted her onto the sorrel's back. When he vaulted up to sit behind her he wrapped his arms around her and held her tight, almost as if he was afraid to let her go.

Renata was uncommonly silent as she let her gaze wander over the vast landscape before them. For a man who had once considered the silence and solitude of the mountains to be heaven, Jake's wish for Renata to speak incessantly was nonsense . . . but he did. He wanted to hear the sound of her voice. He didn't even care what she said. Jake smiled wryly and turned the sorrel away from town.

Renata didn't ask where he was taking her.

Chapter Thirty

The creek cut through Harrison Summers's property on the western border. It wasn't his main water source, for it usually went dry before the main tributary, but Jake remembered it from his childhood as a place of peace and solitude, protected as it was from the rest of the ranch by stone walls on two sides and a steep hill on another. It was in a secluded valley nestled in a triangular hold, the water disappearing between the tall rock formations and the rugged hill. Jake tethered the sorrel and carried Renata down the hill, remembering even after all these years where to step to find secure footing.

Renata twisted her neck to look below. The water was clear and rushing merrily, fed at one end by a waterfall. It wasn't a thunderous waterfall, but a steady trickle of water that produced a soporific sound that grew louder as they descended into the valley.

Still, she remained silent. Jake didn't know if he should take that as a good sign or a bad one. Renata was completely relaxed in his arms as he made his way down the slope. She was looking down at the water as if she already loved the place as much as he did, as if his memories were hers.

"What are we doing here?" She finally spoke as he set her on her feet near the water.

Jake couldn't answer her. He didn't know why he had brought her to this place. Seeing his father had stirred up a lot of old memories—painful ones, for the most part, but not all of them were hurtful. He remembered this place, and riding with his father across the ranch. He remembered the slowly developing sense of belonging that had been so devastating to lose. Over the years, the memories of Corinne and her treachery had overshadowed everything else, until he had almost forgotten the moments of beauty from that time.

Renata looked up into his face. He had always been hard to read, and now it was impossible to tell what was in his mind and his heart. His eyes were dark and hooded, his mouth grim. Perhaps now was the time to tell him about the baby. She was certain she was carrying his child. Would he be happy about it? Would he want her to stay?

Perhaps he wouldn't care for the child at all, and that would break her heart. So she hesitated, unable to pull her eyes away from his face.

"I came here often as a child," Jake said softly. "To swim and to think." He looked out at the water. "It seems everything else has changed, but this place is the same." There was an odd, almost wistful touch to Jake's voice.

Renata could almost see Jake as a child, sitting on the edge of the creek, silent and alone. Had he been a loner, even as a child? She knew without asking that he had been, and the knowledge broke her heart.

He didn't need her. That fact hit her like a painful blow as she looked into his stoic face. She had fooled herself for weeks, because she wanted to believe that to be true. What a fool she had been to believe that a man like Jake would actually need a frivolous girl like her. He needed no one, least of all her.

But her father did need her, and Renata knew with a sudden and heavy weight in her heart what she had to do. She would leave Jake and marry Percival, and her father would be saved from financial ruin. She could fix all her father's problems very simply . . . and she would. It was all she could do for the man who had given her everything.

And then Jake lowered his lips to hers and kissed her. The touch of his lips was light, questioning. It was as if he were testing her. His hands rested lightly on her shoulders, and when she didn't move away he wrapped those arms around her and gathered her close, deepening his kiss.

Her own response was tentative at first, but she soon cast aside her hesitation and melted into his inviting warmth, wrapping her arms around his neck. Renata's hands found the back of his head, and her fingers twined in the hair that was so silky to the touch. Her tongue delved deeply into his mouth, and she was gratified with Jake's response as he moaned low in his throat and crushed her to his chest.

This was the way it was with Jake. All he had to do was touch her, and she forgot everything else. He kissed her, and she pressed her body against his. He placed his hand on her breast and she was moaning, feeling the heat and urgency of his touch in the pit of her belly, in the center of her very soul.

Jake lowered her to the soft grass on the bank of the gently rushing creek and lavished her with kisses. He branded her with his lips as they trailed down her slender throat, kissing the flesh he exposed as he slowly unbuttoned her dark brown dress. He didn't rush, but treasured every caress, every moment. Slowly, he removed her dress and her filmy undergarments, until she was nearly mad with her craving to have him inside her.

*   *   *

Jake wanted to see all of her, every inch of silky skin, every beautiful curve and red-gold hair illuminated in the summer sun. Her green eyes never left his face, and even when he lowered his head to stroke first one breast and then the other with his tongue she didn't so much as blush. She hid nothing from him, not her frenzied desire or her heated response to his touch.

When she helped Jake remove his buckskins she studied him with as much intensity as he had her. Renata ran her hands along his thighs and kissed the scars on his shoulder and along his arms. They were faded now, almost invisible, but Renata knew every inch of his body as if it were her own. Every scar, every muscle.

They explored one another not as strangers, not as if they were seeing one another for the first time, but as if this was, perhaps, the last time.

When Jake held himself over her, his weight supported on his forearms resting on either side of her head, he met her strong gaze with his own. Their eyes were locked as he pressed his manhood against her soft, inviting center, and she lifted her hips to guide him inside her. He moved slowly, deliberately, wanting to make this joining last. When he was deep within her, his shaft buried completely in her warmth, she closed her eyes and took a deep breath. She was completely still for a moment.

Suddenly Jake knew what she was doing. She

was memorizing the smell of the air, the sound of the waterfall, the feel of having him inside her. She was memorizing a perfect moment, and Jake was certain then that she meant to leave.

He wanted to hate her for it, but he couldn't. His love for her went too deep. She had his heart and soul, would have them wherever she went. He lost himself in her body and forgot, for a while, that she wasn't his anymore.

He felt her shudder and she screamed his name. He caught that scream with his mouth, taking a part of her inside him as surely as he was inside her. There were just the two of them, melding their bodies and their souls, giving everything they had to give to become one being that defied the rest of the world.

When Jake convulsed over her he kept his mouth firmly clamped on hers, unable to be gentle with this tender woman, unable to hold back any of his explosive passion.

No matter what, he would never be the same. The heart he had protected for so long was raw and bleeding . . . and it would never heal.

Silently he begged her to stay. Silently he told her how much he loved her. But he was quiet as always, raining lazy kisses on her throat and her shoulders, drinking in the soft touch of her hand against his head and at his back, listening with his ears and his heart to the soft sighs she expelled contentedly.

He rolled onto his side, keeping her in his

embrace. He didn't want to crush her, but neither did he want to let her go. His fingers trailed lazily over her arm and down her back, and he buried his face in her hair. Unconsciously, he was making a memory of his own.

They lay there for a time, the sun warming their bodies. But the chill of knowing that this couldn't last settled over them, and Jake could feel Renata's body begin to tense.

"Jake, I . . ." She finally spoke, but then hesitated. "The stage will be through this afternoon." Her voice sounded oddly detached, as if it belonged to someone other than the woman who had just given herself to him.

"Will you be on it?" Jake's question seemed as chilly as the water looked.

"I . . . I suppose I will be," Renata said despondently. "I don't think we can live on lightning alone."

Jake pulled away from her and stared at her coldly. She was going to leave, taking her baby, his baby, with her. She wasn't even going to tell him. Why was he surprised? Why should he expect anything different?

"Well, you're a city girl. I knew that all along. You don't belong here." His statement was cold and derisive, putting her in her place. "But I guess I should thank you for saving my skin . . . more than once." He managed an icy smile and lowered his head to kiss her belly.

Renata sat up quickly. "I suppose we're even, then, since you saved mine today."

Jake stood and walked into the water until

it was waist deep, and then he splashed cool water over his face and his chest, keeping his back to the bank. "Edenworth's not a bad fellow." His voice was amazingly distant. "I guess you'll like living in a castle. Having all those servants . . ." He felt her behind him before he heard her splashing in the water. Jake prayed that she would stay behind him where she couldn't see his face. He had been able to disguise his voice very well. But his face—he knew if she saw him before he had a chance to drive down the pain, to drive it so deep inside even he forgot it was there, she would know. Renata didn't come close to him, though.

"I suppose it will be all right," she said calmly, splashing the water again. "It gets rather cold there, I hear." Their conversation was taking an absurdly formal turn, and Jake returned to his quiet iciness.

It was easier that way.

Neither of them said a word from the time they left the creek until they found themselves on Silver Valley's only street. Renata found life in town to be preposterously ordinary. People went in and out of the general store; a lady stepped into the dress shop. As they passed the blacksmith's, a loud clanging assaulted them. Renata wanted to scream. Didn't they know that the world had changed?

Jake halted the sorrel in front of the hotel. "Good-bye, Renata," he said without emotion as he lowered her to the ground. He didn't even move from the saddle.

Renata looked up at him. How could he be so passionate one minute and so distant the next? The sun was high in the sky, and she shaded her eyes as she looked up. "You'll stay out of trouble, won't you, Jake?"

He shrugged noncommittally. "Trouble always seems to find me."

Renata bit her lower lip. If she told him about the baby, he would have to keep her. Wouldn't he?

"Renata!" her mother screamed and ran into the street to embrace her. "Where have you been? I've been beside myself with worry. The sheriff was back hours ago, and he said that you were with that . . . that . . . Well, thank goodness you're all right."

Renata extricated herself from her mother's grasp and turned around, but Jake was gone. She glanced down the street and saw his broad, straight back as he rode away from her without a word.

"The stage will be here in two hours," Cecilia said excitedly. "We're almost packed, but you need to get cleaned up and . . ."

"I just had a bath, Mother," Renata said tiredly, her eyes on Jake's back as he stopped at the blacksmith's livery.

"Where did you . . ." Cecilia stopped suddenly, her face reddening with comprehension.

"In a creek. A beautiful creek with a waterfall." Renata pulled her eyes away from Jake and walked slowly toward the hotel with her mother. He didn't want her, he didn't need her, and he certainly didn't love her. But she still loved him. Would always love him.

"A creek?" Her mother's tone displayed her horror. "Good heavens. We'll have to get you in a hot tub. God only knows what . . . what creatures frequent that creek."

Renata allowed her mother to escort her into the hotel and up the stairs. She lowered herself into a steaming bath and finally donned the traveling suit her mother had had altered for her. She did it all without complaint or comment.

It didn't matter anymore.

Chapter Thirty-one

Jake stood in the familiar parlor, his back to his father. Harrison Summers should have been in bed, but even though he was tired, exhausted almost to the point of collapse, he'd announced that he was damned tired of that bed.

Jake remained angry. He couldn't forget the years of isolation, the hate he'd clung to when there was nothing else. But he had come to his father's home of his own free will, had finally been driven to search for answers to questions that had plagued him for more than half his life.

But now that he was here, he couldn't find the words. Dammit, Renata would know exactly what to say. She was so good with people, with words, and he was so inept— yet another reason they were doomed to part. Had been doomed from the beginning.

"I've missed you, Jake," Harrison said, his voice stronger than Jake had expected. The man he remembered as being so powerful was frail and weak. Jake felt a surge of guilt. Renata had been right about that too: Corinne had been slowly poisoning her husband. She had been a sick woman, hungry for money and control. Control over people, like Ben Beechcroft and her daughters.

"Why . . ." Jake's voice was gruff. He didn't want to sound like a hurt child. "Why did you never marry my mother?"

Harrison was silent for several minutes. Jake couldn't see him, but he heard his father's heavy sigh. "I asked her. Many times. Always she said no. She had no need for a white man's ceremony to make her my wife. In her heart she had taken me for her husband, and that was enough for her."

Jake closed his eyes, shutting out the bright light that streamed through the window. Those had been Yellow Moon Woman's words as well: married in the heart. He would always be married in his heart to Renata. Thunderheart Woman.

"When she was in the family way with you I asked her every day. Her answer was always the same. 'Maybe tomorrow, Summers.' That was what she always called me: Summers. She never called me Harry or Harrison. Always Summers." His voice was dreamlike. "God, she was the most beautiful woman I ever saw. But it was her spirit I loved."

Jake turned away from the window and frowned at his father. "If you loved her, why did you let her go?" There was more pain than anger in his question.

"She was never happy here. Not truly happy. She didn't like staying inside the house all the time. Staying in the same place." He smiled at Jake. "You have her restlessness. I can see it." His smile faded. "And it's true that she was never really accepted here. I never suspected that it bothered her until after you were born. She didn't want people calling you half-breed and treating you as less than they would treat a child who had no mixed blood.

"In the weeks before she left she began to say things that should have warned me. She said that I should take a white wife who wouldn't embarrass me. That she was tired of breathing stale air. That was what she called the air in the house—stale air. I realized that she was not as happy as she had once been, but I thought . . . in time . . ." Harrison stared at Jake, who had taken a step forward, a look of puzzlement on his face.

"She . . . left . . . you?" Jake's voice was no more than a harsh whisper.

"Yes." Harrison breathed his soft answer. "Early one morning, when she thought I was still sleeping, she slipped from our bed and gathered you up and sneaked away. God help me, I watched her leave from our bedroom window. It broke my heart, to watch her walk away, but I wanted her to be happy."

"She was never happy after we left this place," Jake said hoarsely. "Never. That's why I always thought . . . that you made her leave. That you . . . sent us away."

Harrison shook his head sadly. "No. All I ever wanted was for Snow Flower to be happy."

"She told me that you needed a white wife who would be accepted by the men who worked for you and the people of the town. A woman who could help you build this ranch into the empire you wanted."

Harrison looked up, and Jake saw tears glistening in his father's eyes. "If I had known that was the reason she left, I never would have let her go. I would trade this ranch and every dollar I have in the bank to have her back with me."

Jake turned away from his father. This was a side of Harrison Summers he had never seen before. He clenched and unclenched his hands, wanting—needing—the hate that had driven him for years.

"Jake. Son," Harrison called softly. "About what happened when you left here . . . all those years ago . . . I'm sorry. I never should have believed Corinne. It was years before I knew what she was really like."

"You don't have to do this," Jake said, but he didn't turn around to face his father.

"Your wife thinks I do."

Jake turned back to his father with a

deep frown. "What does Renata have to do with this?"

"She told me that I should have known you would never attack Corinne. She gave me what for, she did." Harrison was smiling slightly once again. "She's a fireball, that one." Harrison grinned and shook his head. "I wish you'd brought her with you. Is she resting? Corinne and Ben didn't hurt her none, did they?"

"Renata's fine," Jake said sharply. "She's leaving on the stage this afternoon."

"She told me that she was leaving, but I didn't really believe her."

Jake shook his head. This conversation was taking a turn he didn't care for. He'd much rather talk over ancient history than discuss Renata with his father. "It's for the best."

"She loves you, Jake," Harrison said harshly. "And I damn well know that you love her. What the hell are you thinking?"

"She deserves better." Jake found and held his father's dark blue eyes. "Renata would never be happy . . . with me."

Harrison leaned forward, a gleam of anger and frustration in his eye. "Don't you see what you're doing?" He placed both hands on the arms of his chair and forced himself to his feet. Jake saw a glimmer in him of the man he remembered. "Don't be the fool I was. Don't make the same mistake your old man made and regretted all his life. Snow Flower is dead!" he shouted. "I'll never get the chance to undo the mistake I made. If I had told her that morning that I loved her, that I needed her with me . . . maybe she wouldn't have gone away. Maybe she would have stayed here and had a dozen more babies like you. Maybe she'd still be alive." His strength faded and his voice failed as he sat down hard in his chair.

Jake strode back to the window, turning his back on his frail father. Jake wasn't his father, and Renata wasn't Snow Flower. But there was a hollow feeling deep inside him that had been there since he'd dropped Renata off in front of the hotel. He hadn't even had the courage to dismount himself. He'd just lowered her to the ground and gone to the stable for his black stallion. He hadn't even looked back as she'd watched him ride away. But that empty feeling, that hollowness deep inside, had grown with each passing minute. She had a part of him he would never recover. A part of his heart. A part of his soul.

He tried to imagine Renata living in a castle in England, raising her child as Edenworth's. His child.

But it was too late.

He didn't even realize he had spoken aloud until his father answered him.

"It's never too late, Jake," Harrison said with tenderness in his usually gruff voice. "Not while there's a breath left in your body."

"I can't force her to stay," Jake said solemnly.

"You don't have to drive her away, either."

Jake turned to glare at his father. "And what

makes you think I'm driving her away?"

"You're my son. You're your mother's son. I'm afraid you had no choice but to be the stubborn mule you are." He said it with affection, but the insult was there. "Don't be so damn hardheaded that you ruin your life as well as that girl's."

Jake stared at his father for a long time. He shouldn't be listening to a word Harrison Summers had to say. He could hardly remember a time when he hadn't hated the man . . . but this was where he'd come when he'd left Silver Valley. Why? To hear the explanation he'd just listened to? To have someone—anyone—tell him that he was doing the right thing by letting her go?

Jake left without a word, his long strides purposeful.

It seemed the whole town had come out to see her off. For the first time since the fire she was properly dressed. The traveling outfit her mother had purchased and had altered by the dressmaker was an apricot silk and fit well, considering the dressmaker had only had her mother's instructions, and no fittings, to go by.

The color was flattering on Renata, as was the hint of delicate lace at her throat. The skirt flared becomingly, accenting her still tiny waist.

She knew her face was pale and blank. She felt as though she might never smile again.

Her mother was directing the loading of

their trunks, demanding and regal as always, impatient with the clumsiness of the boys who were trying to load the heavy trunks onto the waiting stage. In the bottom of one of those trunks was Jake's buckskin shirt, and Renata's deerskin dress and moccasins.

Renata would have found the scene around her comical if she'd been paying attention. One of the boys dropped a small trunk, and the contents spilled across the boardwalk. As the boy apologized, everyone tried to help, stepping on items of clothing and almost fighting over the slapdash repacking of the trunk, and it took twice as long as it should have.

The stage driver was offered a meal, and though he tried to refuse, insisting on attempting to stick to the schedule, he was escorted to the hotel with the promise of a veritable feast: steak, hot bread, green beans, potatoes dripping with butter. It was the promise of two kinds of pie that finally persuaded him.

Renata watched her parents as they waited impatiently. They didn't seem to notice or care that her life was ruined, that she couldn't manage a smile as her friends bid her good-bye. At least Percival had the good grace not to appear as relieved and eager as her own mother and father. He seemed as dejected as she.

Percival's eyes followed Renata's every move as she hugged Felicia Collins—three times— and said tearful good-byes, to the storekeeper and his scowling wife. The townspeople left him alone, ignoring him blatantly, and for once he didn't mind.

He was so accustomed to being ignored that he almost jumped out of his skin when Gabriel spoke to him.

"You must be a mighty happy man, English," the rancher said in a low voice that held no hint of congratulations.

Percival raised an eyebrow, imparting all his dignity and superiority. "Is that so?"

Gabriel leaned against a post that supported the overhang that shaded the boardwalk. His stance was casual, but there was an intensity in his gaze that made Percival want to step back, though of course he didn't.

"Sure. You've won. She's going with you," Gabriel said nonchalantly, the fire in his eyes anything but casual.

Percival sighed deeply, facing the rancher. "I've won, have I?" he asked in a low voice, a husky whisper meant for Gabriel's ears alone. "Look at her. Look at her!" he insisted when Gabriel's gaze remained on his face.

Gabriel's eyes shifted slightly, and he looked over Percival's shoulder to watch his wife's cousin, who looked openly miserable. Though she was trying to hide it, she was doing a rotten job.

"I've won. She'll divorce your friend and marry me, that's true. But what have I won?" Percival's voice was almost melancholy. "Where is that bloody loggerhead?"

* * *

Two little girls, identical from the top of their dark heads to their blue shifts to the special-made cowboy boots their grandfather had given them, danced around Renata. Sam and Alex, three years old, clutched their peppermint sticks and romped with the endless energy that only the very young can muster. Only they could make Renata smile, though the smile was wistful.

Melanie shooed her daughters away and wound an arm through Renata's. "You could stay with us, you know," Mel offered in a quiet voice. "You don't have to leave so soon."

"I do," Renata said cheerlessly. She didn't want to explain her reasons to Melanie. Her cousin would never understand the reasons why Renata felt obligated to help her father. Renata didn't want Melanie's sympathy, and she certainly didn't want her cousin making a scene as she left Silver Valley. And she would if she knew why Renata was going to marry Percival. "I don't belong here. Jake told me as much."

Melanie scoffed. "Jake's a fool. I swear . . . Where is he, anyway? Shouldn't he be here?"

Renata didn't answer her cousin's questions, and she tried to attribute her melancholy to her delicate condition. That, and her sadness at leaving the new friends she had made in Silver Valley. There was a weight in her chest, a heaviness that was new and uncomfortable, and she didn't know if it would ever go away.

She couldn't possibly attribute it to Jake. He

didn't love her, didn't want her around. He had tried from the moment they'd met to drive her from Silver Valley . . . and at last he had succeeded.

Renata stepped away from the crowd near the stage. Her father paced impatiently, and her mother fanned herself furiously. The preacher who had married her to Jake stood at the fringes of the crowd, his pale face impassive, serene. Janie Boyle was reciting her recipe for white cake to Alice Clark, and Felicia Collins and her mother were deep in a quiet argument. Percival was carrying on an animated conversation with Gabriel, while Melanie chased her daughters. The men who had gathered in front of the general store chattered away about the weather, and for a moment Renata felt herself free of their attention.

She heard it first, a sound like thunder, drawing closer and closer, and she took a step away from the crowd. Her heart was beating faster and faster. What if it was . . .

It wasn't. He had left her like an unwanted sack of refuse on the street in front of the hotel. He wouldn't come back. Would he?

She stepped down into the street. By now everyone had heard the thunder of approaching hooves and had turned to watch. Renata was nearly in the middle of the street. Waiting.

There were dozens of smiles in the crowd when Jake rode in on his black stallion. He was leaning low over the stallion's neck, barreling down the street toward her.

"Unca Jake! Unca Jake!" The two little Maxwell girls jumped up and down on the boardwalk, and Melanie had to hold on to their shifts to keep them from joining Renata. Dr. Parkhurst stepped forward. In a moment he was rushing down the boardwalk, intent on keeping Renata from Jake, who was bearing down on her. Her father was staring at her and didn't see the foot that was thrust out in front of him, bringing him to his knees.

"I'm so sorry." The minister helped Renata's father to his feet, refusing to loosen his hold on his lapels as he looked him up and down. "Are you hurt?"

"Release me, you fool!" her father shouted, and the minister did just that.

But it was too late. Dr. Parkhurst turned just in time to see Jake lean over and scoop Renata off the dusty street, barely slowing the stride of the stallion. They flew past the stage and the stunned onlookers. Gabriel's twins were jumping up and down, clapping and squealing in delight at the exciting display put on by their Unca Jake and Renata. Their cheers were drowned out as the rest of the crowd began to whoop and holler.

William and Cecilia Parkhurst stood in stunned silence, and Percival restrained his own emotions, simply sighing tiredly. Ah, well. 'Twas for the best, he supposed.

In a country that could contain a treasure

like Renata, and a prize like her cousin Melanie, there were certainly other women equally enchanting.

Percival slipped through the crowd until he was at the minister's side. "Nice move, Reverend," he said in a low voice. "I must say, I'm quite impressed."

The minister gave Percival a solemn look, but his face flushed red. A man unaccustomed to trickery of any kind, Percival supposed.

"The Lord and I don't like to see our work undone." The minister must have recognized an unexpected ally in Percival, because he allowed himself a small smile. "Especially when it's been done so well to begin with."

Chapter Thirty-two

Jake slowed his pace as soon as they left the town behind. He held Renata firmly in front of him, her head against his chest, her waist firmly in his grasp.

He'd expected her to protest, but she hadn't. In fact, when he'd reached down to snatch her from the street she'd lifted her arms to him, and that gave him more hope than he ever could have imagined.

The stagecoach should have been long gone, and he'd expected to ride through Silver Valley without stopping. Seeing the Concord actually made him think twice about his hasty decision. What could he say to her? What had he been thinking when he'd stormed from his father's house?

And then she'd stepped into the street, waiting for him. Now she was perfectly still as she rested against him, her red-gold hair falling from its restraints and curling around her face and down her back.

When Jake was certain no one was following them he stopped in the middle of the dirt road. Dust rose from the stallion's stomping hooves, and a light breeze swept that dust away in dancing whirlwinds.

Renata lifted her face to him, a face full of hope and expectation. Her green eyes were as wide as he'd ever seen them.

Jake took her chin in his hand, his fingers so light they barely brushed her skin. What could he say to make her stay? There were so many words . . . and he tried to think of something romantic and powerful, something that would move her to stay with him. But he'd never been good with words. Edenworth could woo her with pretty speeches, but Jake could not.

"Don't go," he whispered harshly.

Renata started to smile. He saw it in her eyes, but she hesitated. "Give me one good reason why I should stay, Jake Wolf," she demanded gently.

Jake looked into her face and knew he would never again be content if she left. She was, to him, the good in the world. She was everything he had lived without: hope, happiness, love. All he could do was allow his heart to speak for him. "You have the stars in your eyes and the sun in your smile, and if you go away you'll leave me in darkness." Jake's eyes held hers. "Stay with me because I love you."

Renata smiled then and threw her arms around Jake's neck. Those were the words she had wanted to hear. He loved her. He couldn't even remember why he had been so hesitant to say the words aloud . . . what had he been afraid of?

"I love you so much, Jake," she whispered into his ear. "And there's yet another reason why I should stay here with you."

"And what's that?" Jake held her close, a hint of a smile forming on his lips.

"I'm . . . in a rather delicate condition."

Jake played dumb. "You're sick?"

"No, I'm . . ." She drew back and looked into his face, her eyes twinkling as she slapped him lightly across the chest. "You know exactly what I mean, Jake. A baby." She bit her lower lip, waiting for him to respond to her news. Jake couldn't stop the smile that spread across his face, and he bent to kiss her lips softly.

"You took your sweet time telling me, Renata Marie Wolf," he whispered as he pulled away reluctantly.

"You knew?"

Jake nodded. "Edenworth told me." His smile faded a little. "I can't believe you told him and not me."

"Well, at the time . . ."

Jake silenced her with a kiss. "From now on, no matter what, you tell me everything. And the next time we make a baby I want to be the first to know."

Renata grinned broadly, and her eyes twinkled like emeralds. "A baby," she whispered. "When you say it . . . it seems so real to me."

How long they sat atop the black stallion, the warm sun beating against their heads, the horse prancing restlessly, Jake couldn't say. He kissed his wife, his Rennie, over and over again, content to hold her against him and kiss her lightly, on her lips, her neck, her cheeks. Time was still, the sun hung in the sky, the winds had stopped, and Renata placed her hands on his face and looked deep into his eyes.

She'd never known a man as strong as Jake, or as tender. He tried to hide that tenderness from everyone—even himself—but she had found it, and she intended to hold on to it forever.

"You were right, you know," Jake said in a lazy drawl.

"About what?" Renata's voice was almost dreamlike. Jake could put her under a spell that made her forget everything else. It was his own special magic.

"Everything. My father, my sisters . . ." A slight frown passed over his face. "They'll need both of us. Corinne was a cruel woman, but she was their mother."

Renata moved her hand to the back of Jake's neck and tangled her fingers in his hair. It was the first time he had actually acknowledged that Corinne's daughters were his sisters . . . his family. "They're very lucky to have a brother like you." She kissed him, and then withdrew abruptly. "Oh, dear."

"What's wrong?"

"I have to go back," Renata whispered, and Jake drew away from her with a frown.

"Back where?"

"I have to see my father before he leaves," she explained.

Jake didn't like it. She recognized the determination in those dark eyes, but he didn't back away from it.

"Write him a letter," he said in a low voice.

Renata shook her head. "I can't. I need to . . . tell him face-to-face." She frowned slightly. Was she betraying her father for her own happiness?

Jake grumbled, but he turned the stallion around and they headed toward town. This time he led the horse at a slow pace, leisurely almost, and Renata leaned back against him and felt the tension in his body.

All eyes turned to them as they approached the stage. The driver was ready to pull out, and Renata's father was shouting at him that his daughter had not yet returned, that he must wait. Her mother was pacing anxiously, away from the rest of the crowd. Sam and Alex saw her and Jake first and waved excitedly as they neared. Soon everyone was watching. And waiting.

Jake stopped near the boardwalk. He looked

down at her, and Renata saw the doubt in his eyes. Did he think she would leave him? Ever? Renata gave him a smile, a smile that she hoped spoke what was in her heart.

The wariness left his eyes, and he slid from the stallion with his usual strong grace. Renata slipped from the horse's back and into his waiting arms without a hint of hesitation or fear. Jake caught her in his arms, careful not to jar her.

"Good heavens!" Cecilia screamed. "He could have dropped her in the street!" Everyone else looked at her as if she were mad, and Renata realized that her mother was the only person there who didn't know that Jake would never let any harm come to her.

"She might have broken her neck!" Cecilia continued her tirade. "Sheriff! Arrest that man!"

Even Percival looked at her mother with disdain. "Bloody hell, Cecilia. Do shut up."

Jake carried Renata to the edge of the crowd, refusing to put her down until she whispered into his ear, asking him to. With a scowl, he set her lightly on her feet.

"Renata," her father snapped. "Let's go. The stage is waiting."

Renata looked at the faces in the crowd around her. Felicia was chewing on her bottom lip, and Janie Boyle wrung her hands in a rare display of anxiety. Donnie Boyle and the others frowned mightily, and the minister seemed to be saying a silent prayer. Suddenly Renata knew that all the delays—the dropped luggage, the sumptuous meal, her father's tripping—had been deliberate, and she smiled at her friends. They had known all along what she and Jake had refused to see. Renata was smiling brightly when she answered.

"I'm not going." Her voice was serene, strong and loving. "I'm sorry. I know you were counting on me, but you'll have to find another way. You're smart and strong; you'll find a way without Percival's money."

Jake stepped between Renata and her father, glaring down at the little man. He would have been a formidable sight if he hadn't had a giggling three-year-old attached to each buckskin-clad leg. "You were trying to sell your daughter?" His voice conveyed his anger and disbelief.

"No." Her father shook his head. "It wasn't like that. I only wanted Renata to have the best of everything." He took a step away from Jake. "You're right." He looked from Jake to Renata. "I'm sorry." He sounded sincere, but Renata was still suspicious. Evidently, so was Jake, who refused to back away. "We'll find another way, your mother and I. We can sell the house. We don't need so much room anymore."

Her mother pushed her way through the crowd. "Renata Marie Parkhurst . . ."

"Renata Marie Wolf." At least a half-dozen voices corrected her, Renata's and Jake's among them.

"You would let your parents starve . . . lose

their home and position in society . . . what an ungrateful girl you are," Cecilia snapped.

"You'll survive, Mother," Renata assured the ranting woman lovingly.

"How much do you want for her?" Jake leaned closer to Renata's parents. "If Renata's for sale, I'd like to buy her. How much?" He was seething, and her father took another step back.

"It's not like that . . ." he insisted.

"Bloody hell." Percival pushed his way forward. With a haughty look of disdain he brushed a few grains of dust from his impeccable attire. "I'll give you the bloody money. This is what I get for meddling in others' financial affairs." He turned to Renata and took her hand, ignoring the deadly stare Jake turned his way.

"At last I see before me the woman who compelled me to . . . shall we say . . . arrange a bit of financial disaster in order to win her . . . by fair means or foul."

Renata glared at him, but she felt too wonderful to be really angry. "You ruined my father just to . . ."

"I know, I know. I've learned my lesson, really I have." He was as dismal as a little boy who'd been caught with his hand in the cookie jar, but there was no real regret in his eyes or his voice. "Besides . . ." Percival's gray eyes twinkled. "Jake understands." He looked up at Jake, who continued to stare at Percival's hand. "Don't you, old fellow?"

Jake reached out and took Renata's hand from Percival's grasp. "Yes."

Melanie pried one of her daughters from Jake's leg and Gabriel disengaged the other. Jake looked down at the girls and smiled.

It was Alex who looked with disdain at their hands grasping one another so naturally, Renata's fingers a sharp contrast as they rested against Jake's bronzed skin.

"Unca Jake, do you like my cousin Renata?" Alex asked suspiciously.

Jake squatted so that he was face-to-face with Alex, and a moment later Sam's almost identical face was pressed close as well. "Yes, I do," he whispered conspiratorially. "She's going to stay in Silver Valley with us."

Alex's face lit up. "She's not leaving?"

Jake shook his head and the girls danced up and down.

Renata's mother's shoulders slumped as Renata and Jake turned away. She followed them, her short steps light on the boardwalk.

Jake vaulted onto the tall stallion, and Renata lifted her arms to him. With a smooth and easy motion he pulled her up to sit in his lap, and she settled there with a smile on her face.

"Oh, dear." Renata saw her mother wring her hands. "I know I've made mistakes. But I did so want Renata to be a lady."

Jake glared down at her. "Mrs. Parkhurst, whether Renata lives in a castle or a cave she will always be a lady."

With that they turned and rode away from

the crowd, the stallion moving at its own slow pace. Renata leaned against her husband's broad chest as he drew her even closer to him, and she heard the satisfied murmurs of her friends behind them.

Her mother's voice transcended them all. "Did he say a cave?"

Epilogue

Jake bought a parcel of land from his father, a parcel he had refused to accept as a wedding present. It was on the western border of the Summers ranch, a fertile tract that included a secluded valley with a rushing creek and a gentle waterfall. Jake started his horse farm, and before his son was born had built a sprawling ranch house. There was a courtyard in the center of their home, and double doors from the dining room, the library, and the master bedroom opened onto the green sanctuary. Sometimes, on a still night, the sounds of a waterfall could be heard from that quiet courtyard.

Jacob Summers Wolf was born six weeks after Melanie and Gabriel's son, James Gabriel Maxwell III, whom everyone called Little Max. Renata confidently declared that he and her own son would grow up as best friends. She was as certain of this as her dream of coming to Colorado and finding a rancher. Harrison's ranch would one day go to Little Jake.

Renata somehow convinced Yellow Moon Woman to live on the farm with them. Jake never asked what she had said to the old woman to make her agree to leave her mountain home. No doubt she had spun a tale of the disasters that would befall all of them if the old Cheyenne woman didn't come to live with them. Yellow Moon Woman was more readily accepted by the townspeople than Jake could have dreamed. Renata would have it no other way.

The relationship between Jake and his father was slow to mend, but it did. Renata was there, seemingly forever between them, as long as they needed her. And then she backed away and watched. Harrison Summers spent long hours talking with Yellow Moon Woman, remembering old friends and old ways, and cooing over Little Jake. It was Little Jake, in the end, who managed to bring his father and grandfather together.

Renata set her sights on Jake's sisters, determined to bring the older girls out of their shells and see that they married properly. Harriet and Gilda blossomed slowly under Renata's watchful eye. But Lina was her favorite, and the two of them were as close as any sisters before Little Jake was born and over the years. Lina watched Little Jake and the four babies who followed him when Jake and Renata disappeared into the mountains for a day, or two, or three . . .

There wasn't a resident of Silver Valley or the surrounding area who didn't claim to have known all along that Jake was an upstanding citizen—a man of sterling character.

For Renata, Jake learned to dance.

Jake loved working with the horses, though he never took to the tedious bookkeeping required to run a business. But occasionally it was necessary.

Sometimes, on a busy afternoon, as Jake sat at his desk and scowled at the papers before him, Renata would sneak into his study and slip into his lap. She would smile at her husband, declare that he looked as if he needed a kiss, and lift his spirits with a smile that rivaled the sun for its brightness.

NORAH HESS
Kentucky Bride

Kentucky Woman

NORAH HESS

Winner of 5 *Romantic Times* Awards!

Norah Hess's historical romances are "delightful, tender and heartwarming reads from a special storyteller!"

—*Romantic Times*

Spencer Atkins wants no part of a wife and children while he can live in his pa's backwoods cabin as a carefree bachelor. Fresh from the poorhouse, Gretchen Ames will marry no man refusing her a home and a family. Although they are the unlikeliest couple, Spencer and Gretchen find themselves grudgingly sharing a cabin, working side by side, and fighting an attraction neither can deny.

_3518-9 $4.99 US/$5.99 CAN

Heart's Landing
Robin Lee Hatcher

Winner Of The *Romantic Times* Storyteller Of The Year Award.

Vivacious Brenetta Lattimer is as untamed and beautiful as the Idaho mountain country where she has been raised. Only one man can tame her wild spirit—handsome Rory O'Hara, who has grown up with her on Heart's Landing ranch.

But fate has taken Rory away from Brenetta, and when they are brought together again, she feels her childhood crush blossom into an all-consuming passion. Brenetta thinks she will never allow another man to kiss her lips as Rory has so hungrily done, until her scheming cousin Megan plots to win Rory for herself.

Despite the seeming success of Megan's ruthless deception, Brenetta continues to nourish in her heart a love for the man who has awakened her to the sweet agony of desire.

__3621-5 $4.99 US/$5.99 CAN

JESSIE'S OUTLAW
Cheryl Anne Porter

A lonely orphan, Jessie Stewart never imagines that her dreams of happiness will be fulfilled until a wounded man appears in her root cellar. Exasperating, infuriating, and unbelievably handsome, the stranger has secrets to hide and enemies to flee. Whoever he is, whatever he has done, Jessie longs to help him, no matter how great the danger to her life or her virtue. As deadly gunrunners pursue the desperate pair across the scorching New Mexican desert, the sassy girl will have to dodge bullets and the law and silence the desperado's protests with her sweet lips if she ever hopes to unleash the wild, tantalizing ecstasy of their love.

_3541-3 $4.50 US/$5.50 CAN